Isaiah reentered Hezekiah's sickroom and found the king just as he had left him, lying still as death with his eyes focused on the beamed ceiling above him. Hezekiah's hands, long and thin, lay clasped tightly on the coverlet, clenched in pain and fear.

"My king," Isaiah said gently, Hezekiah did not move, but the prophet saw his eyelids flutter slightly. "Hezekiah, listen to me. Yahweh has sent us a sign. You will recover. You will not die, not now!" Isaiah bent over him and watched as a sparkle of hope came into Hezekiah's dark eyes.

ISAIAH

THE PROPHET-PRINCE

CONSTANCE HEAD

LIVING BOOKS
Tyndale House Publishers, Inc.
Wheaton, Illinois

Living Books is a registered trademark
of Tyndale House Publishers, Inc.

Third printing, December 1988

Library of Congress Catalog Card Number 87-51339
ISBN 0-8423-1751-1
Copyright 1988 by Jeannine Clarke-Dodels
Printed in the United States of America

CONTENTS

ONE

The Prisoner

The prisoner was an old man, though it would have been hard to guess how old, for the hair that swept back from his high forehead was still more brown than gray. And although his beard was somewhat grayer than the hair of his head, his eyes seemed to sparkle with the glow of youth. A strange color they were, too: grayish-green in a land of dark-eyed people.

Hanun, the guard, surveyed his charge curiously, longing to ask him who he was and what he had done to deserve confinement in King Manasseh's prison, but fear held him back.

The prisoner was no ordinary malefactor. He was a man of dignity, as anyone could tell by looking at him. His clothes were good; the brown linen robe he wore was decorated with elaborate bands of stitchery in gray and red around its hem. Some woman's hands had worked on it with patience and care. Somewhere there was someone who loved him—a wife, a daughter, perhaps? Hanun wondered, nervously fingering the ugly manacles he had been ordered to place on the prisoner's wrists.

"Do not be hesitant, young man." The prisoner's

voice was deep and without any trace of age. "You have a task you must perform. I do not blame you for it." He held out his hands, and Hanun saw that the traditional mark of prophets of Judah's God, Yahweh, was branded on the back of the prisoner's right hand. *Perhaps this explains why he has been arrested,* Hanun thought. King Manasseh had forbidden the prophets of Lord Yahweh ever to preach or teach in public. Yet the mark on the prisoner's hand was obviously an old scar, one he had borne for many years, starkly white in his sun-bronzed skin. There were other men in the kingdom who bore the prophet's brand, men who were silent now that Manasseh reigned, men apparently determined to forget what they had been in some earlier, better time.

In the old days, before Manasseh ruled, the whole land had acknowledged Yahweh as the one true God, and Hanun as a boy had been brought up to revere him and to respect his prophets. But now, while Manasseh's many other gods had their devotees, Yahweh, the Lord God of Israel and Judah, had seemingly become mute.

Hanun wished he could ask the prisoner to explain it all, for there was a look of understanding and patience and kindness in the old man's compelling gray-green eyes. And there was so much that Hanun wondered and wanted to know about God—and the gods.

Although prison rules strictly limited conversation between guards and inmates, the young man realized that this was an opportunity too valuable to ignore. "You were once a prophet of Yahweh," he offered hesitantly, more a question than a statement.

"I was, and still am, and will be while my life endures," the prisoner answered. "And so I have been brought to this place. But this . . . this circumstance will pass, as other trials have passed." The prisoner's voice was calm and steady as Hanun fastened the dreadful manacles about the man's wrists.

He was still speaking when Hanun noticed that the

man had another very interesting mark in the soft flesh of his inner arm. Just above the veins of his left wrist was tattooed the design of King David's star. The guard's curiosity mounted. "What is that on your arm?" he blurted out.

The prisoner smiled. "That," he said gently, "is a mark I had put on me when I was just a boy. Sixty years ago, no, almost seventy now. I'm afraid it's become rather faded after so long a time."

"But . . . it's King David's star. King Manasseh has it on his arm—just like yours. I've seen it," Hanun announced. "And I think the old king did, too. I've heard folks say it's the sign of the royal family."

"Yes, so it is." The prisoner looked pensively at the design on his arm and at the manacles encircling his wrists. Light from the one tiny west window streamed in and seemed to wrap him in an almost unearthly aura. Inexplicably, Hanun found himself in awe of this man who bore the sign of Judah's royalty, yet was also a prophet of Yahweh and now a prisoner as well. *It cannot be*, Hanun thought, *yet he has to be: Isaiah, the king's grandfather.*

"You know me," the prisoner spoke even as Hanun was thinking.

"You are Prince Isaiah?"

"Yes."

Hanun felt deep shame sweeping over him. *This should not be*, he thought. *This man is one of our country's most honored men. He is a great, and powerful servant of Yahweh. Whatever he has done, he cannnot have deserved to be treated like a common criminal. And besides, he is the king's grandfather.* "My prince, when King Manasseh discovers you are in here," Hanun began, "I'm sure he'll let you out at once. It's some kind of terrible mistake, sir, I'm sure. Here, let me remove those manacles."

Isaiah pulled away. "Let them be," he said. "There is no mistake. Manasseh already knows I am here. I am a prisoner by his order." The prophet's voice remained calm, but there was deep sadness in it now. "Eventually, he will kill me, too. I know that. But I have lived long already, and I am not afraid. Remember that, young man. Do not mourn for me. Mourn, if you will, for worse troubles that are to come—but not for me."

Had Hanun himself been sentenced to die at that instant he could not have been more stunned. "But, sir . . . my prince," he stammered helplessly.

"Isaiah—that is my name. That is all you need to call me. No titles. And your name?"

"Hanun."

"Yes. Well, Hanun . . ." Isaiah seemed for a moment lost in thought. "I am blessed indeed that Lord Yahweh has placed you as one of my guards, for there is something you can do for me."

The young man shivered. He was under orders not to converse with prisoners, yet here was Isaiah about to ask for some favor—Isaiah the magnificent, the great and wonderful prophet about whom Hanun had heard all his life. Hanun had always looked up to Isaiah, though he never dreamed they would meet face-to-face.

Recklessly, for a fleeting instant, the guard tried to put into words something of the tumult stirring within him. "Prince Isaiah," he stammered, "whatever you wish . . . if I am able." He did not want to put himself in danger, yet faced with an apparent injustice of staggering proportions, his own safety suddenly did not seem important. He was ready to risk his own life for Isaiah. He wished he could tell him so, but he could not.

"If you can, get word to my wife," Isaiah said. "She must be frightened and concerned about me. Our home is in the country, outside Jerusalem, on the north road toward Gibeah. Tell her . . ." He hesitated. "Tell her where I am and that whatever happens, she must *not* come into the city."

Hanun nodded. To locate the prophet's wife would

probably be simple enough. To convey Isaiah's message would, perhaps, be more difficult. The news of his imprisonment and the fact that he seemed to believe his very life was in danger would surely come as an unwelcome shock to the prophet's lady.

"Naamah is very courageous," Isaiah continued, as if reading Hanun's thoughts. "Yet this, no doubt, will be the hardest trial she has ever had to bear. Tell her that no man could have wished for a better wife than she has been to me these many years."

In his words there was finality and all the sadness of parting because Isaiah knew he was going to die, and the woman he had loved through a long lifetime would not be beside him when his time came. Years before they had lost their only daughter, gentle, lovely Hephzibah, the mother of the impossible Manasseh. Naamah had wept bitterly for Hephzibah, and now Naamah would weep for Isaiah, too.

"I must stay on duty through the night," Hanun told the prophet, "but in the morning I'll go and find her."

In her wide bed, the woman Naamah stirred uneasily, the night sadly still as she lay awake longing for Isaiah's return. In the old days she had slept alone many times when Isaiah was off on his travels or visiting at the king's palace. But in these last few years he had never left her, not until this morning. Though she did not want to admit it, she was deeply frightened. She wanted to know where he was, and, more than that, she wanted him home beside her. Though she was a courageous woman, Naamah did not relish being alone without knowledge of her husband's whereabouts.

She was not entirely alone. In the next room slept Ethan and Zina, the young couple who had, almost, taken the place of Naamah's own children. Ethan was young and strong and would staunchly protect the household should a thief break in, but Naamah's fears were not allayed by this thought. The danger she dreaded seemed to lurk within the shadows of her own room, the room she and Isaiah had shared for so many years.

This time he is gone forever. She felt the dreadful prospect inside her, and it was a thought without hope. "Lord Yahweh," Naamah whispered, "give me strength and protect my dear one!" Naamah believed in Yahweh's authority, his strength, and his ability to infuse in his followers courage and endurance beyond mere human powers. If only she could concentrate completely on the idea of Yahweh's protecting love! If only she could have complete trust that Isaiah would be safe.

But, she thought as she turned uneasily in her bed, *Lord Yahweh has never guaranteed any of us safety or happiness or anything of that sort. The Lord is our guide through trouble, but he has never promised that the troubles won't come.*

Finally, as the light of earliest morning crept into the room, Naamah drifted off into a dreamless sleep.

Through the long night, as Hanun patrolled the hall of the king's prison, Isaiah slept well. Several times during those seemingly endless hours, the guard peered into the prophet's cell. In the reflection of the pale moonlight that streamed through the one tiny window, he saw Isaiah lying still and peaceful on the wretched straw pallet that was his bed. Oblivious to the chain that bound his hands together, the discomfort of the hard floor, and even the chill that permeated the building's old stone walls, the prophet slept. *But it is only his first night in prison,* Hanun thought, *and heaven only knows how long he will remain here.* The entire situation seemed unreal. As the guard paced the hall, he thought of what he knew about King Manasseh and meditated on Isaiah's prospects for release.

Manasseh was a youth in his midteens, a man fully grown in the eyes of the law, yet willful and headstrong with the temper of a petulant child. Wildly irresponsible, he enjoyed to the fullest all that it meant to be king without any apparent concern for the sacred duty of his office.

Still, he would not kill his own grandfather. Certainly not, Hanun thought. It was simply inconceivable that any man, anywhere, could contemplate such a deed.

Very early the next morning Hanun set out on the north road to find the home of Naamah. The summer air was sweet, and the world in the light of early morning had never appeared so lovely, yet as he walked along, he felt deeply troubled. No matter how he had rationalized through the night, it was true that King Manasseh had absolutely forbidden the prophets of Yahweh to speak publicly or teach or write. For those who disobeyed, the prescribed penalty was death, and the sentence had been carried out already, more than once.

After more than an hour's journey, Hanun reached Isaiah's house. It was just as the prophet had described it, a stone dwelling of considerable size, lying comfortable and still in its own little valley. As he approached, he found himself wondering about the woman inside. *What is she like, and how will she bear the news?*

The voice of the young woman, Zina, roused Naamah from her brief slumber. "My lady, there is a stranger here from the city. He says he must see you. He brings word from Prince Isaiah."

Naamah sprang out of bed with an energy that belied her years. Hurriedly, with no real concern for appearance, she slipped on the dress she had worn the day before and tied a scarf over her long gray braids, which were much disheveled from her tossing and turning in the night. It was not a messenger she wanted to see, but Isaiah himself. Messengers had a way of bringing bad news. Yet how bad it was, she scarcely dared to imagine.

13

Then Hanun told her. The guard was prepared for weeping, and indeed, for a few moments, tears welled up in Naamah's eyes. But to his surprise, she did not dissolve into the spasms of grief he had expected.

"I must go to him," she said.

"But, my lady, Prince Isaiah said you must not."

Naamah sighed deeply. "Yes, he would say so. But I will go."

"It would be dangerous for you, my lady," Hanun protested. "Believe me, I feel confident the king will release him in a few days at most, and you'll have him safely home again."

Naamah shook her head. "Isaiah has always, always taught us we must have hope," she said slowly. "Lord Yahweh is with us through every trouble, and there are better days coming someday when the reign of peace comes to earth at last. I have always believed him and hoped, but now I am sure we shall not live to see it, neither myself nor my husband. Manasseh will kill him, and I . . . I will live on a while, but what will my life be without him?" Naamah's words were delivered in a slow, steady voice, sadder than if she had wept openly.

"He told me," Hanun said, groping for words of comfort, "that he could have wished for no finer wife than you."

Naamah closed her eyes. Through her mind a thousand images floated: memories of herself and Isaiah when they were both young, of their children—Jashub, Maher, and Hephzibah—and of Prince Hezekiah whom they had loved as if he were their own child—Hezekiah, who grew up to be king and who had married Hephzibah.

"Gone, all gone," she whispered. Naamah had always been a strong woman. Her confidence in Yahweh's plan for eventual good was very much a part of her, deeply embedded in her consciousness. It had sustained her through many heartaches. Yet now she felt the deepest emptiness of her long life, emptiness that only Isaiah could have filled. In other times of trouble, he had always been there to comfort her, to hold her close beside him.

Naamah's hands felt icy cold though the room was warm. She was shaking inside, her heart pounding uncomfortably. "Tell him I want to come to him," she said. It was hard to find the right words to say to the young stranger for Naamah was very reserved, one who usually kept her deepest thoughts to herself. "Will you see him again this evening?" she asked.

Hanun nodded.

"Tell him I love him," she said softly. "Of course, he knows, but tell him anyway." She paused. "Now if you will tarry, Zina will bring you food and drink before you must make your long walk back to the city. But I must beg you to excuse me."

She arose with the dignity of a princess, though unlike her husband, Naamah was not a born aristocrat. Without another word she left the room, and Hanun was left to contemplate the mystic beauty revealed in the love that bound Naamah and Isaiah.

A few moments later the young woman, Zina, entered with a plate of cheese and fruit and a cup of wine, which she placed on the table before Hanun. "Lady Naamah says you must eat," she announced.

Hanun, hungrier than he realized from his long walk, had no objection and consumed the food eagerly.

Zina lingered. She was very young, and her great dark eyes were pools of fear. Nervously her fingers toyed with the scarf that hung about her shoulders, pleating it into countless little folds. "Prince Isaiah—he is in trouble?" she asked hesitantly.

Hanun nodded. As he briefly explained the situation, the stunned look in Zina's eyes deepened. "Lady Naamah is dressing for a journey," she said when Hanun had ended his story. "She says she is going back into the city with you. Do you think that is wise?"

"No! She can't do that!" The guard rose with haste,

protesting loudly as he strode toward the door, his breakfast unfinished. "I must go at once." Nervous chills overcame his instilled sense of etiquette.

Once out of Naamah's house, Hanun practically ran. To allow her to return with him would be disastrous. Surely she would realize this when she found he was gone and, upon reconsidering, would keep herself safely at home. Then, as he walked along, a new thought worried him: perhaps she would attempt the journey by herself. It was a long walk for an old lady, and though Naamah seemed spryer and stronger than most women of her age, it would simply not be safe. Perhaps he should have stayed and tried to reason with her. His worries mounted. Perhaps the girl Zina might also try to make the journey, and since she was young and attractive, it would be even more unsafe for her now that Manasseh reigned. The old respect for Lord Yahweh's laws seemed to be disappearing fast.

Later that day as he tossed fitfully on his cot in the guardroom, Hanun was assailed by the fear that Naamah and Zina would come. But when he went back on guard duty in the late afternoon and there was still no sign of them, he felt somewhat reassured that Lady Naamah had realized the folly of the journey and had not attempted it after all.

Isaiah listened to Hanun's report of his visit.

"She wants very much to come to see you," Hanun concluded.

"Yes," Isaiah replied. "Yes, and I long to see her, too. But I fear for her."

It was at that moment that the door of Isaiah's cell opened and Kadmiel, one of the other guards, escorted Naamah in with a large basket over her arm.

"There he is, lady," Kadmiel said roughly. "As the king said, try to talk some sense into him."

Naamah ignored Kadmiel and Hanun as well. "Isaiah, my love!" she exclaimed. In a moment she was sitting beside him on his straw pallet, her arms about him, her head nestled against his shoulder. Embarrassed, Hanun looked away as Isaiah tried to embrace her. Those terrible manacles bound his wrists, and he lifted both hands helplessly.

"Chains," he said with a faint smile. Naamah grasped his hands and held them in her own.

"Ethan and Zina came into town with me," she said. "We're all going to stay at the city house so we can be close by until we've gotten you out of here. I've brought you some things." She opened the basket and began to extract its treasures. "Your good cloak and a nice pillow. No, better yet, *two* pillows," she announced with forced cheerfulness. "And some cheese and olives and a fresh loaf of bread Zina baked this morning just before we left."

Isaiah tossed the cloak around his shoulders. Though it was summer, the stone interior of his cell was uncomfortably cold. "You are good, Naamah," he whispered softly.

By duty, Hanun was obliged to stand guard, but he felt he must at least allow them a measure of privacy. Discreetly, he withdrew into the hall, beckoning to Kadmiel to join him. But even there he could hear their voices through the open doorway.

"Now, tell me everything," Naamah was saying as she again grasped his shackled hands in hers.

"Everything . . ." Isaiah sighed. He did not seem inclined to talk. There were a thousand questions Naamah wanted to ask, but it was better, she knew, simply to be still and listen to what he would tell her. Naamah had always been a wonderful listener, and over their long years together this man had at times poured out his heart to her. But, she remembered, there had been other times when she could not draw him out at all, when, in his passion to speak for Lord Yahweh, he had seemed so far away, so far beyond her.

Isaiah had always spoken of peace, yet in his boldness, at times, he had been far from peaceful. He had never hesitated to advise the kings of Judah—whether they wanted his advice or not. Countless times he had reprimanded the late King Hezekiah and implored him to change his policies and then grieved with him over his well-intentioned failures. Yet throughout those stressful years, there was the indestructible bond of devotion and loyalty between Isaiah and Hezekiah.

The crowning irony of it all was Manasseh—the fruit of the union of Hezekiah and Hephzibah. Manasseh carried in his veins not only the blood of the kings of Judah but also of Isaiah the prophet. Yet he felt nothing but contempt for his heritage and hated what he had sprung from. As a child he had frequently been sullen and full of rage, and now as a young man, in many ways he threatened the well-being of the kingdom he had inherited.

"Everything," Isaiah repeated. "Well, I came to the palace yesterday morning. I felt I had to talk to Manasseh, to try to reach him somehow. After all, he is our grandson. We talked, and when I refused to stop speaking about our God, he ordered me here. In due time, he plans to kill me, I am quite sure. He is the king, and I have broken his law."

"No, my love! No!" Naamah gasped. Isaiah had put into words the fear she had tried so hard to still. He did not reply, but he held her hands tightly. There was strength, courage, and love in his grasp. She clung to him, knowing that in moments she must let him go, perhaps forever. A host of haunting memories beset her. So much sorrow had she shared with Isaiah, but so much joy also. And occasional anger. Yes, that too, for when they were young, Naamah had sometimes found fault with him and tried to change some of his habits to suit her own ideas. But time had wiped away these youthful dissatisfactions. The love that had always existed between them grew deeper with the years. If the passions of their youth had faded, something yet more lovely had remained.

We have had so many years together, she thought, *more than most couples ever have. If he were sick, hopelessly ill, I could part with him with less pain, knowing his troubles would be ending. But he is still well and strong and might live years longer . . . and I need him.*

Aloud, to Isaiah, she could say nothing at all.

"Naamah," he said after long moments of silence, "I do not want to leave you. You know that. But all must die. We have always known that one of us would precede the other. Is that not so, my dearest?"

She nodded. "Yes, but it is so needless," she whispered. This was the agony of it all—that this man who had always lived for peace, who had spent his whole life deploring violence, should die violently.

"No, Naamah. Lord Yahweh's plan is never needless."

"Lord Yahweh's plan! It is Manasseh's plan—our despicable grandchild's evil plan—not the plan of our good God!"

"Manasseh is only the instrument through which my death shall come."

Naamah could find no answer. She was very tired, not merely from her sleepless night and her long walk into the city, but also from the far deeper weariness of despair. If only she could close her eyes and go to sleep in Isaiah's arms and awaken in a world where they would both be free—a world where Manasseh would not exist at all.

When Hanun entered a moment later, he found them still sitting there, side by side, comforting each other wordlessly by their nearness to each another. "Lady Naamah," he whispered.

Isaiah stood up, knowing that the time of parting had come. Reluctantly, Naamah also rose.

"Do not condemn Manasseh too much," Isaiah remarked solemnly. "He is—he always was—a child of the shadows. My heart aches for him."

"My heart aches only for you," replied Naamah. It was all she could say before Hanun escorted her from the cell, through the long hall of the prison, upstairs and out to the court of the guard, and then to the palace gate. In those moments, Hanun and Naamah spoke not a word.

Isaiah must live, Naamah thought as she walked through the twilight to the city house where she would find temporary refuge. Her heart beat rapidly though her steps were slow.

There must be a way, she thought as that night she lay sleepless in a lonely bed. "Lord Yahweh, help me!" she cried.

And in the stillness came the answer: Naamah must talk to her grandson.

Manasseh will certainly listen to me, she reasoned. It was with this thought in mind that she arose with the first light of dawn to prepare for a journey to the king's palace. *Perhaps none of us ever talked to Manasseh enough when he was a child, though Isaiah tried if anyone ever did.* The boy Manasseh had been an elusive little imp, subtle and stand-offish, unwilling ever to open his heart to those who wanted to love him. Naamah had found him utterly baffling in those days, so different from any of her own children, and so unlike his father, the demonstrative, enthusiastic Hezekiah.

But whatever else, Manasseh has never lacked for intelligence. He's a grown man now, Naamah thought, *but I can still reach him. I'll turn his heart back to Lord Yahweh. Perhaps it was for this mission I was born, for this Yahweh has given me such a long life, all for this: to teach my grandson about God's good purposes—and to save the life of my beloved Isaiah.*

Naamah's heart fairly sang with hope as she set out

that morning, thinking of the joys and sorrows of years gone by. And now, with the Lord's help, she would unfold these things to Manasseh that he, too, might understand and love the roots from which he sprang.

TWO

The Dawn Days

As Isaiah once again adjusted to the quietness of his cell, he also became more acutely aware of how dark his place of confinement was. The flame of love between Isaiah and his beloved Naamah had brightened every corner for the few moments she was there.

In the darkness Isaiah smiled. Naamah had always brightened his life, even when she was a young girl scarcely aware of his existence. As far as Naamah was concerned, Isaiah was simply one of the numerous children—the oldest son—of Prince Amoz, an aristocrat with close ties of kinship to the royal house of Judah. Amoz's estate, just outside Jerusalem, adjoined that of Naamah's father, Yosef, and Naamah was a childhood friend of Isaiah's younger sisters. Together they had giggled and shared secrets as little girls have always done, generally ignoring the slightly older Isaiah, who was growing up in their midst.

Isaiah remembered that it was during this time he acquired the wooden storage chest that would always remain one of his most prized possessions. The sturdy box had been made by one of Prince Amoz's tenants, who gave it to his landlord some years earlier in payment of rent. Designed to hold clothing or bedding, it was crafted of cypress wood, substantial and practical, but rather ugly. Amoz, with a houseful of princely furniture, deposited it in the loft of one of his barns, and completely forgot about it, until young Isaiah found it—dusty, neglected, and empty. . . .

"There's an old chest in the loft, Father. May I have it?" Isaiah's eyes sparkled with the inexpressible joy that sees the usefulness and the beauty in something nobody else wants.

"That old cypress box that Ben-neriah made?" Amoz looked askance at his little son, who was covered with dust and cobwebs from prowling about in the loft. "Whatever would you want with that?"

"To keep things in . . . important things."

"Well, I suppose there's no harm in it," Amoz assented. The box found its way from the barn to an honored spot at the foot of Isaiah's bed.

Isaiah's mother frowned. "It's so unsightly," she said.

"I'll fix it up," replied Isaiah, lovingly caressing its lid. The soft wood, already scarred and battered, seemed to invite carving, and in his mind he envisioned it adorned in splendor. But youthful dreams are often far from reality. It was with more zeal than artistry that the boy spent many happy hours whittling a curious hodgepodge of designs into the box's surface. Across the lid, in bold uneven characters was his name, Isaiah. There were palm trees and pomegranates and King David's star with numerous variations—and incomprehensible squiggles that defied description.

Inside were Isaiah's potsherds—discarded bits and pieces of broken dishes. Papyrus, imported from Egypt, was expensive and used only for the most important writing, but potsherds were excellent material for recording little notes of every sort. Isaiah collected them avidly because there was so much he wanted to write down.

As he thought back over the years, Isaiah could not remember a time *before* the poems, the songs, had started to come to him. But he did remember vividly how he had first become aware of the value of the written word. He was just a tiny lad then. It was several years before his acquisition of the cypress box. . . .

"I made a song!" Isaiah, breathless with excitement, came running into the house to find his mother. "Listen, Mama!"

It was a simple ditty, something about green hills and blue skies, but Maacah listened with pride, and later that evening, Amoz listened, too, impressed with his little son's uncommon gift for the metrical sounds of words.

"Let's write it down," Amoz said, and the child Isaiah watched in wonder as his father inscribed his words in black ink on a clay potsherd.

It was the first of many. They were not all his own, for often in the early twilight, his mother would sing to him and to the younger children, age-old songs from across the generations. The young mother's voice was sweet and clear.

"Let's write down all the words, Mama," Isaiah said as he sat on the floor at his mother's feet, listening to a fascinating ballad of the Israelites' wanderings in the wilderness. His little sister slept in her mother's lap and an even smaller brother lay in a cradle nearby as Maacah sang. Isaiah suddenly slipped away and quickly returned, clasping in his hands a big potsherd, a piece of a recently broken dinner plate, smooth and unmarked. "We can put a lot of words on this," he said hopefully.

Maacah, blissfully illiterate, did not share her son's passion for the written word. "Why under the sun would anyone want to do that?" she asked. "We know the words already."

"But, Mama, if they're written down, they won't be forgotten. Ever."

"Child, you know I can't write. Your father will have to teach you, and then you can write down whatever you please."

So Amoz had taught the boy to read and write, a task that proved rewarding, for learning seemed to come effortlessly to young Isaiah. He breathed in the wonderful business of the written word. There simply weren't enough things written down to satisfy him. By the time Isaiah was nine or ten, Amoz was borrowing precious scrolls from the palace archives to bring home to his son.

Isaiah loved history, especially the stories of the kings who had ruled in centuries past, many of them his own ancestors. He loved, too, the tales of even earlier times, of the time when Lord Yahweh first created mankind and the earth was new and unspoiled. His memory for details, for the orderly succession of events, was superb, and he was a natural-born story teller.

Amoz and Maacah sometimes overheard him retelling stories to the younger children, and their hearts glowed with pride in their firstborn son. "He will be a fine scholar," Amoz often said. "And if ever he has to work for a living, he could be a scribe."

"Or a musician," reflected Maacah.

If there was anything Isaiah loved as much as reading and writing, it was music. No one taught him to sing. The melodious tones were simply there, a gift. No one taught him to play the various musical instruments that Amoz bought for him in the little shops of Jerusalem. Isaiah had only to touch a stringed instrument of any sort and in a few moments it was at home in his hands, and the air was filled with sweet music.

"He is like King David," Amoz remarked. If anyone dared to say that a prince should devote himself to more important things than music, there was always the example of the great psalmist king to be called to mind.

Young Isaiah learned all of David's psalms, and as he sang and played them, it gave him special delight to remember that it was his many-times-great-grandfather who wrote them nearly three centuries before. Across all that long span of time, the same God had been watching over the land of Judah, promising steadfast love forever to his people. It was a wonderful thought, something Isaiah found marvelous to ponder.

As Isaiah grew to young manhood, his voice changed from its clear boyish treble to a beautiful, deep baritone. His body grew tall, taller than most of the men of Judah, and though he could not be considered really handsome, he was most definitely striking in appearance, with thick, light brown hair that swept back from a high, aristocratic forehead. His mother worried that his nose was too long, too prominent, that he was too thin and bony, and that his skin was too pale. But no one could deny the fascination of those deep-set gray-green eyes, so sparkling with life and enthusiasm.

Amoz saw to it that young Isaiah went often to the king's palace so he could learn the ways of courtly life and make friends with the other young aristocrats. Those were the days when Isaiah's uncle, the prince regent Jotham, ruled Judah. Jotham was a big, hearty, essentially good-natured man caught in a difficult position of regency for his ailing father, Uzziah, who had leprosy.

Although a royal leper, Isaiah's grandfather did not have to suffer the degradation of wandering about the countryside, shunned and despised, begging for sustenance. However, he was still an outcast from society, dwelling alone in a little house far from the royal palace with a few faithful servants to attend him, sentenced to a living death.

Isaiah had never known his grandfather well. Though he did recall occasional childhood visits to the king's palace before Uzziah's illness, he could scarcely remember what his grandfather looked like. Yet frequently he worried about him.

Sometimes Isaiah's father and Uncle Jotham would talk about it. "He is well taken care of," Jotham often said. "I have done everything possible that I can do for him. He does not really suffer. Lepers don't, you know. But he is almost blind, and the servants say he is terribly disfigured. I wish he would let me visit him, but he refuses." Prince Jotham sighed deeply. "His mind is as clear as a young man in the prime of life. That is the greatest tragedy of all."

To young Isaiah, listening to his uncle's reflections, this seemed a strange remark. Surely to be clear of mind, to understand what was going on around him, could only be a blessing. Isaiah remembered asking his father about it as they journeyed home to Amoz's estate outside the city wall.

Prince Amoz, the child of one of Uzziah's concubines, had never really been close to his father, neither did he feel the deep grief and guilt of his half brother, Jotham the regent. Yet Amoz understood well what Jotham meant. "It is sad for the old king to be so aware of his illness, to know he will never get well. To live without hope is worse than death."

"Why doesn't Lord Yahweh heal him?" asked Isaiah. It was an enigma to him. God was good—God wanted the best for his children—yet he let the old king live on and on, an outcast from his people.

"I truly do not know," Amoz answered. "There are some things we just don't understand."

A most unsatisfactory answer, Isaiah thought, and if he let himself ponder it much, he worried.

Once he even discussed the matter with Jotham's son, Ahaz. It was a day he long remembered, a beautiful, warm spring afternoon when the palace gardens were full of flowers and the sky above them was full of puffy little clouds. Isaiah and Ahaz, cousins, sat at the edge of the fish pond in one of the palace courtyards. Ahaz, a few years younger than Isaiah, a handsome boy with striking red hair, was idly tossing pebbles into the pond while Isaiah played his lute and sang one of the old psalms about Yahweh's protective love:

> "Yahweh is my light and my salvation.
>   Whom shall I fear?"

Ahaz did not care much for music. He could not carry a tune, nor bring harmonious sounds from any stringed instrument.

Isaiah sang on alone.

> "Yahweh will hide me in his shelter.
> He will conceal me under
>   the cover of his tent.
> He will set me high upon a rock."

Suddenly Ahaz interrupted and asked in an angry voice, "If Yahweh cares so much for all of us, then why is our grandfather so sick? Tell me that, Isaiah!"

Isaiah's song broke off, and he placed his lute carefully on the grass at his side. Anguish filled his young cousin's eyes.

"You don't remember him like I do," Ahaz went on. "I have always lived here in the palace and used to see him every day before he got sick."

Isaiah sighed deeply. The standard answer, of course, was that illness and all sorts of other disasters—famines, plagues, and war—were punishments sent by the Lord Yahweh. Throughout most of the history of Israel, which Isaiah had studied so carefully, this explanation made very good sense. Yet it was hard to see how it applied in the case of King Uzziah. He had been one of Judah's best-loved kings and a loyal follower of Yahweh. Could it be that Yahweh himself could not help what had happened?

"He was a wonderful man," Ahaz continued. "A good

man. I loved him so much." The young prince's lips trembled. These were things he scarcely ever spoke about. Isaiah marveled that his cousin would reveal such feelings to him, for he knew that Ahaz didn't even like him.

"Sometimes," Isaiah said, mustering thoughts he scarcely understood himself, "I think things just *happen*. In the beginning when Lord Yahweh formed the earth, there was chaos everywhere, but he took it and changed it into an orderly, beautiful world. Only there's still some of that chaos around, and sometimes it works against Yahweh's plan."

"You know what I think?" Ahaz replied, completely unimpressed by Isaiah's statement. "I think there are many gods out there, and if Lord Yahweh won't help, then you find one who will."

"Oh, no!" Isaiah protested. "Those others are just idols, and our grandfather forbade their worship long ago."

"Yes, and look what happened to him," Ahaz countered.

Suddenly Isaiah realized that this cousin of his, moody, sullen Ahaz, would most likely be king someday. A wave of dismay swept through him. Things might be difficult indeed, if ever Ahaz ruled in Judah.

THREE

Here Am I! Send Me!

Life was pleasant and uncomplicated for Isaiah in that long-ago time of his youth, and then suddenly, in the year that King Uzziah died, an event occurred that changed the course of his entire life.

The newly crowned King Jotham was holding a great festival at Lord Yahweh's temple beside the royal palace. Multitudes gathered in the temple courtyard to pray and sing, looking forward to the feasting and celebrating that would follow after sacrifices were offered and the festal meal distributed to the crowd.

With the favored few, the high-ranking priests and the immediate royal family, Isaiah entered the temple. The air was heavy with the smoke of incense. Priests chanted, and the very walls of the building seemed to reflect the radiance of Yahweh's holiness.

Then without warning, Isaiah suddenly saw a vision of Lord Yahweh and his seraphim. They were *there*—actually present in the temple. The chanting of the priests was replaced by the voices of the six-winged seraphim calling to each other, "Holy, holy, holy is Lord Yahweh the Almighty. The whole earth is full of his glory."

Isaiah instantly fell to his knees, trembling. He had never heard or seen anything like the glorious display he now witnessed. In view of the splendor which surrounded him, he suddenly saw himself as wretched and filthy before Almighty God, the Holy One of Israel.

"Woe is me!" The words tumbled out of Isaiah's mouth. "Woe is me! For I am lost. I cannot even praise Yahweh, for my lips are unclean. I am altogether unclean before my holy God, and I live in a whole company of unclean people. But my eyes have seen the King, the Lord Almighty."

As if in answer to Isaiah, one of the seraphim took a pair of tongs, lifted a glowing coal from the sacrificial altar of the temple, and flew toward the trembling young prince, who remained on his knees.

His heart pounding in his chest, Isaiah stiffened in fear as the seraph brought the burning coal nearer and at last touched it to Isaiah's lips with a searing hiss. The poet-prince winced with the pain but did not cry out.

Immediately the seraph spoke. "Behold, this has touched your lips. Your guilt is removed, your sin forgiven."

Isaiah felt numb, and then an indescribable joy arose within him.

Then came the voice of Yahweh himself. "Whom shall I send, and who will go for us?"

The question sent shudders through Isaiah's body, but with all the fervency and optimism of youth, the poet-prince immediately responded, "Here am I! Send me!"

How many times in the years that followed had Isaiah tried to describe what he had seen that day in the temple! It was beyond explanation. Sometimes he could hear the voice of Yahweh whispering within him, but never in his long life would he see another vision with seraphim and smoke and glowing coals. Perhaps it was but a dream, yet perhaps it was the divine ecstasy that goes beyond the grasp of human words. Isaiah never really knew.

He only knew that something had happened, something had irrevocably changed him and filled him with a sense of commitment to Yahweh's service that he would never lose.

After his vision, he sought out a colony of "sons of the prophets." For many weeks he lived there with other disciples of an aged master prophet named Oded, seeking to understand what Yahweh's calling meant. Isaiah was, and would always be, an aristocrat, while most of the "sons of the prophets" came from among the very poor, the illiterate, and, regrettably, often the ignorant.

His weeks at the camp were a time of testing, of preparation for more important things. Life was no longer pleasantly uncomplicated. Isaiah had been chosen to be the carrier of Yahweh's message to the court of the kings of Judah. He who was born to the royal family could speak where no ordinary man could.

During the summer of his spiritual awakening, Isaiah decided to have the mark of Yahweh's service branded on his right hand. This was the usual practice for men committed to the prophetic vocation, and although Master Oded had been most reluctant to allow it in Isaiah's case, the youthful prince was so determined that at last Oded relented. The brand—the curious symbol of entwined letters standing for "belonging to Yahweh"—was burned indelibly into Isaiah's flesh, the visible sign that he meant to live by his decision forever.

Like all the young princes of Judah, in his early boyhood Isaiah had had the star of King David tatooed on his left arm. This was the symbol of royalty, the indication of his princely birth, and no man who ever bore the royal star had also borne the slave brand of Yahweh. Yet Isaiah was proud of both symbols, as different as they were in significance. Together they reflected much of the essence of what he was: the prophet-prince.

The kingdom of Judah had never had a prophet-prince

before, and the Judeans were unsure at first what to think of Isaiah. His own father, Prince Amoz, was stunned and seemed hurt by Isaiah's commitment to Yahweh's service. His mother determined to act as though it had never happened. Isaiah's Uncle Jotham, king at last after so many years of regency, vaguely admired his nephew's sense of dedication and otherwise ignored him. But Jotham's son, Ahaz, the crown prince, was openly scornful.

Still, Isaiah was young and full of hope. Yahweh had chosen him to bring the message of spiritual awakening and reform. It was so simple, so wonderful! And with Yahweh's help, he, Isaiah ben-Amoz of Jerusalem, would be the agent who would bring it all about.

How it was best to go about his mission, young Isaiah was not at all sure. Prophets did not necessarily have to make predictions, but certainly they had to speak forth for Lord Yahweh and try to make people see that true devotion to God was not just a matter of going through the right rituals at the temple, chanting the right prayers, and celebrating the right holidays. It was, rather, a matter of how one treated his fellow human beings, and in the world around him, Isaiah clearly saw that human beings often treated each other very badly indeed. To follow Yahweh's will meant striving for right relationships among men. It meant striving for peace.

If true peace were ever to come on earth, people simply had to learn to walk in better ways, and it was his mission to guide them there. With all his heart he was trying, yet shortly after his call to Yahweh's service he sadly began to realize that his efforts were yielding few results.

Still, there was no turning back from his commitment. The symbol branded on his hand was only the outward reminder that he had promised his whole life to Lord Yahweh. It was never going to be an easy life, Isaiah knew, and sometimes as the months and seasons slipped by, he felt his optimism giving way to despair.

How long, O Lord? he often wondered. Yet he knew full well Yahweh's answer: "Forever, while your life endures."

It was during the frequent discouraging periods of those early years that the Lord sent Isaiah consolation and hope in the form of Naamah, the neighbor girl he had known all his life. As their friendship grew, Naamah became an understanding and devoted partner. Isaiah was not yet twenty when he married her; she was several years younger. Love—enduring and steadfast love—was one of Yahweh's greatest gifts.

Naamah was no meek creature without a mind of her own. She was, rather, a strong-willed, deep-thinking young woman. She was deeply devoted to Yahweh, and from the moment she learned of Isaiah's commitment to the prophetic task, she was just as devoted to Isaiah himself. While his own relatives found his choice of vocation incomprehensible, Naamah understood him. In her, too, there were longings to be a prophet of Yahweh, dreams that as a woman she could scarcely hope to fulfill.

Isaiah called her "my prophetess." She was the only woman he ever really wanted, the only woman he would ever love.

Just to look at them, they were an unlikely pair. The wife of tall, slender Isaiah was short and plump, a dusky, dark-complexioned girl with very straight black hair wrapped in a neat little knot at the back of her neck. To most men's eyes Naamah was deemed uncommonly plain, almost homely. And Isaiah was, in the words of some, *difficult.* Commitment to Lord Yahweh's service meant that he frequently made trips into Jerusalem, preached on street corners, and sometimes sang to get the crowd's attention—all very unprincely behavior.

Isaiah's parents and Naamah's, who had taken delight in arranging the match, were nonetheless surprised that the young couple seemed so genuinely devoted to each other.

As the eldest son of Prince Amoz, the young prophet had no immediate worries about the matter of providing a living for himself and his bride. Amoz was the owner of vast tracts of land, and when Isaiah married, his father's gift was a large and comfortable farmhouse and acreage in the country, a few miles north of Jerusalem.

There were dependent tenants, who lived in smaller cottages close by to tend Isaiah's fig and olive trees, and shepherds to watch his flocks in the nearby hills. While the income from these various enterprises was always sufficient to maintain Isaiah's household respectably, his personal gains would never be large because he had no head for business nor any interest in the accumulation of personal wealth.

In time Naamah proved to be far more competent than her husband in the management of their property, and he gladly let these responsibilities fall into her hands. *How fortunate it was*, Isaiah thought, looking back across the years, *that Naamah persuaded me to teach her the basic fundamentals of reading and writing!*

It was early in their marriage when Naamah first had the yen to master the unwomanly skills of literacy, a day when she and Isaiah were moving into their new home, that she had her first encounter with Isaiah's cypress box. There it sat, battered, scarred, and ugly, in the center of their spacious bedroom. The bride Naamah stared at it with obvious distaste. Unquestionably, it couldn't stay where it was. She nudged it with her knee and was surprised to realize it was quite heavy. "Isaiah! Whatever do you want to do with this old chest?" she called. He was in another room, moving furniture, helping to get things settled. "Don't you think it could go into a storeroom somewhere?"

Isaiah dashed into the room in defense of his prized possession. "No, indeed, dear. That stays beside my bed." Carefully, he pushed it to a place against the wall by his bedside, and Naamah heard the rattle of pottery. Curiosity struggled with her inbred restraint. Obviously the box was not a clothes chest, and she longed to see inside it to see what valuables it might contain.

Yet Isaiah was not inclined to open it or to explain its contents. He was not a secretive man. He simply assumed that Naamah had already looked into the box and found nothing of interest since she was illiterate like most women.

For the first time in the brief days of their marriage, the young couple had reached a communication impasse. As Isaiah turned to leave the room, Naamah, hurt and frustrated, burst into tears. "Well, if I have to live with it, you could at least tell me why it's so important."

"Didn't you look inside?"

"No, certainly not."

Isaiah returned to the box and lifted its lid. There were the potsherds and a few small scrolls neatly wrapped in woolen cloths. A deep wooden tray held jars of ink and carefully cut reed pens.

Naamah peered at the box's contents, lifted one of the potsherds and held it uncertainly, unsure which way the letters ran. Deep longings stirred within her. Here on these fragments of clay was the fruit of Isaiah's service to Lord Yahweh. Here, in characters beyond her comprehension, was the very essence of her husband's soul. Naamah felt a deep sadness entirely out of harmony with the joyous love she had for her young husband. "Do you think I could ever learn to read and write?" she asked softly.

The question took Isaiah by surprise. His mother and sisters had never shown the slightest inclination toward literacy. It was something women really didn't need. Of course, there were some women who had mastered the arts of reading and writing. Only recently Prince Ahaz had boasted that *his* bride, Lady Abijah, had acquired these skills in her childhood. "It is most convenient," Ahaz had commented, "since we're able to send each other little secret messages."

Naamah's voice interrupted Isaiah's train of thought. "I think I could learn," she said timidly, "if you would teach me." Carefully she replaced the potsherd and closed the lid of the box. "You could start by telling me what it says here on the lid."

On the lid in the straggling, hesitant carving of his boyhood, was simply inscribed his name, Isaiah. Somewhat startled, he realized she could not read even that. This young woman, who was just as much a thinker and a child of Lord Yahweh as he, stood cut off from the whole wonderful world of the written word.

"Of course, I'll teach you," he said. Who was he to object to the shattering of tradition in a good cause? There was, after all, a reason for everything in Yahweh's plan. Perhaps Yahweh had a reason for Naamah to learn to read and write.

Ironically, in spite of her initial eagerness to learn, Naamah did not take rapidly to literacy. Isaiah was patient, and Naamah made progress, but her attention tended to wander.

"It's so *hard!*" she exclaimed one afternoon as she and Isaiah sat at the large table where he regularly worked on his own writings. "So many words seem to be spelled just alike, or almost so, and you just have to guess. And some of the letters look so much like others."

"It will get easier if you really work at it," he assured her.

Naamah was not really sure she liked this sort of work, but neither did she want to disappoint Isaiah. As she sat quietly, here eyes strayed from the little scroll spread out on the table. She contemplated the young man who was her husband. His hands, resting lightly on the scroll, were long-fingered and graceful, a musician's hands, yet on the right one there was that deep scar, the brand of Lord Yahweh's prophets. Isaiah had spoken to her about it only a few times—of his determination to have it, of the terrible pain in receiving it—but most of the time the mark was ignored.

Now Naamah grasped Isaiah's hand and gently caressed it. "How does it really feel to have this on you?" she asked finally. While Naamah admired Isaiah for choosing to bear the mark, she was very conscious of it, aware of this visible sign that he was somehow set apart by God from ordinary humanity for a specific purpose. This was something wonderful and made her love him even more. How she longed to be able to tell him so!

"You mean, am I conscious of it all the time?" Isaiah replied. "That worries you, doesn't it, my love?"

"Yes, I suppose it does."

"How does it feel?" Isaiah repeated. "Well, it is a great responsibility and sometimes a great burden. There are times when I feel unworthy of it, for who am I to have presumed to enter the service of our God? And yes, a few months ago, when I first had the mark put on me, I was conscious of it every waking moment. There were even times when I was sorry I'd had it done. But I've grown used to it now, and I'm glad it's there as a reminder of what Yahweh expects of me. I'm sure you understand that, don't you?"

Naamah nodded but did not reply. She simply lifted Isaiah's hand to her lips and kissed it, saying by her action what she could not say in words. It was a precious moment to be cherished forever.

There were many other precious moments. Isaiah remembered times when he and his bride would lie in each other's arms on a comfortable pallet on the rooftop porch of their new home, watching the brilliant sunset as summer's scorching heat subsided. To see the sky grow dark and the first stars emerge from its deepening blackness was a pleasure both Naamah and Isaiah had loved since childhood. In the spreading panorama of the heavens, Lord Yahweh seemed very real, nearer than he ever seemed at family festivals or in the crowded courtyards of the temple.

By the autumn following their marriage, Naamah was pregnant, and Isaiah, delighted with the prospective birth of his first child, was also beginning to think about his service to Yahweh. The masses of Judah might never be reached by his preaching, but there were always the faithful few, the people who really listened and wanted to follow in God's path—"The Remnant," Naamah called them, the faithful, righteous Remnant. And though few in numbers, there was a chance their ranks might grow as others turned to follow the better way.

With this thought in mind, Isaiah traveled almost daily into the city of Jerusalem, spoke publicly wherever he could find an audience, and sat at the council table of King Jotham as was his right as a prince of Judah.

In due time Naamah gave birth to her first child. They called him Shear-jashub—"A Remnant shall return." It was such a strange name that people could not help but comment upon it, and Isaiah was always pleased to have an opportunity to explain. But it was quite a long name for a little boy, so when Naamah took to calling him simply "Jashub," Isaiah really didn't mind.

The boy was a happy, healthy, lovable child, dark like Naamah. Isaiah, who had come from a house full of younger brothers and sisters, was immeasurably pleased to have a child of his own.

By the time Jashub was walking, he idolized his father and would have followed him everywhere if he could.

Naamah, happy and deeply occupied by the time-consuming tasks of motherhood, slackened her efforts at learning to read. There were so many more important things to do! *There will be time for that later,* she rationalized. Isaiah, busy with his daily trips to the city, did not pressure her.

Alarming rumors of war continued stirring at King Jotham's court. Plans surfaced for Judah to join a coalition with other small kingdoms in a concerted effort to overthrow Assyria, the mightiest nation on earth.

Young as he was, Isaiah could see the foolhardiness of these schemes and spoke vigorously against them in public and at the king's council table. But those who really counted, Jotham and his advisors, seemed unmoved.

Perhaps to atone for disregarding his young nephew's pleas, Jotham presented Isaiah with a house near the royal palace, safely inside the walled city of Jerusalem. The king had recently acquired the property in payment of a debt and had no real use for it himself. Why not give it to Isaiah? "So you won't have to travel so many miles every day," Jotham told him. "Bring that young wife and son of yours and settle in Jerusalem."

Isaiah's first reaction to the house was one of considerable confusion and surprise. As much as he disliked the thought of acquiring additional property, he did not dare refuse the king's gift.

The old house was built of stone, constructed perhaps a century or two earlier, although no one seemed to know its exact origin. An unpretentious front door opened directly onto a much-traveled street near the palace. Inside there was one very large main room with an imposing stone fireplace. Steps along the interior wall led to a trapdoor that opened onto the flat rooftop. As was true of many houses in the land of Judah, the roof area provided another floor of living space and promised to be the most pleasant part of the house.

Behind the house was a large, enclosed courtyard with all the conveniences of city life, even a latrine in a tiny closet of its own. Further back on the property was a stable for the household animals, a superior arrangement indeed, since more often than not the stable room adjoined the family's living quarters.

Upon inspecting the property further, Isaiah decided that it did have possibilities. In many ways he was a city-dweller at heart. He loved Jerusalem. And since his real mission in life was to serve as a spokesman for Yahweh at the king's court, the city house would be infinitely more convenient. Perhaps he could convey his country place back to his father or to one of his younger brothers.

But he had not considered Naamah's reaction.

The next day they left little Jashub with Isaiah's sister and went into Jerusalem to look at their newly acquired house.

Isaiah opened the front door proudly, and Naamah contemplated the large, empty room in dismay.

"It has no rooms," she said softly, as if stunned. "It's all open. Where would we sleep?"

"On the roof in good weather, I suppose, and down here when it's cold. Look at this splendid fireplace."

"We have three fireplaces at home," Naamah said "and seven rooms. Where would Jashub sleep here? On the roof, with us? And the other ones yet to be born? On the roof? Oh, no, Isaiah! We have a good house with *rooms* and *walls* and lovely trees outside, and open fields. You would bring your family here to be crowded together in one room? No, Isaiah! No." Her dark eyes blazed. She was a small bundle of resistance, adamant and determined.

"But, Naamah—"

"Walls and rooms are so very necessary," she adamantly continued. "When you write you must have peace and serenity. Where would you write here? On the roof, I suppose? And in bad weather?" The scorn in her voice was evident. It was her way of covering deeper emotions.

He had not anticipated Naamah's opposition. On most occasions she was as acquiescent as wives were traditionally supposed to be. Or was that because they rarely disagreed? "Not just for me, Isaiah, but for Jashub and our other children yet to come," she continued, "and for yourself and your mission for Yahweh. Oh, Isaiah, I beg of you, please do not bring us to this house!"

A little woman with a will of iron was Naamah.

"What am I to tell the king?" Isaiah asked, his defenses crumbling.

"Oh, we must keep the place, I suppose," Naamah remarked. "We can stay here occasionally. Better yet, maybe you can lend it to your brother. Tell the king you are grateful for his bountiful kindness but your wife prefers the country."

"He will laugh me to scorn," Isaiah replied. Jotham would indeed make Isaiah the object of his ricicule. He would laugh at the foolish young husband much too willing to listen to his wife. But that would be the end of it. Isaiah did not mind ridicule if it meant keeping Naamah happy. Her dislike of the house was so intense he would never want to force her to live there.

He was obliged to keep the place, but for the time being he loaned it, for nothing, to the younger brother next to him in age, who now had a bride of his own and was delighted with a city house.

Occasionally in those early years, Isaiah and Naamah and their family visited and slept on the roof—in good weather. Little did they realize how important the city house would become to them in the future.

FOUR

In the Days of Ahaz

King Jotham died young, and in contrast to his father's years of isolated anguish, Jotham's death was mercifully sudden, the result, no doubt, of massive heart failure.

And now Ahaz, twenty years old, was king, and the land of Judah began to change overnight. Isaiah watched, appalled, as the worship of many gods, illegal during Jotham's reign, suddenly became open and widely accepted. In the high places throughout the countryside, new altars were erected to the old Canaanite god and goddess, Baal and Ashtoreth. Judeans who had been at least nominally true to the precepts of Yahweh now turned openly to these less demanding fertility deities, who not only permitted but encouraged every sort of licentious behavior.

Worst of all was Ahaz's enthusiastic sponsorship of his own particular favorite, Molech, the fire god of the Ammonites. A bloodthirsty figure of frightening proportions, he was yet one whom Ahaz, for reasons that Isaiah could not comprehend, considered a specially powerful protector.

Isaiah's daily walks from his country house to the city

were a time of meditation and preparation for his work, preaching to the people in Jerusalem. Ahaz himself seemed unreachable. Although the prophet continued to visit the palace, there was such a deep chill between him and the king that real communication was almost impossible.

Yet, oddly enough, on one matter of vital importance, Ahaz and Isaiah agreed. Both of them deplored needless war. Jotham's plans for joining the anti-Assyrian coalition of the Westlands hung in abeyance.

And then, one evening, despite all the discouraging new trends in Ahaz's kingdom, Isaiah returned home almost buoyant with new hope. "The king announced today that he is going to refuse to bring Judah into the coalition!" Isaiah exclaimed as he seated himself on a bench near the fireplace. He motioned Naamah to his side.

"I hope," said Naamah, "that this is as good as you think."

"Of course it's good! Judah has nothing at all to gain from such a foolhardy scheme. We're not a tributary state. I can understand, even though I feel they're terribly wrong, why King Rezin of Syria and King Pekah of Israel want this international uprising. Their kingdoms are under a terrible burden of tribute payments to Tiglath-pileser of Assyria. For them and for their people, rebellion offers a glimmer of hope for something better— very small, faint hope, yet somehow to them it seems better than nothing."

"But Judah has never had to pay tribute," Naamah said. "I can't see why Pekah and Rezin and all the rest of their allies ever thought Judah would join in their schemes."

"King Jotham was a man of war," Isaiah answered, "and he was surrounded by a whole council of men of war—Elkanah the prime minister, Azrikam the chief steward, and General Ben-tabeel—all of them. They say war is good for a country. I remember that before Uncle

Jotham died, Elkanah made a ridiculous speech about how a war would pull the people of Judah together, give us a spirit of unity, and that Yahweh was on our side. Oh, what fools! What fools they are!" Isaiah's voice rose passionately. "Lord Yahweh gave us life, and when man destroys it, he is destroying God's most wonderful gift!" The prophet's eyes flashed. "'I set before you life and death: choose life.' That's what Moses said to our people long ago."

Isaiah's burst of oratory was broken as little Jashub, not quite three, entered the room. Shouting with delight, he ran into his father's open arms. Isaiah gathered him onto his lap and bounced him about happily while Jashub chattered the nonsense that Isaiah adored.

Before Naamah's eyes the impassioned, young prophet was transformed into a doting father whose worries were momentarily erased by the presence of his little son. It was as good a time as any, Naamah reasoned, to announce her news.

"Isaiah, we are going to have another child," she whispered softly.

"Jashub!" Isaiah turned to the child in his lap, who was too young to comprehend Naamah's message. "Did you hear that? You're going to have a little brother or sister. You're going to *be* a brother, and that's something wonderful!"

Jashub looked confused. "Brother," he repeated uncertainly. Isaiah held him close in his arms.

No one, least of all Isaiah and Naamah, anticipated the disastrous results of Ahaz's refusal to join the anti-Assyrian alliance. Though news traveled slowly, it was only a few days before the Judean envoy, General Bentabeel, was in Samaria at the court of the Israelite king, Pekah, to report Ahaz's decision. A week or two later a joint force of Israelites and Syrians invaded Judah, cutting a wide path of devastation across the country. After annihilating a Judean force at Gibeah, the invaders headed straight toward Jerusalem.

"If Ahaz won't cooperate, we'll remove him and find a king who will," was Pekah's ultimatum. He even had his handpicked candidate: Ahaz's envoy-turned-renegade, Ben-tabeel, a man with only the remotest connections to the royal family of Judah.

From the villages and countryside near Jerusalem, people swarmed into the strong-walled city. Among them was Isaiah's family, for which the city house was waiting, a place of comparative safety in a land where things were rapidly falling apart. Isaiah left Naamah at the city house with his brother and sister-in-law while he set out with a servant and little Jashub on one more trip to the country place. Valued posessions had to be rescued if possible: clothes, dishes, and above all, Isaiah's cypress box. The prophet and his servant borrowed an ox cart to transport the household goods. Sadly, Isaiah went about the heartrending task of deciding what was worth saving—mostly Naamah's things—while Jashub dashed about happily, thinking the entire business of moving was a wonderful adventure.

On the way back to Jerusalem Lord Yahweh gave Isaiah a message for King Ahaz. True to Yahweh's word, Isaiah found Ahaz surrounded by a group of courtiers, inspecting the water supply at a particularly vulnerable point—the conduit on the highway to the Fuller's Field. Isaiah knew he must try to reach his royal cousin now. That morning he had heard rumors of the most disturbing sort. Ahaz, too insecure and panicky to wait out the forthcoming seige of Jerusalem, was planning to appeal for help to Tiglath-pileser and send him tribute gifts. It was the most foolhardy act Isaiah could imagine. Jerusalem had the resources to withstand a long seige, and as soon as Tiglath-pileser got wind of the anti-Assyrian uprising, he would move his troops westward anyway. Pekah and Rezin would have to abandon Jerusalem and return home to defend their own kingdoms. All Ahaz had to do was wait.

With little Jashub beside him and God's power emboldening him, Isaiah walked fearlessly toward the king. "Hear me, Ahaz!" he cried out. "Take heed, be quiet, do not fear, do not let your heart be faint! Rezin and Pekah are only smoldering stumps of firebrands, torches almost burned out! Trust in Yahweh to protect Jerusalem, and don't go crying to Tiglath-pileser!"

"I am not interested in your opinions, Isaiah," Ahaz responded. "I know what I must do and I plan to proceed. The Assyrians can save us. They are our only hope."

"No!" Isaiah pleaded. "No! You must have trust in Yahweh's plan! If you have no faith, you cannot be firmly established as king. Ahaz, ask for a sign from Yahweh your God! Let it be as deep as Sheol or as high as heaven! Yahweh will certainly show you the truth."

Ahaz was rapidly growing angry, but he kept his composure well. If there was anything he did not want, it was a sign from Yahweh proving him wrong. "I will not ask!" Ahaz's reply was bold and forthright. "I will not put the Lord to the test!"

Once again Isaiah spoke the words of Yahweh, words which would create controversy for years to come. "Like it or not, Yahweh will give you a sign," Isaiah began. Then all of a sudden he was talking about the forthcoming birth of a child who would be called Immanuel. "And before Immanuel is two or three years old, Israel and Syria will be devastated by the Assyrians! But they won't stop there. If you call on them to aid us, they will wind up pillaging Judah as well!"

With that, Isaiah walked away, leaving Ahaz to ponder the import of his words.

Who was this Immanuel? Ahaz's young wife, Lady Abijah, was pregnant, and in the days to come, as

Isaiah's cryptic saying was widely quoted, misquoted, and discussed hundreds of times, many people felt the reference was to Ahaz's heir, soon to be born.

Yet there was another very real possibility. Since Naamah, too, was pregnant, perhaps Isaiah meant the reference to apply to his own child. Or, some said, Immanuel could be just anyone, any baby born in this time of trouble. Hope grew upon speculation. Immanuel would be a wonder-child, a heaven-sent deliverer. To the ordinary people that idea was the most appealing of all, for if ever Judah needed a deliverer, it was now.

Pekah and Rezin's forces set up seige around Jerusalem. Inside the city Ahaz nervously waited for response to his appeal to Tiglath-pileser.

Isaiah, meanwhile, preached daily, and his speeches were not encouraging. "The spoil speeds, the prey hastens!" A large wax-coated tablet with this warning inscribed on it stood in front of the city house. Those who stopped to ask what it meant received a lecture on foreign policy.

According to Isaiah, the Assyrians were not really Judah's friends. No matter what Ahaz might claim, Yahweh was very much opposed to entangling alliances. The best that could be hoped for now was Judah's reduction to the status of a tributary state. The worst, which to Isaiah seemed far more likely, would be Judah's total destruction as a kingdom. And if the worst happened, it was Yahweh's will, since the king and his advisors had defied him so openly.

Weeks dragged by and turned to months as the Israelite and Syrian troops surrounded and besieged Jerusalem. Then at last came the news Ahaz waited for. Tiglath-pileser's forces had attacked Damascus, Resin's capital city. The enemies outside Jerusalem withdrew to defend their home territories. Judah was safe, at least for the present. In spite of Isaiah's warnings, it seemed that Ahaz was not so unwise after all.

On a winter morning, a few months later, Lady Abijah gave birth to Ahaz's son. He was not called Immanuel, but Hezekiah, meaning "Yahweh is my strength." At this point in time, though he had not abandoned his allegiance to Molech, Ahaz was feeling very friendly toward Judah's own national God.

It was a time to be encouraged, and Isaiah knew from the moment he learned of Hezekiah's birth that this child was destined for some great role in Yahweh's plan. Was it too much to hope that he would indeed grow up to be the greatest of all Judah's kings?

Day by day, as Isaiah communed with Yahweh, he wrote innumerable fragments of poetry, seeking to put his hopes clearly into words. Someday, in Yahweh's own good time, such a prince would be born, the Prince of Peace who would inaugurate a whole new way of life on earth. This prince would usher in a golden age when all people would come to recognize the true God and live in harmony with each other. It might be Hezekiah. Isaiah was not sure.

When Naamah sent a copy of one of Isaiah's poems by courier to Ahaz and Abijah, the prophet was momentarily upset. The verses were too lavish, too bold in their predictions of the prince's greatness. He had meant to do it over, to tone it down. After all, it was really rash to describe a newborn infant as "Wonderful Counselor, Mighty God, Everlasting Father, Prince of Peace."

But once the little scroll with these words and more had been sent to Lady Abijah, Isaiah knew he could not change what was written. Abijah—and Ahaz—were delighted with the scroll, and perhaps that in itself was a good sign.

Isaiah's own hopes also grew that little Hezekiah might indeed turn out to be the prince of the promise.

Yet when Naamah's second son was born a week or so later, the name Yahweh gave the prophet for this child carried no such rosy hopes for the future. It was rather a warning for the immediate present: Maher-shalal-hash-baz—"the spoil speeds, the prey hastens." These were the very words of Yahweh inscribed on the placard in front of Isaiah's house that stood throughout the seige of Jerusalem. But now the seige was over. Jerusalem seemed safe. Isaiah's family had returned to their home in the country some weeks before the child was born.

Naamah did not like the name at all. "It's such a long name," Naamah complained. "Much worse than Shear-jashub. It's not a name—it's a whole sentence!"

"It's a warning to our people about what will happen if the Assyrians decide to take over Judah," Isaiah said, "and that's certainly what they'll do unless Ahaz and his advisors are very careful to meet all their tribute demands. Yahweh will not go on protecting a heedless nation much longer!"

When Isaiah made up his mind about something, there was no dissuading him. The infant's name was Maher-shalal-hash-baz. But from the very start, Naamah simply called him Maher, meaning "Speedy." It was not at all what the prophet had intended!

"I think you should name the next one," Isaiah commented to his wife one evening as they sat on the steps of their country house, watching little Maher, now three, darting about gleefully while Jashub chased after him. "Though I must admit, Maher does live up to his name!"

Naamah, who was pregnant again and very near her time of delivery, smiled. "I have been thinking about that. This one's going to be a girl, I feel almost sure, and if so, I want to call her Hephzibah."

"'My delight is in her.' That's perfectly charming! So will the Holy One of Israel himself say of the new Jerusalem when the golden age finally comes!" Isaiah was obviously pleased. Once again, but in a much more positive way, his new baby's name would provide the theme for an important message to the people of Judah.

And Hephzibah it was, for Naamah's prediction of a girl turned out to be correct. But even while Isaiah and Naamah looked forward to the coming of better times, the present realities of life in Judah were far from easy. Although peace had come to the kingdom, it was a fragile, difficult peace, accompanied by the hardships of heavy taxation, since King Ahaz was now a permanent vassal of Assyria. Tribute payments had to be made annually, and every Judean subject felt the hard economic pinch of living more simply.

It was a chastisement from Lord Yahweh for the foolish policies of the king and his advisors, Isaiah declared. Yet he wondered why the ordinary people had to suffer far more than the wealthy. Was it because so many of them had turned wholeheartedly to Baal and Ashtoreth, finding the wild, orgiastic rites of the fertility gods an escape from the harsh realities of daily living? Or was it because the king himself still revered the fierce Molech as his special patron, and countless Judeans, seeking to please the king, worshiped Molech as well?

Ahaz introduced a whole host of new deities imported from Assyria, the land of his overlords. Since Assyria was the strongest nation on earth, there was a widespread feeling that these other gods were more potent protectors than Lord Yahweh. Yet only Yahweh expected his worshipers to try to live righteously. The other gods made no such difficult demands.

"I will never understand you, Isaiah," Ahaz remarked on one of the rare occasions when the two of them were alone in the king's council chamber. "And you will never, never understand me! I don't care what you preach to the people in the streets. I know you are Yahweh's prophet and I am not about to risk his wrath by trying to keep you silent. Say what you will, but be aware that you will never change me!"

"No," Isaiah responded. "I cannot change you. Only Yahweh himself could do that."

For a moment, there was stark silence. Then Ahaz said, "I have tried to be a worthy king. I will always try." It had been several years since he had so rashly placed Judah in the irrevocable position of a tribute-paying state, yet he still seemed to believe that he was the savior of his kingdom.

Isaiah didn't answer.

"You are most useful to me," Ahaz continued, "in teaching my son his lessons. Hezekiah is a good pupil, is he not?"

"Yes," Isaiah replied. "He does very well."

Isaiah enjoyed his role as Prince Hezekiah's tutor. Daily he came into Jerusalem, bringing Jashub and Maher with him. The three boys studied together and became the best of friends.

"When I see him, he always seems so quiet," said Ahaz, "but his mother tells me he is bright and quick to learn."

Hezekiah was not at all quiet around Isaiah. His reticence in the presence of his father was based on fear, uncertainty, and a complete lack of understanding. Ahaz had no idea what his little son was really like. "He is all that his mother tells you," Isaiah answered, "and more. Your Hezekiah is the hope of Judah."

Ahaz smiled faintly. He was seated in the wicker chair that had replaced the elaborately carved ivory throne he had long since sent as a tribute gift to Tiglath-pileser. His hands were clenched on the chair arms. Tension and anguish reflected in his eyes. "My cousin," he said with surprising gentleness, "I hope you are right! Lord Yahweh knows—all the gods know—I hope you are right! Now, leave me!" he added, not with anger but with heavy resignation.

Without another word Isaiah discreetly withdrew.

It was as close, probably, as the prophet had ever come to understanding his cousin, the king.

The following summer, Ahaz, in an attempt to bargain with deity, offered up his newborn second son as a sacrifice to Molech.

It was an act of frightened desperation, born of fears that reached back into his own childhood. He became obsessed with the idea that he could only remain in Molech's good graces by sacrificing his own child.

He could not bring himself to give up Hezekiah, the child of the promise. Hezekiah was eight years old—bright, healthy, and handsome. And although Ahaz scarcely realized it, he loved his firstborn far too much to place him in fiery arms of the idol Molech. Instead, he sacrificed his infant son, Azrikam, and in doing so broke the heart of Lady Abijah, the child's mother.

For days Abijah wept bitterly for her lost little one, struggling to face the horrible reality of what Ahaz had done. It was a memory that she would have to live with the rest of her life, a terror so overwhelming that she longed to be dead herself. She worried about Hezekiah, young and vulnerable, stunned by the tragic death of his little brother. Might it be possible to spare him some of the long term pain by sending him away to a safer place?

So Abijah, who had always prided herself on her ability to read and write, wrote to Isaiah. Her little note spoke more than many long scrolls, and the prophet determined to keep it forever among the treasures of his cypress box.

Greetings to Prince Isaiah from Abijah the wife of Ahaz. Isaiah, please come and take Hezekiah my son home with you, and teach him of a better world than what he finds here.

Isaiah came. Ahaz, remorseful and broken by the

terrible thing he had done, did not object to letting young Hezekiah go to Isaiah's country home for as long as the prophet wanted to keep him.

There followed the golden summer of Hezekiah's childhood, a summer when a very frightened, very confused little boy awakened to the reality of Yahweh's protective love.

Hezekiah was a thoughtful child, mature for his years, one who felt deeply the terrible thing his father had done. When he first arrived, neither his friends Jashub and Maher, nor the motherly Naamah, nor Isaiah himself seemed able to reach him. But then the shell shattered. Trembling, in spasms of tears, the child poured out his fears to Isaiah, and Isaiah in return instilled in him the great and powerful hope that he, Hezekiah, was to be given a special role in Yahweh's plans for the future of Judah. He would be the greatest king since David.

Hezekiah never forgot Isaiah's wonderful promises, nor would he ever forget the comfort and assurance he was given when his world was falling apart. Although throughout his life there lingered a shadow of regret that he was the son of Ahaz, Hezekiah became aware of more important things. Lord Yahweh did not blame him for his parentage and neither did Isaiah.

While he knew Lord Yahweh watched and protected him, Isaiah was a present reality. "Always, always remember that I love you as one of my very own," Isaiah often reminded him. For little Prince Hezekiah, this was the most valuable assurance of all.

FIVE

The Turning of the Wheel

There seemed no doubt of Hezekiah's eventual destiny for kingship, but Isaiah was less certain of the future of his own sons. He hoped they would want to follow him as prophets, but he knew that prophecy was a gift that came from Lord Yahweh and was something that could not be forced. At the very least, he hoped they would be directed toward the path of government service. As cousins of the royal family, there would always be a place for them at court. Both Jashub and Maher were intelligent boys and, in their father's eyes, full of potential for greatness.

But neither of them was even slightly inclined to follow in Isaiah's footsteps, either as prophet or statesman.

The prophet did not remember exactly how old Jashub was—perhaps eight or nine—when he first accompanied him through the winding streets of Jerusalem to the shop of Abdon the potter. But Isaiah did recall how even this first visit was an expedition that seemed to interest the boy immensely. A few days earlier, Isaiah had noticed a pile of discarded potsherds outside Abdon's shop, pieces broken in the kiln. What a marvelous source of supply! The normal breakage of dishes from daily use in Isaiah's household was by no means adequate to satisfy his need for writing material.

"You may have all you wish, my Prince," Abdon told him, when Isaiah inquired. "I just throw them on the scrap heap."

Isaiah scooped up a few nice large ones. "I'll come back in a day or so and bring something to carry more of them in. You cannot imagine what a help this is to me!"

Abdon looked amused. "A prince who wants broken dishes! Who would believe it? But I understand, Prince Isaiah. You are using them to inscribe some of your sayings on. You're quite the preacher, I've heard people say, and if your writings read anything like your preaching when you're out there before the crowds, people will be reading them hundreds of years from now."

Isaiah felt a warm glow at these unexpected words of appreciation. When he returned with Jashub a few days later to collect more potsherds, the boy proudly carried two empty baskets, one considerably larger than the other.

"So this is that son of yours with the strange name," remarked the potter, who continued shaping clay on his wheel as he spoke.

"This is the older one, Shear-jashub, but we just call him Jashub most of the time," Isaiah explained.

"My papa let me carry *both* baskets," Jashub boasted, "but on the way home, I only get to carry the little one because papa says the big one will be too heavy."

Jashub was a solemn child, and now he watched Abdon, entranced. The jar on the potter's wheel began to grow, to take shape under Abdon's practiced hands while his bare feet simultaneously worked the treadle, spinning the wheel in a gentle circular motion.

Jashub stood transfixed, watching the transformation of the soft clay into a beautiful vessel. He became so fascinated by the process that he completely forgot about gathering the potsherds into the baskets. After several moments of quiet contemplation he asked, "How does he do that, Papa? How does he make it become so beautiful?"

"I'm sure it's not easy, is it, Abdon?" Isaiah replied. "It takes years and years of practice." More than anything he had ever wanted before, Jashub longed to try his hands on the potter's wheel, but he would not have dared to ask. Abdon was unapproachable, a worker of wonders.

On the way home, however, the boy began to ply Isaiah with questions. "How did Abdon learn to make pottery?" he ventured. This was a serious matter, and Jashub was not about to come right out and say he wanted to try it himself.

"Well," Isaiah said thoughtfully, "I suppose his father, and his grandfather, and his great-grandfather were all potters before him. And so as Abdon was growing up, he learned from his family. That's the way it generally is."

"But what if a boy just wanted to learn, and his father wasn't a potter—could the son learn?"

"I don't think so," Isaiah replied. "Things just don't happen that way. Unless he had an uncle or someone like that to teach him, it would be most unlikely because it usually is a family business."

Jashub frowned and his lower lip protruded in a pout. Isaiah did not help matters any as he went on. "It's like how Hezekiah is going to be king someday because his father is king now."

Jashub wondered what he would become some day, but he was hesitant to put his thoughts into words. As much as he loved his father, he could not imagine himself as a prophet, making speeches about Lord Yahweh and writing down all sorts of things on potsherds. And so, the boy remained very quiet as he walked at his father's side.

Isaiah sensed what Jashub was thinking and felt it was best to let the subject of pottery-making drop. *Just a passing fancy. He'll have forgotten it by tomorrow,* Isaiah thought. "I'm going to make you into a fine scholar," he said cheerfully, "and when you grow up, you can help me with teaching and writing. Or maybe you'll be Hezey's prime minister."

Jashub did not want to be a fine scholar, and he certainly didn't want to be prime minister. He wanted to get his hands on some clay, to have a chance at the potter's wheel.

For months, even years, the dream hovered in the back of Jashub's mind, and whenever he came into town with his father, he hoped for the opportunity to visit the potter's shop to collect potsherds and to watch Abdon at work.

At last there came a day when Isaiah sent him there alone, and Jashub, then eleven, confided his dream to Abdon. The old potter was taken quite by surprise. "Your father is a great aristocrat, my lad, and a prophet besides! I do not think he'd approve."

"Just let me try!" Jashub pleaded.

"Very well, you can try. But it's not as easy as it looks." The potter rose and let the boy take his seat at the wheel.

After many months of observation, Jashub knew well enough what he had to do. But Abdon was right. It *was* harder than it looked. Still, for a first-time effort, Jashub did surprisingly well.

The potter looked pleased. "I believe you have a gift for it, child," he said. "Come back again, and I'll teach you a bit more if your father doesn't mind. But ask him first, mind you!"

Mustering all his courage, Jashub asked Isaiah's permission that very evening.

Isaiah, too stunned to reply, pondered his son's request.

"It can't do any harm," Naamah commented.

"No, I suppose it can't do any harm," Isaiah echoed.

"I'm surprised Abdon would have time for such a thing, but if he's willing, why not? As long as you keep up your studying, too."

Jashub was delighted beyond words. Somehow he felt confident things would work out. He would grow up to be a potter like Abdon, and sooner or later, the whole dreary business of studying, which he didn't enjoy at all, would drop out of his life completely.

Like his father, Shear-jashub was capable of boundless optimism and daring dreams.

Slowly, the cycle of seasons passed. The desolate, damp, grayness of winter gave way to the glories of spring. Then came scorching heat of the long, dry summer and the golden New Year season of autumn—the loveliest time of all. Although Hezekiah had returned to the palace, Isaiah continued to tutor him, along with Jashub and Maher. But with the passing of time, Isaiah remained more and more at his country place.

Prince Hezekiah was a teenager now, compelled to spend most of his time learning the military and diplomatic arts that were not Isaiah's to teach. The prophet at last had sufficient leisure to begin to gather a group of followers, young men who felt the prophetic call and came to learn from a master what the service of Yahweh demanded. Some stayed a few days or even weeks, only to leave disillusioned, knowing that their dreams of a true vocation were ill founded. Others stayed longer, even for a year or two, living in tents around Isaiah's home, studying, reading, discussing, and arguing with heartfelt enthusiasm about the contents of some of the old scrolls Isaiah had collected. Some of them wrote little fragments on the potsherds, and some of the best went into Isaiah's box.

It was clear, however, that Jashub would never be a scholar. Day after day Isaiah's firstborn rose before daybreak to get an early start on his trek to the shop of

Abdon the potter. Night after night he came home, his clothes splattered with dried clay and happiness shining in his eyes. Sometimes he brought with him a bowl or pitcher or vase he had created. His craftsmanship was superb. These were not just useful utensils. They were works of art and beauty, the unsung music of his soul, poured out in a way that Isaiah and Naamah found incomprehensible.

For a long time, Isaiah worried in silence. Then, on a Sabbath morning, when Abdon's shop remained closed and the young man Jashub lay sleeping still and peaceful beside his brother Maher, Isaiah entered his sons' room and gently tapped Jashub's shoulder. "Come outside with me," Isaiah whispered. "We must talk."

Sleepily, Jashub rose and pulled on his robe and sandals while Isaiah waited in the doorway. Outside, the deceptive coolness of early summer morning awaited them. For a while they walked slowly without talking. Isaiah hoped his son would initiate the conversation, while Jashub, puzzled and more than a little worried, waited for his father's message.

"About all this pottery," Isaiah said at last. "Your work is beautiful, son, you know that. But you also know that Abdon has sons of his own, and in time the shop will be theirs. You are nothing more than an apprentice." If there was a hint of anger in Isaiah's voice, it was merely a cover for his deeper disappointment.

"Yes, Papa," said Jashub meekly. "I know."

"Well, don't you ever think about the future? You are *my* son, not the son of a potter, and you're seventeen years old now. It's time you began thinking about what your vocation should be."

"I do think about it, Papa. More than you would ever imagine."

"Well?"

"I don't want to hurt you . . . but . . .," Jashub stammered. "Well, don't you remember when you were young, you ran off to the prophet's camp and got the brand of Yahweh's service on your right hand, and how it nearly broke your parents' hearts?"

Yes, Isaiah remembered, and though the memory was painful, he recalled having told his children about it years before. "They said a prince of Judah could not be a prophet, that I was throwing my life away, that I'd always regret what I'd done." He looked down at the symbol on his hand as if newly aware of it.

"But," Jashub continued, "you have not regretted it. You did what Lord Yahweh called you to do, and so must I."

"But making pottery!" Isaiah exclaimed. "You who are the son of a prophet, my firstborn! Jashub, I've had such great hopes for you! How can you say that Lord Yahweh has called you to pottery-making!"

"Somebody has to make dishes," replied Jashub. When Isaiah did not answer, he continued more fervently. "Not everyone can be like you, Papa. None of these students who come here to study will ever really be like you. And as for me, I'm not like you at all. Papa, I love you so much, but I *can't* be what you are! Please try to understand!"

Yes, thought Isaiah, *I do understand. I am not sure how we'll work it out, but we'll find a way somehow.* He put his arm around his son's shoulders. "There's an old saying," he reflected. "'There is nothing better for a man than to find enjoyment in his toil.' I never realized it before, but I suppose Yahweh does call some men to be potters, just as others are called to be prophets."

"Will you come with me tomorrow and talk to Abdon?" Jashub asked tentatively. There was more he wanted to say, much more, but something held him back.

Isaiah agreed readily and the following day he went with Jashub to Abdon's shop. Through the long night he had prayed for guidance. He could see no real future for Jashub with his hands on the potter's wheel, but he knew there must be an answer somewhere.

Abdon himself had the answer. Leaving his work, the potter escorted Isaiah into the shadowy interior of his home, and the formalities of greeting were exchanged. Isaiah was seated in a comfortable chair, while Abdon's wife appeared with cups of wine for her husband and guest.

"I suppose Jashub has spoken to you about my cousin in Lachish," Abdon said at last in the leisurely, unhurried voice of a man who enjoyed bargaining.

Isaiah shook his head.

"Ah, my prince," said Abdon, "don't be so hesitant. Surely you know of my cousin, Elon the potter, and his charming young daughter, Reba."

Isaiah looked at him, bewildered.

"Reba is fifteen. She is beautiful. She is lovely. She is everything a maiden should be. But alas, she is my cousin's only child. Sons he had, but they died in childhood. Only Reba remains. The man who marries Reba will be Elon's heir, inheritor of the finest pottery shop in Lachish."

"If she is as lovely as you say, she must have many suitors," Isaiah remarked.

"But Elon will accept only a man who knows his craft. He would accept Jashub, I think, if the bride price were sufficient."

"But Lachish is many miles from here, the other side of the kingdom," Isaiah said.

"Lachish is a fine city, second only to Jerusalem," Abdon countered. "And a great prince like yourself should be pleased to see your sons marry well. Reba is well worth the price. Ten shekels of silver, I believe."

A thousand emotions stirred in Isaiah's mind. This was the way it was usually done. Fathers arranged the marriages of their offspring, and more often than not the results seemed to turn out rather well.

"Perhaps," said Isaiah. "We shall see. Maybe Jashub

and I will go to Lachish and meet Elon and Reba for ourselves."

The wheels of Lord Yahweh's plan were turning as surely as the potter's wheel that Jashub was working at that moment in the courtyard outside Abdon's shop.

The following week Isaiah and Jashub journeyed to Lachish. Without haggling, Isaiah handed over to Reba's father the ten shekels of silver for the bride price, and Jashub became betrothed to Reba. A month later, Isaiah's entire family went again to Lachish for the wedding—a festive event with all the traditional singing, dancing, and celebrating that accompanied a marriage feast.

The road home seemed long to Isaiah and Naamah. While Maher and Hephzibah walked vigorously ahead, Isaiah trudged slowly beside Naamah, who rode a little donkey.

"Things are not the way they should be," Naamah said, dolefully. "A young man is supposed to bring his bride home to *his* family. I'm afraid we have lost him, Isaiah."

"Lachish is not the end of the earth," Isaiah replied. "They'll come to see us—I know they will. Things change, Naamah. Jashub has grown up and left us, but he's found a lovely bride and a chance to be what he really wants to be. Yahweh has blessed him greatly."

"How I wish things would stay the same!" Naamah sighed. "Yet I know it isn't good to think that way." With all her heart, Naamah grieved for her firstborn, who had followed such an unlikely road.

"Remember," Isaiah encouraged her, "sometimes as things change they get better."

Naamah did not answer, but in her heart she thought, *O Isaiah, my beloved, I can only pray that you are right!*

"How long am I going to keep missing him as if he were

dead?" Naamah asked a few days later as she and Isaiah reclined on their rooftop porch in the early evening twilight. It was obvious that she spoke of Jashub, and there was a catch in her voice as if she hovered on the verge of tears.

Isaiah held her close. "They'll be back for the Feast of Succoth in the fall. You know they'll come."

The prophet and his wife had had little opportunity for private conversation since their return from Jashub and Reba's wedding. Isaiah's days were full of work with his students while Naamah remained busy with household tasks and the routine business matters of managing their estate. By nightfall, both of them were so tired that neither wished to burden the other with serious worries.

Nevertheless, Isaiah's concerns about their younger son were growing, and this moment afforded a good opportunity to share his thoughts with Naamah. "At least our Jashub found something he wanted to do with his life. I worry more about Maher. That boy has no sense of purpose. Did you realize he's stopped coming to my classes completely since the wedding? Every morning, he takes off out of here, on that horse of his, and he's gone all day long."

"I worry, too," Naamah said. "That horse is as swift and spirited as his name, Barak—lightning."

"I've asked him where he goes, and he says nowhere," Isaiah continued.

"He's hunting. He always takes his bow and arrows with him," Naamah answered. "Remember that wild goat he killed and brought home the day before yesterday? We fed the whole camp of students on it."

"Naamah, we have hundreds of sheep and goats of our own. Do you think I need my son to go out like a scavenger, like some wild man of the desert? I don't like it."

"He thinks he's helping. He's no scholar any more than Jashub is, and he's never going to be a prophet. He must feel very out of place with your disciples. Think about it, Isaiah. They're here because they've heard Lord Yahweh's call, or at least they think they've heard it. Maher knows he hasn't."

Isaiah sighed. "Maybe you could convince him to take more interest in the estate. A young man has to do something with his life."

Naamah, who knew Maher had little interest in the estate, thought it best not to pursue that subject. "Whenever Hezekiah becomes king, he'll have Maher on his council, and he'll be wrapped up in affairs of state, I expect," she offered hopefully.

Isaiah became thoughtful. Even in private, it wasn't wise to sound too eager for Ahaz's death. "Yes, perhaps, but who knows when that will ever be?" he whispered. "Sometimes it is terribly hard to wait for Lord Yahweh's plan to unfold. You know, I've been thinking, the old scrolls say that Moses had two sons, and who has ever heard anything about either one of them? They never amounted to anything."

"Isaiah, my love, don't you realize that there have been millions of people who have amounted to a great deal in Lord Yahweh's eyes but who never got their names into any of those precious scrolls? Most of us will be forgotten someday. But I feel confident you will live on in Judah's history, especially if you can organize your writings."

Isaiah had always hoped that Jashub and Maher would help him with that. Realizing the futility of the idea, he did not verbalize it. He enjoyed writing when the words came easily. He loved working with his students, teaching, studying, discussing, sharing opinions. Yet he deplored the thought of trying to bring order to what must by now amount to hundreds of potsherds in his cypress box. "I'll get to it someday," he answered. "It's going to take a lot of work."

Naamah nestled her head on his shoulder, happy as he

enfolded her in his arms. "Perhaps," she said dreamily, "one of your students would work on them for you."

"Micah wants to," Isaiah answered. "He's the best, the brightest of the lot that are here now, but he's not a young man. He's about as old as I am, and he has a family at home who needs him."

Micah was visiting Isaiah's camp for just a few days. He was a poor farmer from Moresheth, a village on the Philistine border, and had been a prophet for years.

"If only he were twenty years younger!" Isaiah went on. "He might be the successor I've always hoped to find. As it is, I've told him to go home and put his own writings together. He is a gifted man, very close to Lord Yahweh."

Naamah sighed. "Someone else will help," she said, trying to sound encouraging. "If not, someday I'll write your scroll myself." Though she was never going to have a real flair for the written word, Naamah's skills had improved considerably over the years.

Isaiah laughed and kissed her lightly on the forehead. "Little Naamah," he whispered tenderly. "I believe you will!"

SIX

The New King

The last months of Ahaz's reign were a strange time for Judah. Sargon of Assyria, who some years earlier had succeeded to the throne of Tiglath-pileser, sent notice that Assyrian inspectors would be coming to Jerusalem to celebrate the New Year festival. They would also check on the progress that had been made in establishing the worship of the five great gods of Assyria.

Ahaz, even more frightened than usual, planned to give Sargon's men a good show. He decided that the best way to demonstrate his enthusiasm for the Assyrian gods was to have young Prince Hezekiah consecrated as chief priest of Asshur, the foremost of the five great deities.

Hezekiah, now in his late teens, was resolute in his determination to remain true to Yahweh. Aided by Isaiah, he fled from his father's court and hid for a few days in a cave on the prophet's estate. It was there, under less than ideal circumstances that he decided to marry Isaiah's daughter, Hephzibah. It was a genuine love match.

Then, with his future entirely uncertain, the crown

prince of Judah fled with his bride to the obscure village of Moresheth, taking refuge with Isaiah's friend, Micah.

When King Sargon's inspectors arrived in Jerusalem, Ahaz had the temple in readiness for them. There was no hint of Yahweh worship anywhere, and cultic paraphernalia of the five great gods of Assyria was abundantly in evidence. The inspectors, thoroughly satisfied, returned to Sargon's court.

Even though the inspectors had gone, Hezekiah did not return to Jerusalem. Autumn turned to winter, and the crown prince, unaware that he was soon to be king, determined to remain as far away from his father's palace as possible, lest he be forced against his will to support the Assyrian cult.

Ahaz's death, like that of his father Jotham, came suddenly. He was still a young man, not yet forty, and to those around him he seemed the picture of health. Yet one winter morning he collapsed while dictating a letter, and before nightfall he was dead.

There were few to mourn for Ahaz. No one really missed him except Lady Abijah, who had always loved him in spite of everything he had done to hurt her. But even Abijah knew that things would improve for the kingdom of Judah now that Ahaz was gone.

Hezekiah came home to the acclamations of a hopeful nation. Never in Judah's long history had a new king been so enthusiastically welcomed. Never had the kingdom's hopes been higher. Most of all, for Isaiah, it was a time of rejoicing, the beginning of the new age he had dreamed of and spoken about since Hezekiah was born.

There are a few times in almost every life when one's entire being is caught up in a sense of happiness—the pure, unalloyed joy that is one of Lord Yahweh's most precious gifts. For Isaiah, Hezekiah's coronation as King of Judah was such an event.

It was a warm yet wintry afternoon when Hezekiah

ben-Ahaz mounted the great bronze platform that stood before the golden doors of King Solomon's Temple. There he knelt before the multitudes assembled in the courtyard to receive from Isaiah the holy oil of anointment upon his head.

Next came the crown, a rather plain circlet of gold, adorned with a few well-polished, deep green stones from the mines in the south. Ahaz had worn it, and there was not sufficient time to have a new one made. *But,* thought Isaiah, *how different it looks on Hezekiah!* Although there was an undeniable physical resemblance between father and son, in all things that really mattered Ahaz and Hezekiah would be, had to be, entirely different.

Ahaz—the unsure, the fearful, the fainthearted—was dead, and Hezekiah his son reigned in his place. All the hopes that Isaiah had cherished over the years seemed to crystallize in the sacred moments of Hezekiah's coronation. Words he had written long ago flooded back into his mind, words proclaiming the dawn of the new age and the coming of the great prince who would be its ruler.

> The king will reign in righteousness.
> He will be like a hiding place from the wind,
>   a covert from the tempest.
> Like a stream of water in the desert,
>   like the shade of a great rock
>   in a weary land.

The crowd had sung Isaiah's songs that day, sung them to the handsome, dark-haired young king whom Isaiah himself was privileged to anoint. Isaiah remembered every word.

> There shall come forth a shoot
> from the tree of Jesse,
>   a branch shall grow out of his roots.
> And the Spirit of Yahweh shall rest upon him,

the spirit of wisdom and understanding,
   the spirit of counsel and might.
He shall not judge by what his eyes see,
   or decide by what his ears hear,
But with righteousness he shall judge the poor,
   and decide with equity for the meek.
Then none shall hurt or destroy
   in all my holy mountain,
For the earth shall be full of the knowledge
      of Yahweh
   as the waters cover the sea.

Would Hezekiah live up to these marvelous expectations? With all his heart, Isaiah hoped so. Yet the young man who had stood before him was very human. Isaiah knew Hezekiah's shortcomings well. He was too easily excitable, given to impulsive decisions, sometimes beset by deep melancholy, sometimes too emotional, too easily given to tears. And though he was certainly intelligent, he was far from being a careful thinker for he was easily influenced by those around him. *Like it or not,* Isaiah realized, *he had something of Ahaz in him.*

Yet Hezekiah's dedication to Yahweh was unquestionable. From childhood he was determined to be a king like David, the greatest of all the kings, whose reputation for Yahweh's favor none of his successors ever rivaled.

Isaiah loved his own sons, of course. He loved them deeply—Jashub the craftsman, happily working at his potter's wheel, and Maher the hunter, the outdoorsman, galloping across the Judean hills. They were good men, Isaiah reflected, these sons of his body, unimaginative, earthbound, yet decent and solid. But Hezekiah, the son of Ahaz, would always be the child of Isaiah's heart.

On the morning after the coronation, Lady Hephzibah, Hezekiah's young wife, awoke early. In the predawn light of the royal bedchamber she sat up in bed and gazed in silent awe at the figure who lay sleeping beside her. In the stillness the full reality of her husband's new role swept through her. He was Lord Yahweh's anointed one, set apart from all other men for the sacred office of kingship. When she had lain in his arms the night before, he had seemed no different than the young husband she had already loved for many months. Yet he *was* different. The kingship—the purpose for which he was born, which had seemed so unattainable a few months before—was now his.

Better than Hezekiah himself, Hephzibah knew of her father's hopes and dreams for this young man. All her life she had heard the wonderful poems Isaiah had written about the coming of the kingdom of peace. All of them were full of references to the glorious prince who would rule that kingdom and whose reign would bring a sense of harmony on earth unlike anything yet experienced in mankind's history.

Hephzibah recalled a few lines from one of her father's most fanciful and charming songs.

> The wolf shall dwell with the lamb,
>> and the leopard shall lie down with the kid.
> The calf and the lion and the fatling together . . .
>> and a little child shall lead them.

Exaggeration, perhaps, but what a wonderful way of describing the coming of true peace on earth! Into Hephzibah's reverie crept the realization that her love for Hezekiah had originated at least to a certain extent in her conviction that he was indeed the promised prince of the peaceable kingdom.

It was almost a disturbing thought, for in a few months of marriage Hephzibah had learned to know Hezekiah very well indeed, and she realized more clearly than anyone else that he was no supernatural hero. He was idealistic, well-intentioned, and unquestionably devoted to Lord Yahweh's service as he understood it. But he could also be opinionated and stubborn and all too easily swayed by the ideas of others. *He is so young—only twenty-five,* thought Hephzibah, who was herself even younger. Suddenly, she felt the weight of centuries upon her shoulders.

The room was growing lighter. Determined to think only happy thoughts, Hephzibah nestled back down beside Hezekiah. She let her mind wander to the marvelous jet blackness of Hezekiah's hair as she twined a strand of it between her fingers along with a tress of her own. Hephzibah had always considered her own light brown hair entirely nondescript and unsatisfactory. She hoped that their children, when they came, would all inherit Hezekiah's coloring. *Strange how these things turn out,* she thought. In a land where hair and eyes were usually dark, Hephzibah was, like Isaiah, uncommonly fair. *And many people say that my father is a most attractive man.*

As the young woman's mind wandered, her earlier apprehensive thoughts were dispelled. Whatever her husband turned out to be, she knew that she loved him. Perhaps that was sufficient.

At that moment, Hezekiah stirred. Pulling her close, he embraced and kissed her. "My lord king of Judah!" Hephzibah whispered, half-serious, half-whimsical.

Hezekiah put his finger to her lips. "Such language is proper in public, I suppose," he said, "but you are, as the old story says, flesh of my flesh and bone of my bone. So, since I am the king, you are my lady, my favored lady forever and forever, my beloved."

One thing about Hezekiah, Hephzibah though, *he has never had any difficulty putting his feelings into words.* She cherished him for it, though for her such expressions came harder. "Forever, my beloved," she repeated thoughtfully. She hoped with all her heart it was true yet feared that nothing human could truly last forever.

Hezekiah was wide awake now and sitting on the edge

of the bed. "Your father is coming to have breakfast with us this morning," he said. "I must go and prepare myself while you have your maids deck you in your most beautiful array."

"For breakfast?" Hephzibah sounded dubious.

"Oh, Hephzibah, my love, today is the beginning of a glorious new time for Judah. Today the world begins anew!" Hezekiah rose and pulled back the curtains of their bedchamber windows, opened the wooden shutters, and looked out on the enclosed garden beyond. The grayness of winter hung over the brown landscape. The air was misty, thick with fog. Although he was a child of winter, born in the winter and now beginning his reign in the midst of winter, he had always hated the bleak pervading gloom that went with the season.

The day of the coronation had defied expectations with its warm and sunny skies. Even though the morning after was overcast and gray, he resolved not to take it as a bad omen as he reclosed the shutters to keep out the chill air.

"In a few more weeks, spring will be here," he said with a determined note of hope in his voice. "And the world will *really* begin anew! Wait till I tell you—and Isaiah—what I have planned!"

With that he withdrew to his own rooms adjoining Hephzibah's, leaving his bride to wonder what great pronouncements he had in store.

Less than an hour later they gathered at a lavish table, spread for breakfast in Hezekiah's private suite. Hephzibah, sensing the importance of Hezekiah's festive mood, was dressed in a lovely soft woolen gown of deep violet. Delicate gold chains graced her neck, and a golden belt encircled her slender waist. Her long hair, neatly coifed in braids and piled atop her head, was covered with a filmy scarf of soft lavender.

Across from Hephzibah sat Isaiah, clad in a simple, unadorned robe of light brown wool, topped by an equally plain mantle, also brown. He looked serious, almost worried.

One additional place was set, and Hezekiah, seeing his wife's and father-in-law's curious glances, explained. "I have sent my mother a message to join us."

Even as he spoke, Lady Abijah entered—Queen Abijah now, for the title of queen was given by tradition to the king's mother, never to his wife. She was dressed plainly in dark attire for she was still in mourning for Ahaz. Yet there was about her an air of serenity and peace. She smiled at her son as he rose to embrace her and then at Isaiah as he bowed gallantly and pronounced the correct ceremonial greeting. *She is truly a noble lady,* Hephzibah thought, *queenly, one who has suffered much, but one to whom Yahweh has given great inner strength and courage.*

When they were all comfortably seated at the table, Hezekiah began. "I had a chance to look inside the temple yesterday morning before the ceremony, and it is even worse than I had realized. My predecessor's Assyrian idols and paraphernalia are in abundance everywhere, and most of the holy vessels used for the worship of Yahweh seem to have disappeared."

"He didn't destroy them," Abijah put in. "The incense burners, the table for showbread, all the plates and vessels and utensils were packed away somewhere in the storerooms just before the Assyrian inspector's visit last fall. If he had lived, I believe he would have restored everything." Hezekiah's mother possessed a determined loyalty to Ahaz's memory. While she was a devoted daughter of Yahweh, Queen Abijah had come to understand Ahaz far better than anyone else. "He had to hide the things he did not want the Assyrians to find," she continued. "Otherwise they would have taken them as tribute."

"Perhaps so," Hezekiah said. "In any case, we are going to find them and bring them out now. We are going to restore the temple to what Lord Yahweh wants it to be. I plan to start on this project right away, so that when spring comes we can have a great festival and invite all of Judah and the Israelites from the north, too, if they'll come."

"We could celebrate Passover," said Abijah. "The fourteenth of Nisan it was in the old days, in the early spring. Only there might not be enough time to get ready because it's less than a month's time."

"We could try." Hezekiah's enthusiasm mounted. "But the temple must be thoroughly purified. Those Assyrian idols in there will have to go! And we must reconvene the priests and the Levites. I spoke to a Levite, Mahath, yesterday. He promised to help me get these people together and retrain them in the proper rituals. And we have to have singers for the choir and men who can play musical instruments. Isaiah, you'll help me, won't you? I want you to organize the music."

Isaiah should have been happy. He loved music, and the prospect of such a glorious occasion as Hezekiah described pleased him. Yet a strange uneasiness also stirred him. He looked around the table. Hephzibah's eyes sparkled with pride in her young husband. Queen Abijah's face, too, reflected her pleasure. Hezekiah himself fairly glowed with enthusiasm.

"Hezekiah, my king," Isaiah said somemnly, "I am delighted with what you are planning to do, and you know I will help you. Yes, certainly Lord Yahweh will be pleased to have the old rituals restored. I only want you to remember, there are other more important things."

"But what could be more important?" Hezekiah seemed genuinely surprised. "Through all the years as I grew up and saw what my father was doing, I longed for this day when I could begin to set things right in the house of the Lord!"

"We all know that King Ahaz did great wrongs," Isaiah replied, "and we are looking forward to changes for the better. But remember this, Hezekiah: There is nothing on earth more important than *peace*. In spite of everything else, King Ahaz was basically a man of peace. However, you will be a better ruler than your father because you faithfully serve Yahweh. Yet I beg you, do not depart from the one thing Ahaz did *right*. Do not ever break the peace with Assyria! Do not send Yahweh's people to certain death!"

"Isaiah!" Hezekiah exclaimed, "What ever makes you suspect such a thing? I am only interested in reform at the temple, in purifying the worship of Lord Yahweh! King Sargon's inspectors were here last fall. It may be years before they return. The Assyrians won't care what we're doing. I certainly have no intentions of breaking the peace with Assyria."

"And may you never!" said Isaiah. Unrest stirred within him, and he realized that it probably sprang from Hezekiah's casual mention of inviting the Israelites to worship at the restored temple. While it was probably true that King Sargon would remain unaware or unconcerned by a local revival of the worship of Judah's God, how would he react to the King of Judah meddling in a territory to which he had no right? It seemed risky. It might even be dangerous.

Yet Isaiah was pleased with his son-in-law, the king.

A restored temple, free from idols and devoted to Yahweh, the one true God—what a thought!

SEVEN

Not According
to the Sanctuary's Rules

Nothing seemed to dampen Hezekiah's enthusiasm for carrying out his great plan for reform. "King Sargon has plenty of other, more serious things to worry about," he assured everyone. "As long as Judah is loyal to the tribute payments, why should he bother to notice how we worship? It may be years before he even hears of it."

Hezekiah's reasoning seemed logical enough, and even Isaiah began to feel some of his son-in-law's enthusiasm as he threw himself into the task of helping the singers and musicians prepare for the anticipated festival of rededication.

Carefully packed away in the temple storerooms were hundreds of musical instruments—harps of all varieties, cymbals, tambourines, and trumpets. As news of the king's appeal to the priests and Levites spread, men converged on the temple, eager to offer their services. Isaiah found himself very busy interviewing them, distributing the instruments to those who showed skill and listening to auditions of prospective choir members.

The chief priest, Azariah, who might have been expected to take a more active role, was a doddering old man of good intentions but very little real ability. He gladly allowed Isaiah a free hand with these matters which, strictly speaking, should have been priestly business.

Meanwhile, Mahath the Levite and his men cleansed and purified the temple building and piled up a number of small stone and clay idols they had found inside. Hezekiah ordered these figures—representing not only Assyrian gods but also the local Baals and Ashteroth—smashed to pieces.

There was also the matter of Nehushtan, the bronze serpent reputed crafted by Moses himself in the time of Israel's wilderness wanderings. Coiled on a bronze pole, Nehushtan had long held an honored place in the inner sanctuary, and King Ahaz had not disturbed it. It was not supposed to be an idol but simply a reminder of Yahweh's power in healing the Israelites of a plague many centuries before. It had long been customary on various feast days to take Nehushtan from its place in the temple and parade it through the streets of Jerusalem. Unfortunately, many citizens, ever willing to add another god to their collection of deities, had bowed eagerly and worshiped it.

"Nehushtan must go!" Hezekiah said, looking almost frightened as he gave the order one morning at the temple.

"But, my lord," protested the aged chief priest, Azariah, "it is *holy!*"

"Moses made it. It has historical value. We can't possibly destroy something so ancient, so revered," Mahath the Levite put in. "Yahweh would be angry."

"Lord Yahweh will be more angry if we allow it to remain," the young king responded. Personally, he found the bronze serpent far more disturbing than the idols that were so blatantly in opposition to Yahweh's commands. Nehushtan was indeed ancient and historic and reputed very powerful. While Hezekiah rather doubted its origin, in the time of Moses it was a thing that had long been revered even by Yahweh's loyal followers. Though he tried to sound firm, Hezekiah was inwardly more frightened than he wanted to admit.

Isaiah, who had overheard the discussion, joined the group who surrounded Hezekiah. "The king is absolutely right. Nehushtan must go because people have forgotten its original use and made it into a false god. It doesn't matter that it's ancient. It has been around entirely too long already. Break it into pieces!"

Grateful for his father-in-law's support, Hezekiah smiled warmly.

That very day Nehushtan was removed from the sanctuary and broken into bits. The fragments, along with those of the other discarded idols, were carried outside the walls of Jerusalem to a refuse dump in the Valley of Kidron.

The reform was making wonderful progress, and Hezekiah stood firm in enforcing his first really controversial decree. *Now,* he thought, *to the matter of inviting those Israelites to our festivities.*

Israel, to the north of Judah, had become something of a no-man's-land in recent years. The once-flourishing capital city, Samaria, had been destroyed by Sargon's forces a few years earlier, and nothing was left there but a heap of ruins. Most of the native population, also worshipers of Yahweh, had been deported and scattered by the Assyrian conquerors in places far to the east. Meanwhile, other people, uprooted by the Assyrians elsewhere, were being brought into Israel to fill the population gap. Judeans spoke of their former northern neighbors as the "ten lost tribes of Israel" and looked askance at the newcomers, who were not really Israelites at all.

As Hezekiah and Isaiah discussed the king's proposed invitation to the Israelites, they were joined by Eliakim, a young man on whom Hezekiah had come to rely who was well-informed.

"In spite of the rumors we've heard," Eliakim reported, "there are still a number of Israelite natives in the villages in the north. And among the new people, there are many who worship Yahweh and would be eager to come if we invited them."

Isaiah listened to these remarks with considerable dismay. "Of course they'll come—droves of them—for the free food and entertainment. Hezekiah, be reasonable! We don't need those people. And there's no way to get ready for them by the fourteenth of Nisan. Forget about Israel! This festival should be for our own people, the people of Judah."

Hezekiah listened but remained unmoved. Isaiah's opposition was something he had not anticipated, and he scarcely knew how to deal with it for he loved Isaiah. From the time that Hezekiah was a child, Isaiah had been to him the father that Ahaz never was. For years Isaiah had encouraged Hezekiah's dreams and looked forward to the time when Hezekiah would be king. It had not occurred to Hezekiah that there would ever be disagreement between them, and it hurt him deeply.

"I have made up my mind!" the king exclaimed adamantly. "I will send couriers throughout Israel. If the fourteenth of Nisan is too soon, we'll have our Passover one month later, the fourteenth of Iyar! And our neighbors to the north will be here!"

Isaiah tried repeatedly to warn Hezekiah that the Assyrians would likely look upon this action as a dangerous political move. But Hezekiah would not change his mind.

As each day passed, it became clearer that Hezekiah was moved only by advice he really wanted to hear. Isaiah tried not to think too much about this as he concentrated on preparing the music for the upcoming ceremonies, but he was worried. Meanwhile, Hezekiah visited the temple daily to check on progress. More and more often as days went by, he was accompanied by Shebna, a young nobleman who had become his close companion. Shebna, who was a few years older than the new monarch, was dynamic and intelligent. On the surface he seemed a man of ability and promise, an ideal confidant for King Hezekiah. In the days of Ahaz Shebna had outwardly accepted worship of the Assyrian gods, but now he made it clear that he intended to be loyal to Yahweh only, as he had always wished to be.

Isaiah did not trust Shebna, and yet he felt guilty for distrusting him. The man certainly seemed devoted to Lord Yahweh and to Hezekiah, but there was something disquieting about him. Isaiah eyed him with apprehension whenever he came with the king to listen to choir practice. He was perhaps too suave, too polished. Obviously he wanted power, and Isaiah found himself increasingly uneasy in his presence.

At home, it was Maher who provided a listening ear for Isaiah's speculations. "Son, why don't you come to the palace more often?" Isaiah asked him one evening over supper. "I feel sure Hezekiah would give you a place on his council if only you'd be there. You were his best friend before he became king."

Maher shrugged. "I am still his friend."

"That is not what I asked you. You have been to the palace only a few times since the coronation. Shebna is there every day."

"Shebna wants to be chief minister," Maher answered, "and no doubt he will be as soon as Hezey sees fit to announce it." Maher had put Isaiah's apprehensions into words.

"It might have been you, son," Isaiah said somberly.

"No, Papa. Hezey knows I am no courtier. The tragedy of it all is that it should be *you*. There is no one in all of Judah better qualified for the job, and you know it as well as I do. But Hezey is going to listen to the advice he wants to hear, and Shebna gives it to him."

Isaiah knew entirely too well that what Maher said was true.

Not long afterward, the first of Hezekiah's messengers returned from Israel with news of the people's surprising reaction to the festival invitation. "Most of them just laughed," the messenger reported. "They said they had never heard of Passover and they weren't going anywhere they couldn't worship their other gods along with Yahweh."

"Never heard of Passover!" King Hezekiah was astonished. He had heard of Passover all his life—not that it was actually celebrated in the days of Ahaz, but the story of Moses and the Israelites and their escape from Egypt was a part of his ancestral heritage. "Haven't they ever heard about how the death angel struck down the firstborn of every Egyptian household but passed over the Israelites?"

"A few of them did seem to know about *that,* my king." The messenger was obviously embarrassed. "And they asked why we were having the festival in the wrong month."

"To give them time to get here!" Hezekiah's frustration was obvious. He rose from his chair and paced about the audience hall. "We try to do something great for the service of Yahweh and nobody appreciates it!"

"Don't worry so, my king!" It was Shebna, as smoothly solicitous as ever. "If they don't come, it is their loss, not ours. But I believe they'll come, some of them. Enough to be useful for our purposes, no?"

Hezekiah smiled. Shebna knew that along with the king's plan for the festival went the hope that he would be able to ask some of the local leaders of Israel how strong Assyrian control was there. Sargon had many problems in many parts of his far-flung empire. Rumor had it that he was far to the east, suppressing difficulties in other territories. If ever there was a time to rejoin the Judeans and Israelites into one grand united kingdom, as it had been in the days of David and Solomon, perhaps the time was now!

Once his imagination was aroused, Hezekiah could very easily give way to wonderful fantasizing. Within a few years, he speculated, a new Israelite state might be established, a kingdom far larger than little Judah. A united kingdom might effectively topple Assyria's strangle-hold over all the Westlands. And the king, of course, would be Hezekiah himself! Had Isaiah not always told him he would be as great a ruler as David?

As Hezekiah dreamed, Isaiah walked into the audience hall. "I heard the Israelites are not interested in our Passover," he said without preamble. "So much the better, my king. I believe the hand of Yahweh is at work in this entire matter."

Hezekiah shook his head. He knew Isaiah would never understand because Isaiah valued peace so much. And empires were not built by keeping peace.

Hezekiah was delighted and Isaiah considerably distressed when, over the next few days, messengers returned from Israel with news of a more enthusiastic response from the villages they had visited. In the northernmost reaches of Israel there were still considerable numbers who belonged to the old tribes of Zebulun, Asher, and Issachar. Among these people the invitation to the great festival elicited favorable reaction. Even though the journey would take a week or more, quite a few announced their intention to come.

The days spun rapidly on. As the fourteenth of Iyar approached, Jerusalem was full of visitors, mostly Judeans, but also some Israelites, whole families of them. The city dwellers of Jerusalem opened their homes to the visitors, not merely kinsmen and friends but strangers as well. The Israelites were made to feel at home in the general air of festivity that reigned in Jerusalem.

In Isaiah's household there was no room for any Israelites. Maher, who was planning to be married soon, had recently established himself in the old city house, long ago abandoned by Isaiah's brother for more comfortable quarters. There he played host to his parents and to Jashub and Reba, who came up from Lachish with their infant daughter. The house was crowded, but the spring weather was delightful, and the visitors had no objections to sleeping on the roof.

The morning of the fourteenth of Iyar dawned warm and clear, and shortly after daybreak the streets filled with people, all pressing eagerly toward the temple courts. Isaiah's musicians and singers were in fine form, and as the music began, the priests began the lengthy and messy business of slaughtering the hundreds of lambs provided by the king for the feast. These would be roasted on the great altar, and while some portions were to be set aside as burnt offerings for Yahweh, most of the meat would be eaten by the crowd.

In the royal kitchens, teams of servants were busy baking the traditional unleavened bread and preparing baskets full of greens and bitter herbs for distribution to the people.

It was a day of wonderful festivity. Since the actual meal would be long in coming, many of the worshipers joined in the singing, while others, carried away by the holiday mood, began dancing in the temple courtyards. Though it was an extremely good-natured crowd, there was noise and confusion everywhere.

King Hezekiah grew tense as he observed the numerous livestock still penned behind the temple, waiting for ritual preparation. "Why is everything taking so long?" he exclaimed to Eliakim and Shebna.

"Don't worry, my king," Shebna replied calmly. "Things like this simply take more time than you think they will. We won't be dining until nightfall, but that's the way it's supposed to be."

Suddenly Mahath the Levite, out of breath and obviously distraught, came dashing up. "My lord, the people out there, some of those Israelites—they're doing something *unclean*!"

For a moment Hezekiah imagined the worst. Could some of his guests be transforming the festival into a fertility rite? Were there devotees of Baal and Ashteroth among the masses from Israel, determined to serve their own gods even here in the courts of Lord Yahweh's temple?

"What is it, Mahath?" he asked fearfully.

"They're eating *leavened* bread!" The Levite could not have been any more aghast had he been reporting a full-fledged orgy. "Heaven knows where they got it, but a lot of them have little loaves of it and they're passing it around. *Leavened*! On Passover! We'll have to make them leave! They'll pollute our feast!"

Hezekiah almost laughed. "We'll certainly not make them leave!" he said decisively. "Remember, Mahath, these people don't know any better, but the fact that they came at all shows they want to learn!" Even as he spoke, angry cries resounded from the nearby courtyards. Obviously some of Mahath's assistants had taken matters into their own hands, and the Israelites were not taking kindly to being evicted.

Hezekiah's festival was on the verge of turning into a bloody riot.

"Shebna, quick, go tell the trumpeters to sound an alarm!" the king commanded. "We'll settle this right now!"

Shebna obeyed, and the mournful ram's horn trumpets sounded through the temple courts as Hezekiah strode rapidly toward the king's bronze platform and mounted the steps. Suddenly the crowd became very quiet.

"Hear me, O Lord Yahweh!" the king declared in a loud voice. "We have not been perfect in keeping the rules of your holy day, and we admit our errors. But may the Lord pardon everyone who sets his heart to seek

Yahweh, God of our ancestors, even if not according to the sanctuary's rules!"

The crowd was silent for a moment. Then some among them burst into loud, joyous shouts of "Amen!"

The crisis had subsided. Isaiah, standing with the choir, felt a glow of pride in Hezekiah's masterful handling of the situation. He believed that the king should not have invited the Israelites, but since he had, at least he knew what to do with them. The king stepped down from the royal platform, whispered briefly to Isaiah, and the choir resumed its singing. The day was saved. There would be joy and feasting well into the evening, and a sense of real affection prevailed for the generous and open-minded king.

There will never be another Passover like this one in all the years to come, Isaiah thought.

At the end of the specified week of festivity, Hezekiah announced that since everyone was having such a joyous time, the celebration would be extended another week. For all the nobles as well as the king himself, this meant contribution of more sheep to feed the hungry crowds, but no one grumbled publicly.

"Lord Yahweh must be pleased by the great revival." "He will certainly reward us with special blessings!" These were the comments heard hundreds of times.

That was exactly what Hezekiah was hoping for.

And as the festivities continued, he found ample time for discussions with the leaders from Israel. The future held prospects of wonderful success. No matter what Isaiah kept saying about the value of peace, Hezekiah grew increasingly eager to begin building his empire.

EIGHT

The Waters under the Earth

"Whatever has Gaza done to us?" stormed Isaiah. "Hezekiah, I can't believe you mean it—sending out this call to arms! There is no reason under the sun to attack a neighboring state that is just sitting there, minding its own business!"

It was early summer, just a few weeks since the unseasonable Passover. The king and his father-in-law were alone in one of the royal gardens. Hezckiah, delighted with his newly announced military objective, relaxed on a bench in the cool shade while Isaiah paced nervously up and down before him, his wrath mounting.

"It's not as simple as you think," Hezekiah explained. "The Philistines of Gaza and all those other little city-states of theirs along the coast have always been our enemies. Right now there are Judean prisoners of war being held in Gaza, forced to serve as slaves. Those Philistines have raided our border villages for years, but the late King Ahaz was so busy kowtowing to the Assyrians that he never did anything about it. We cannot let our people remain in bondage! Besides, I have it on good authority that Gaza is woefully underdefended. Some of the Israelites are joining with our forces. This could be the first step toward the new Judah!"

It was difficult to counter Hezekiah's enthusiasm. "You have never been to war," Isaiah remarked. "You do not know its horrors. To young men like you it seems a grand adventure, but to the rest of us it is murder!"

Isaiah suspected, though he did not dare to say so, that the king's eagerness for military action was rooted in his desire to be as different from his father as possible. It did not escape Isaiah's notice that Hezekiah almost always referred to his predecessor as "the late King Ahaz" rather than "my father."

"You've never been to war either, Isaiah," Hezekiah countered.

"No, but I remember when Rezin and Pekah invaded. I remember the thousands of our people slain, the devastation, the looting, the unspeakable cruelty of it all. Yes, I was safe inside Jerusalem, but I saw enough."

"But, this time Judah is going to win! How can you possibly care if those idol-worshiping Philistines are slain? Isn't that a sign of the wrath of Yahweh upon them?"

Isaiah was silent. He had often said that military defeat was a sure indication of Lord Yahweh's anger. The history of Israel and Judah was full of incidents that fit the pattern perfectly, right up to and including Sargon's recent destruction of Samaria, the Israelite capital. Still, Isaiah could not endorse Hezekiah's plan. "Whenever there is war, there are losers on both sides," he said. "You know that you might very well be killed yourself. And no sons yet!"

"If I am killed, then you will be king!" Hezekiah replied. "Always remember, you are the nearest living heir to the throne."

"I don't want to be king! I want you to live and prosper for long years to come and leave many children to keep your memory alive—my grandchildren."

Hezekiah looked deeply troubled. "Lord Yahweh

knows," he whispered, "it's not Hephzibah's fault. We're trying. Hephzibah has even offered some of her servant girls, too—just as Sarai offered Hagar to Abram."

To acquire a collection of concubines was, traditionally, the king's perogative, but Hezekiah looked embarrassed as he spoke. He was deeply in love with Hephzibah, and the girls he had taken into his bed recently meant nothing more to him than the hope of producing an heir, which seemed increasingly unlikely.

Isaiah sensed his deep concern. "Lord Yahweh promised King David there would never fail to be a son to inherit the throne of his father," the prophet reflected.

Isaiah left the king's presence feeling slightly better. Yet their conversation had not been a happy one. Isaiah grieved over Hezekiah's taking concubines. This was something he had not heard about before. He wondered how many there were but was afraid to ask.

And still Isaiah remained apprehensive about Gaza. Hezekiah's impending attack on the Philistines was definitely not the way to usher in the peaceable kingdom.

A few weeks later the Judean troops returned from the conquest of Gaza, laden with spoils and bringing with them a host of liberated captives. All Jerusalem celebrated, gleeful with the excitement that follows a sudden victory of a longtime loser. Hezekiah, who had conquered one Philistine town, was as much acclaimed as if he had conquered half the world.

Of course, there had been Judean losses, but they were few indeed. There was a vast amount of loot taken from the Philistines, including horses and chariots and a large supply of weaponry—all a great boost to the king's plans for further military activity.

Joah, the king's chief recording secretary, charged with writing an official report of the campaign, looked up from the little scroll he had just begun to prepare as Hezekiah entered the room that served as the scribe's office. "Listen to this, my king. 'Lord Yahweh was with Hezekiah, and wherever he went forth he prospered.'" Joah read his own words with obvious pleasure. "'He defeated the Philistines as far as Gaza and its territory, from watchtower to fortified city.'"

"Splendid! An excellent beginning, but give it much more detail!" Hezekiah was as enthusiastic as usual. "And look at this, Joah! Prince Isaiah has written us a victory poem. See that it goes into the record."

Like most of Isaiah's writings, the lines were inscribed on a potsherd, or rather on two potsherds since the entire text did not fit on one.

> "Wait, O gate; cry, O city;
>   Melt in fear, O Philistia, all of you!
> For smoke comes out of the north,
>   and there is no straggler in his ranks.
> And the firstborn of the poor will feed,
>   and the needy lie down in safety."

Joah read the text aloud, questions hovering in every line. "Maybe the last part goes first," he suggested after a moment. "And whatever does he mean by 'out of the north'?"

"Presumably it sounded more poetic than 'out of the northeast,'" Hezekiah answered.

"But he almost seems to be mourning for the Philistines! Not that he means it that way, of course." The scribe was clearly dissatisfied with Isaiah's effort.

"Believe me, Joah, from Isaiah, *this* is a victory poem!" Hezekiah placed the potsherds on the scribe's table and walked away. "It is more than I expected from him."

Hezekiah firmly hoped that Isaiah was beginning to see the necessity of military action in a good cause.

Meanwhile, Isaiah was hoping just as strongly that, having had his little adventure, Hezekiah would be content to stay at home and pursue a more peaceful course.

Hezekiah's next great project, while it had military overtones, at least did not involve an overt attack on any of Judah's neighbors. What Jerusalem needed most desperately was a better method for bringing water into the city. For years King Ahaz and his advisors had talked of digging a tunnel deep under the earth, through solid rock, to bring the waters of the pool of Siloam into a reservoir inside the city. But Ahaz finally decided it couldn't be done. The logistics of the whole scheme defied his experts, and besides, it was too expensive.

Hezekiah, inspired by his father's failure, was determined to go down in history as the builder of the Siloam Tunnel. For weeks the palace buzzed with activity as various self-appointed authorities came before the king's council with their schemes for bringing the waters under the earth. A large part of the difficulty lay in concealing the tunnel's entrance outside the walls. If it were too easy to find, enemy forces could utilize it to slip into the city. Anyone familiar with Judah's history knew that King David's troops had first seized Jerusalem by entering through an underground water passage.

Hezekiah wanted a far more sophisticated system which would involve cutting through many feet of solid rock with pickaxes and chisels—a long laborious task. After a lengthy deliberation, it was decided that a group of quarrymen would begin at opposite ends, working toward each other. Then came a great deal of careful measuring above ground, with the king in the thick of it all, obviously enjoying the entire project.

"There is always the danger that the two groups won't meet exactly, but once they begin to get close, each side will hear the pickaxes of the other, and then they can work in the direction of the sound."

Hezekiah, who by now considered himself the tunnel

expert, was eager to explain the project to Isaiah and to show him its progress. One afternoon he persuaded the prophet to accompany him down a flight of stone steps into the underground recesses of the tunnel's entry point inside Jerusalem. The noise of the laborers' tools almost drowned out the king's voice as he and Isaiah approached.

There were about ten or twelve quarrymen at work, chipping away diligently at the seemingly impenetrable barrier of hard stone. They were not slaves but free men, who were being well paid for the job. Suddenly an awareness of the king's presence seemed to sweep through the entire team, and they stopped their work to salute him cheerfully. "We have come further than the men outside the city, my king," one of them said. "Yesterday my brother measured. He's an impartial observer. He says we're going to win!"

"Perhaps!" Hezekiah answered. "It is a close race. Both sides are coming along very well!"

"But you're for *us*, aren't you, my king?" another of the men called. "For the Insiders?"

Isaiah was surprised at the familiarity with which Hezekiah's people spoke to him. It was something Ahaz never would have permitted, and it was heartwarming.

"You know the king can't take sides!" Hezekiah answered with a laugh. "Just remember, there's a bonus for every man on the team that cuts the most distance, and a special gift for the man whose pickaxe knocks through the first hole at the connecting point."

"Which side are *you* for, Prince Isaiah?" The workmen continued their banter, obviously enjoying the break from the ardous task.

Isaiah smiled. "Oh, I haven't even thought about it."

"No predictions?"

"Absolutely no predictions," he answered. Yet as he and Hezekiah turned away and the quarrymen resumed their labor, Isaiah felt a distinct satisfaction. The tunnel would be a success, something to benefit Jerusalem for years to come.

"When they finally do break through the rock," Isaiah said, "you should have them carve an inscription, deep into the stone, so it will be there forever."

"I suppose we could," Hezekiah answered. "What would you have it say?"

"Oh, have them tell how they built it. Give plenty of details. Someday our descendants will want to know about this. Even if scrolls are lost and potsherds are broken, stone remains forever, and there it will be, the monument of King Hezekiah, who brought the waters under the earth into the city."

Hezekiah liked that idea. Yes, there would definitely have to be an inscription.

As the friendly rivalry of the Insiders and the Outsiders continued and the two parts of the tunnel grew closer together, the king decided upon a plan for the further improvement of Jerusalem, a thorough inspection of the city walls, with repairs wherever needed and installation of several new watchtowers.

"The late King Ahaz allowed our local defenses to fall into a deplorable state of repair," Hezekiah announced one morning to a full gathering of his council. Isaiah was there, along with Shebna, Eliakim, Joah, and several other close friends of the king. Among the less frequent attendants was Maher, a young man still very much at loose ends. Two weeks earlier, his bride of less than a year had died of a miscarriage. Sensing the aimlessness of his life and unwilling to seek his father's advice, lonely Maher had gone to his boyhood friend Hezekiah and asked if there were some way he might enter the king's service.

Isaiah was puzzled by his son's sudden interest in affairs of state and was surprised by Hezekiah's announcement at the council meeting that Maher would be in charge of rebuilding Jerusalem's fortifications.

"Our predecessor," Hezekiah said, using another of his unaffectionate terms for Ahaz, "always said Judah was too poor for any great schemes, yet I have found his secret storehouses full of treasures. Times are good. There have been abundant crops for several years now. Taxes continue to be paid, and if we lack funds, we'll simply have a special levy for our repair project. We must have the stongest defenses possible in case Jerusalem should be attacked."

Shebna nodded enthusiastic agreement, as did Maher.

"Who, may I ask, is likely to attack Jerusalem?" Isaiah interjected. "Not the Philistines, after what we did to Gaza! Certainly not the Israelites. Egypt is far away, and from all we hear, the Black Pharaoh has plenty of trouble at home trying to hold together two kingdoms so different as Egypt and Ethiopia." Hezekiah was pleased that Isaiah was so well-informed on the current state of world affairs.

Isaiah continued, "Besides, as long as we keep up our tribute payments to Assyria, we have their guarantee of military protection from enemies anywhere. Hezekiah, my king, please don't put a further tax burden on our people to pay for unnecessary defenses!"

"Defense can never be called unnecessary! And we may not need a special levy. Prince Maher has agreed to supervise the rebuilding project. I'm sure you trust your son's judgment, Isaiah?"

The prophet shivered with apprehension. He swallowed hard, and said nothing. Across the table sat Maher, looking happy for the first time since his young bride's death. Yet, if there was anyone whose judgment Isaiah did not trust at all, it was Maher's. How well he remembered Naamah's efforts several years earlier to interest the lad in the routine details of managing the family estate. Maher had responded with obvious boredom, if not actual distaste. Since Isaiah had no real gift for business matters himself, he had not blamed him, yet now Maher was about to be put in charge of a great amount of public funds. Sometimes Hezekiah, even with good intentions, used no sense at all.

"Well, Isaiah?" The king broke the prophet's stunned silence.

"My son is honest and loyal, and I know he will serve you to the best of his ability, my king." Isaiah's voice was formal and polite. He knew he was going to be spending a great deal of time behind the scenes helping Maher with this project.

But, of course, there was always Naamah, who for years had collected rents, supervised purchases, kept all the household accounts, and who knew more about such things than either her husband or son would ever know. *Naamah is going to have to help us both,* Isaiah thought. *And like it or not, we're going to have to move back into the city house for a while.*

That evening Isaiah told his wife the situation. Naamah was willing to do what she could. "Certainly Maher will need help! Whatever was Hezey thinking of, giving him such an appointment!" she exclaimed indignantly. "Yes, we'll have to move back into that dreadful house for a time so we can be close to the palace. I'll do what I can, but if it gets too much for me, we'll find help somewhere. We can't let Maher spend our people's money like there's no end to it, and we can't let Hezey raise taxes!"

Once Naamah was motivated, there was no limit to her energy. For a woman whose accounts had always been kept in shekels, it would be something of a shock to deal with *talents* of gold and silver, far greater sums than she had ever thought about. But Naamah coped admirably. For weeks thereafter, the prophet's city house bustled with activity as Naamah discreetly checked figures, estimated costs, and sent her son scurrying about Jerusalem recruiting workers for the great repair project.

Isaiah, helped, too. He persuaded many workers that it was better to work for lower wages than to face a greatly increased tax burden.

As for Maher, even though it was somewhat galling to him to realize that his parents, especially his mother, were doing the job the king had assigned to him personally, he did not complain. He seemed, rather, to enjoy the prestige that his position gave him.

Work was well underway on the repair of the city's fortifications when the Siloam Tunnel at last reached completion. While it was the Insiders who finally covered more distance, it was one of the Outsiders who made the first hole at the breakthrough point in the stone. All Jerusalem was jubilant. Hezekiah distributed the promised bonuses and announced that an inscription would be carved on the tunnel's wall as Isaiah had suggested. The Insiders were given the additional honor of composing the inscription and chiseling it into the stone.

A few days later, the leader of the Insiders brought the king a neatly written sheet of papyrus with a copy of the inscription upon it. Hezekiah read it aloud with glowing satisfaction. Seated in the public audience hall of the palace, he was gratified that there were many bystanders to hear him as he read.

"In the days of Hezekiah the king, the tunnel was driven through. And this is the way in which it was cut through: While each man worked toward his fellow, and while there were still three cubits to be cut through, there was heard the voice of a man calling to his fellow, for there was an overlap in the rock on the right and on the left. And when the tunnel was driven through, the quarrymen hewed the rock, each man toward his fellow, axe against axe, and the water flowed from the spring toward the reservoir for twelve hundred cubits, and the height of the rock above the heads of the quarrymen was one hundred cubits."

Hezekiah smiled, pleased that he could accomplish something noble for Yahweh's people.

NINE

Naked and Barefoot

For nearly a decade there was peace in the land of Judah, not so much because of Hezekiah but as the result of circumstances beyond his control. Through much of this time, the king kept his couriers scurrying back and forth to distant lands, seeking allies for his great anti-Assyrian scheme. Feisty King Merodach-baladan of Babylon was always scheming, hoping to restore Babylonian glory. The Assyrians saw to it that he was no more than a local overlord in Babylon, but Merodach-baladan was biding his time, looking for an opportunity to rebel.

As for the Israelites to the north, while they were friendly enough to Hezekiah's rhetoric on a reunited kingdom, their poor, underpopulated little country was not worth trying to annex, and Hezekiah knew it. To attempt to join Israel with Judah in one kingdom would be more of a burden than a gain for the Judeans and would lead to Assyrian reprisals much too soon. Hezekiah had to be patient. There would be time enough for his rebellion when, and only when, Judah could count on some reliable military aid.

Meanwhile, the cycle of living and dying went on.

Queen Abijah, Hezekiah's mother, died suddenly. She had not been ill, though she had often complained of a weariness. One evening she went to bed early and died in her sleep. Her maids did not discover her body until the following morning.

Had she been a different sort of woman, many would have suspected foul play, but no one hated Abijah. She was kinder and far more respected than most royal ladies of history.

Hezekiah wept bitterly, consoled only by the fact that his mother's parting had been so easy, so painless. Hephzibah grieved deeply, too, for in many ways she and her mother-in-law had been kindred souls, these two ladies who had loved Judah's kings. Abijah was far more serious, more a thinker than Hephzibah ever cared to be. Hephzibah was spirited, more creative, happier— but with good reason. She had a husband whose affection for her was strong and true, but Abijah had only had Ahaz.

In accord with her often-expressed wish, Abijah was buried beside King Ahaz in the garden of Uzziah. Gradually, her memory faded, except in the heart of her son, where she would live forever, eternally beautiful.

Maher married again, then his young wife died along with her premature infant. Deeply discouraged and grieved, Isaiah's younger son vowed he would not marry again, that he was somehow accursed. He determined to seek consolation outside the bounds of marriage. If he were careful and found his harlots outside of Jerusalem, his parents need never know. Maher was discreet, though sadly troubled. At the king's court he continued to hold a succession of appointments, but none were so significant as his supervision of Jerusalem's fortification repairs. Somehow, probably through Hephzibah, Hezekiah realized that most of the important planning on that project was done by Naamah.

Maher continued to enjoy the courtesy title of prince,

though technically, unlike his father, he was not a true prince in the sense of being a born descendant of a reigning monarch. Hezekiah was not one to bother with fine distinctions such as that. The land of Judah was woefully short of princes.

Jashub, the potter of Lachish, could have had the title, too—if he had wanted it. However, Jashub and Reba, his wife, had no interest in such matters. Their pottery business in Lachish was thriving. Jashub as an artisan was far more prosperous and happy than his rootless, unmotivated brother. In rapid succession, Reba gave birth to five children—three girls and then two boys. Yearly, at Passover, the whole family came to visit Isaiah and Naamah, and in the autumn, the prophet and his wife usually went for a few days to Lachish for the festival of Succoth. Jashub's neighbors were much more impressed by the fact that his father was a prophet of Yahweh than by his kinship to the royal house. The potter, who was not one to trade on family ties, doubted if any of his neighbors even realized that his sister was Lady Hephzibah, the king's wife.

As the years passed, Hezekiah who never really forgot his early dreams of regaining Judah's independence, began to hear some rumbles from the southwest.

Ashdod, one of the little Philistine city-states, which by itself could have never hoped to achieve anything at all, was beginning to organize a plot against Assyria. The real power behind the whole scheme was the indomitable Pharaoh Shabako, the Ethiopian prince who had by now firmly welded Egypt and Ethiopia into one kingdom and was looking for new worlds to conquer.

Was King Hezekiah of Judah interested?

Indeed, Hezekiah was interested. All of a sudden, Jerusalem was full of Philistines, Egyptians, and Ethiopians, envoys to the king's court. At public meetings of the royal council, matters seemed innocuous enough. Pharaoh Shabako was interested in bettering trade relations with Judah. But behind closed doors, war, not trade, was the major subject of the foreigners' conversations with Hezekiah.

Isaiah the prophet worried over the situation. *Don't Hezekiah and his advisors realize that Pharaoh Shabako's promises of aid are a ploy in his own empire-building schemes? Why exchange one master for another? Egypt would be no better than Assyria, possibly much worse.*

Isaiah did something he had not done since the most demonstrative days of his youth. He started appearing in public and at court, clad in a kilt of rough sackcloth. It was the traditional garb of Lord Yahweh's prophets, but Isaiah, though he always dressed rather plainly, had long felt that such excesses were unnecessary. Now something drastic had to be done to get people's attention.

But even in sackcloth, the prophet found that no one paid him much attention at all. Busy people hurried by him as he stood on a street corner near the palace. He heard a few remarks. "That's Isaiah. He and the king are on bad terms again." "It's shameful for a prince of Judah to go around looking like some poor beggar." "What does he think he's trying to prove?"

"Listen, my people!" he cried out in a loud voice. "Hear the word of the Lord:

"'Woe to the rebellious children,' says Yahweh,
'who carry out a plan, but not mine;
and who make a league, but not of my spirit,
that they may add sin to sin!'"

A small crowd was beginning to gather, and Isaiah saw among them faces he had known for many years. But he also saw a number of strangers, men of the Egyptian-Ethiopian entourage. He hoped they would understand him. He continued:

"The Egyptians are men, and not God;
and their horses are flesh,
and not spirit.
When the Lord stretches out his hand,

the helper will stumble, and he
who is helped will fall,
and they will all perish together!"

There was angry muttering among the foreigners in their own tongue. At least one of them understood what Isaiah said and was attempting to translate to his fellows.

Undeterred, the prophet continued.

"Egypt's help is worthless and empty,
therefore I have called her
'Rahab the Dragon' who sits still!"

Suddenly a small rock, well aimed by someone in the crowd, struck Isaiah's bare chest. Stunned, he grasped at the strickened spot and felt blood, warm and sticky, oozing into his hand. Then another rock sailed just over his shoulder.

"Stop, you fools!" someone in the mob shouted. "He's the king's kinsman! He's a prince!"

There was angry scuffling among the bystanders while Isaiah, even more aroused and angry, preached on.

"You are a rebellious people,
lying sons!
Sons who will not hear
the instruction of Yahweh.
You say to the seers, 'See not,'
and to the prophets,
'Prophesy not to us what is right,
Speak to us smooth things,
Prophesy illusions.
Leave the way, turn aside from the path.
Let us hear no more of the Holy One of Israel!'"

No one really listened. Another rock whizzed past him, barely missing his forehead. Then, suddenly, as if from nowhere, Maher was beside him. Maher, who had been at home in the city house a few doors away, had heard the shouting and ventured forth out of curiosity, scarcely expecting what he found.

There was surprising energy in the unambitious young Maher. Angrily, he pushed through the crowd to his father's side. "Papa, come with me," he whispered gently, draping his own cloak around Isaiah's bare shoulders.

The mob dispersed, and Maher led his father away. "Isaiah is a brilliant man and a true servant of Yahweh," he heard someone say, "but he always was a bit peculiar."

"Downright crazy, if you ask me," said another.

They have not seen anything yet, Isaiah thought sadly. *They must listen to me. Hezekiah must listen.* Suddenly Yahweh spoke to his heart, telling him what he must do.

Isaiah spent the night at the city house, and the next morning he ventured out into the street, clad only in a scanty linen loincloth. Even his feet were bare. A lesser man in such a state of undress would have immediately been suspected of drunkenness or sudden loss of reason, but because of Isaiah's reputation, those who saw him realized he must be enacting a message from Yahweh.

"Hey, Isaiah, did you lose your sackcloth in the big fight yesterday?" called a stranger in a rude voice.

"Wait till the king hears about this!" another shouted.

"What are you trying to tell us now?"

"I am telling you," Isaiah replied, "what Lord Yahweh himself told me. If Judah is so foolish as to join in the revolt of Ashdod and count on help from Egypt, its people will be defeated and dragged off as captives to Assyria, naked and barefoot, even as I am now!"

All morning, as he walked through the streets of the city, he preached the same message again and again to throngs of the curious. No one was throwing rocks today. They were listening, many of them shocked and silent in the face of Isaiah's bold action.

It was only the beginning.

He returned to his country house that evening, and Naamah greeted him in disbelief. "Isaiah! Whatever has happened?" She put her arms around him and felt how cold he was. "Your clothes!" she gasped. "Even your sandals! And you've been hurt, too." The wound on his chest, while not deep, looked worse than it was. "Oh, my darling!" Naamah fluttered about, dashing to their bedroom to grab one of Isaiah's robes from a clothes chest. "Here, put this on," she urged, "and tell me what has happened."

Meekly, Isaiah did what Naamah requested. At home, he would wear ordinary clothes, he decided but in public, until Hezekiah broke off all negotiations with Ashdod and with the pharaoh, he would go about in loincloth only.

"But it might be months!" Naamah protested on hearing Isaiah's plan. "In fact, who can say that Hezekiah can ever be deterred from his Egyptian schemes now that all those men from Pharaoh's court are actually here?"

"I know what I must do," Isaiah replied calmly. "Yes, it might take months because our Hezey is a dreamer, and he's stubborn and unrealistic and surrounded by bad advisors. But I'll reach him. And with Lord Yahweh's help, Judah will be preserved." There was a faraway look in Isaiah's eyes, a look of determination mixed with inexpressible sadness. It was one of those times when Naamah found him most unreachable. Indeed, not since the naming of Maher-shalal-hash-baz had he done anything so rash as this!

But I know I cannot stop him, Naamah thought. The coming months were going to be hard, full of strife. Yet how much worse if Hezekiah did join in the rebellion against Sargon and all the survivors of Judah were dragged off into captivity, naked and barefoot!

Since Naamah knew that Isaiah would not be deterred from doing what he felt Yahweh wanted him to do, she determined to be patient, always ready to welcome him into the warmth of her arms when he came home from facing the scorn and ridicule of the world outside.

The next morning the prophet went to the palace and

requested an audience with the king. One of the palace doorkeepers conducted him into a small, curtained-off, empty room adjoining the royal audience hall and told him to wait.

He waited. Time dragged heavily on. Isaiah sat on the floor, leaned his back against the wall, closed his eyes, and prayed for guidance. Quite miserable and distinctly cold, he was still confident that he was following Lord Yahweh's will.

After what seemed an interminable period of time, Isaiah heard someone approaching. "You'll have to see him to believe it, my king!" Shebna's loud voice sounded excited. "I had him whisked out of sight the moment I saw him coming. It's a shameful thing, very tragic!"

"He *does* have on a loincloth, doesn't he?" Hezekiah seemed concerned.

"Well, yes, but that's absolutely all." Shebna pulled back the curtain as Isaiah rose to his feet. For a moment the king regarded his father-in-law in silence. Hezekiah, who always dressed impeccably, looked even more splendid than usual in a white linen robe topped by a wide, jeweled collar. The outfit was obviously Egyptian, a gift from Pharaoh Shabako.

"Come with me, Isaiah." Hezekiah spoke gently as if addressing a sick man, one who had taken leave of his senses. "We will speak together in private, you and I and Shebna."

Isaiah followed without a word. He was glad that Shebna was there, for he was the leader of the pro-Egyptian agitators, the source of much of Hezekiah's misguided policy.

A few moments later, seated in Hezekiah's private suite, Isaiah explained to the king as clearly and rationally as he had ever spoken in his life the folly of rebellion against Sargon.

Hezekiah listened thoughtfully, but Isaiah could not guess what the king was thinking. The air was heavy with tension. The prophet's spirit ached to reach the king with Yahweh's message. Isaiah tried to imagine himself in Hezekiah's place. What an awesome responsibility it would be to make decisions that might determine the whole of Judah's future! Isaiah wanted so desperately to help him.

As the prophet spoke, the king would not meet his gaze directly. Hezekiah seemed confused. Yet much of what Isaiah said about Assyria and Egypt seemed to make sense to the king. "I have given Pharaoh no promises," he said at last. "I am waiting to see what happens at Ashdod before committing Judah to anything. At present, I am simply keeping our options open. Now, Isaiah, will you let me give you some decent clothes to wear home?"

Isaiah shook his head sadly. "Yahweh has commanded me to go about like this until you break off with Egypt completely."

"Then go!" Hezekiah was suddenly angrier than Isaiah had ever seen him.

Isaiah went, but he knew this was not the end of the matter. It was, he feared, only the beginning.

As anyone could have predicted, Assyria sent forces to besiege Ashdod. The fact that the king did not lead them in person showed how insignificant the Assyrians considered the whole uprising to be. But Ashdod was better prepared for resistance than Sargon expected. Shabako had actually come through with the military aid he had promised. For months, Assyrian troops battered away at the walls of Ashdod with little visible success.

In Jerusalem, where practically everyone was caught up in the fervor of Ashdod's continuing battle, Isaiah continued walking about in his loincloth. The strange protest became accepted. People scarcely noticed him except to comment that if and when the Assyrians retreated from Ashdod, Isaiah would be proven a false prophet.

Hezekiah continued to stall on the matter of alliance

with Egypt. He could not forget Isaiah's warnings nor ignore his ongoing demonstration. Time dragged by. The seasons passed, and Hezekiah, sorely missing Isaiah's presence, at last summoned him back to the palace.

"Have you any new word from Lord Yahweh?" Hezekiah began, trying to act as if the ill will between them had never existed, as if their last visit had been but a few days rather than many months before.

"Only what you have heard from me already," Isaiah said. "Ashdod, of course, will fall to Assyria. You have done well to keep on paying tribute, Hezekiah. But the danger continues. Do not fail now."

"I have been watching you." Hezekiah rose from his chair and paced nervously about. "Day after day, I have had reports about you, Isaiah. And now I am beginning to believe you. No one would do what you have done without the strongest confidence that God is with him. Shebna still thinks our best hopes are with Pharaoh Shabako. You cannot imagine the pressures that man puts upon me! But I am going to follow you." The last sentence was delivered in almost a whisper.

Isaiah looked up at him, surprised and happy. A thousand thoughts stirred through his mind. He knew Hezekiah had made one of the most difficult decisions of his life, giving up his dreams in favor of an alternative he now believed to be Yahweh's will. The prince of the promise, in his confusion and wavering more like Ahaz than he would ever care to admit, had passed the test after all. Peace, for now, was preserved in the land of Judah.

"Have you any clothes I might borrow to wear home?" Isaiah asked. Perhaps that said it all. "Nothing elaborate, please. The simplest things you can find."

"Oh, Isaiah!" Hezekiah exclaimed joyfully. "I wish you would let me deck you out in splendor! Let this whole city see you high in the king's favor as you have always, always, been."

Isaiah shook his head, and Hezekiah knew his offer was in vain. The king rang for a servant and sent him scurrying to find a plain, unadorned robe and a pair of sandals.

A few days later came the news that the Assyrians had taken Ashdod and that the city's surviving inhabitants were being deported to distant lands. Now the evidence was conclusive: Sargon was unstoppable. Isaiah was vindicated. Judah was safe.

"But Sargon is an old man," Shebna whispered to Hezekiah later that day as the two of them discussed the news in private. "He will not last too many years longer, and when his son, Sennacherib, takes over, *then* will be the time for rebellion. We still need to keep in touch with Pharaoh, my king! The time is coming when Assyria will fall."

"Has Lord Yahweh given you the gift of predicting the future?" Hezekiah asked with a tinge of irony in his voice. Shebna was so tiresome, yet he knew how to play upon the king's deepest hopes for Judah's independence. Hezekiah could not ignore him.

"Wait and see, my king," Shebna said smugly. "Young Prince Sennacherib is a weakling from all I've heard."

"Old Sargon isn't dead yet," Hezekiah retorted, "and while he lives Judah will continue a loyal tributary. After that . . . well, we'll wait and see."

TEN

A Sickness unto Death

Weeks slipped by into months, the seasons ran their course, and Isaiah was blithely unaware of Hezekiah's long range plans. In Assyria, old King Sargon stubbornly clung to life while Sennacherib, who was no weakling at all but a fiercer man than his father had ever been, waited impatiently for him to die. In Egypt the Black Pharaoh, well-informed of world events, was also waiting. Shabako truly believed the death of Sargon would be the first step that would reduce the Assyrian empire to a shambles, and when that happened, Egypt would be there to replace Assyria as ruler of the world.

From Jerusalem, Shebna maintained close contact with the Egyptian court. Judean envoys traveled frequently to Egypt, and when Isaiah was so bold as to ask the purpose of these trips, Shebna assured him it was simply a matter of promoting commerce between Egypt and Judah.

There was, in fact, a measure of truth in Shebna's statement. Hezekiah's chief minister was deeply involved in a number of merchant ventures with Egypt and was very rapidly amassing for himself a vast fortune.

Even with the heavy taxes he was compelled to pay into the tribute fund, Shebna managed to live luxuriously, more so than King Hezekiah himself. The chief minister's horses and chariots, imported from Egypt, were the talk of the city. Few men could afford to keep a horse anymore, but Shebna had a stable full of them, along with not just one but several elaborately decorated chariots. His daily rides to the palace always attracted the envious glances of the crowd and sometimes there were angry murmurs. Maher, whose horse had finally died of old age, could scarcely contain his resentment whenever Shebna's chariot raced past him.

Then, as if he already had everything that a man could need on earth, Shebna began construction of an ornate mausoleum. He wanted to be assured that at his death he would have an elaborate burial in a tomb carved out of solid rock on a hillside near Jerusalem. Some of the quarrymen who had worked on the Siloam Tunnel were employed for the project, which promised to be long and laborious.

The wastefulness of the whole enterprise bothered Isaiah more than anything else Shebna had done, and his instinctive distrust of the chief minister grew deeper than ever. By far the most capable man in Hezekiah's immediate circle of advisors was Eliakim ben-Hilkiah, moderate and sensible, a staunch supporter of peace. *What would it take to persuade Hezekiah to replace Shebna with Eliakim?* Isaiah wondered.

Then one morning after a brief session in the king's council chamber, Shebna invited his associates to come out and see his rock-cut tomb, now nearing completion. "It is so grand," he boasted, "that it will be a pleasure to be dead in it."

Hezekiah rode along with Shebna in his best chariot while Eliakim, Isaiah, Maher, Joah the recording secretary, and several other men of the court followed in other chariots of Shebna's fleet, making a splendid parade to the chief minister's monument.

When they reached the mausoleum on the outskirts of Jerusalem, they found a feast awaiting them. Shebna's servants had spread a lavish table in the shade of the overhanging rocks, and there the visiting dignitaries were invited to sit and enjoy their host's bounty. There was food enough to feed a hundred or more guests, not just the small group of already well-fed aristocrats. The wine flowed freely, too, as the large silver goblets at each man's place were not allowed to become empty. Isaiah watched with astonishment as Shebna quaffed several cups of the strong sweet wine in short order and rapidly grew more talkative.

"This is only the beginning of what can be done in Judah," he said, "once we openly acknowledge Pharaoh as our friend and stop the payments to Assyria! Every one of you can have splendid things like these, and much more, once we're rid of the tribute obligation—as soon as Sargon dies—may it be soon!" With the last sentence he raised his goblet to toast his dreams.

"Soon!" Hezekiah responded with an eagerness that chilled Isaiah.

Suddenly all of the prophet's pent-up outrage burst loose. The rules of hospitality forgotten, he rose from Shebna's table. The power of Lord Yahweh came upon him, and the righteous wrath of the prophet poured forth.

"Hear me, Shebna! Thus says the Lord: What have you done here, that you have hewn here a tomb for your-self on the heights, carved a habitation for yourself in the rock? Behold, Lord Yahweh will hurl you away violently, strong man! He will seize a firm hold on you and whirl you around like a ball into a wide land, and there you shall die! And there shall be your splendid chariots, you shame of your master's house! You will be cast down from your of-fice, and in that day the Lord will call Eliakim ben-Hilkiah and clothe him with your robe and bind your belt upon him! The Lord will commit your authority to his hand, and he shall be a father to the inhabitants of Jerusalem and to the house of Judah!"

"Isaiah! Stop!" It was Eliakim, obviously surprised, embarrassed, almost frightened. In spite of their differences, Eliakim and Shebna were friends. "My king! I know nothing about this!" he added.

Isaiah did not stop. "Thus says Lord Yahweh: I will place on the shoulder of Eliakim the key of the house of David. He shall open, and none shall shut; he shall shut and none shall open!"

"Isaiah, please stop!" cried Eliakim.

Shebna, everyone noticed, was saying nothing at all. If Eliakim was frightened, Shebna was absolutely terrified. At last he managed to speak, not to Isaiah, but Hezekiah.

"My king, let me resign my office! Give it to Eliakim! I don't want it any more. Lord Yahweh knows I am his loyal servant! If I have offended, forgive me!"

"Very well," Hezekiah said, hesitantly. "I have been planning some changes anyway. Eliakim, you are now chief minister. Shebna, I will speak with you in private later today. But for now, do not worry! Let us enjoy our feast, and let us all be at peace among ourselves again!"

Isaiah nodded solemnly. Though shaken by the power of Yahweh at work in him, he would have much preferred to go home. He was not at all happy about how he had handled the situation. Yet if a tirade could remove Shebna from office, then it was justified.

Several days later Isaiah learned the outcome of Hezekiah's private conversation with Shebna and realized his outburst had been in vain. While Eliakim now held the title of chief minister, the king created for Shebna a new position—chief secretary. The chief minister's duties would entail local administration— keeping the palace and court running smoothly. Foreign policy would still remain in the hands of the expert on that subject—Shebna.

Fully recovered from his fright, Shebna felt infinitely pleased with himself. He could even afford to be condescendingly polite to Isaiah since the prophet had been completely foiled. In his new office Shebna could look forward to enjoying more power than ever before. He could hardly wait for Sargon to die!

After some months, the news of the old king's death and the accession of his son Sennacherib came at last. The new king of Assyria made it clear to all his vassals that he anticipated special gifts to celebrate the beginning of his reign. Instead, as planned throughout the Westlands, widespread revolt broke out. Hezekiah was in the thick of it, with Judah entirely committed to the rebellion. Once again, Jerusalem was full of envoys from Shabako.

Hezekiah felt that soon Egypt and Assyria would be locked in a struggle to the death, and Judah, as an ally of Shabako, would be the beneficiary of Assyria's collapse. The long-awaited dream of freedom from tribute was drawing nearer and nearer.

Isaiah, however, was torn between grief and anger. All his struggles of the past years, even his long and unforgettable protest demonstration in the loincloth, had accomplished nothing after all. His attempt to have Shebna removed from his position of influence had been equally fruitless. The pro-Egyptian party had triumphed, totally disregarding Yahweh's wishes for his people. Judah had sinned, King Hezekiah had sinned, and the whole land would bear the consequences.

After all that had happened before, how could Hezekiah have done such a reckless and misguided thing? The prophet understood well enough that no king deliberately destroys his own kingdom. And surely no person as genuinely decent as Hezekiah would deliberately pursue a policy that would lead to the death of thousands of his own people.

Yet the king faced a more imminent defeat—his own.

All Jerusalem was talking about the king's grave illness. It came so suddenly and caused wide-spread apprehension. Hephzibah feared for her husband's life, and she frequently wept like a child on Naamah's shoulder. She saw the illness not only as a threat to her beloved Hezekiah, but as a loss of dreams for Judah. Here, at a time when it seemed the kingdom might be able to break free from the Assyrian yoke, the godly and ambitious king lay near the gates of death.

The prophet of Yahweh, the father-in-law of the king, knew he must quickly visit Hezekiah.

Isaiah walked briskly up the great ramp to the king's palace and, as always, was admitted without question. Through the long, quiet halls he walked to the king's private apartment where a lone guard sat in the hall outside the open door.

The strangeness of the king's bedroom immediately struck Isaiah as he stood in the doorway. Someone had pushed Hezekiah's great ivory bed out into the center of the room, and there, beneath a tumble of fine woolen coverlets, surrounded by a mass of pillows, lay the king. His eyes, wide open, stared at the ceiling beams high above him. His dark face mirrored his unspoken agony. There was a look about him—the aura, Yahweh forbid, of death. Isaiah sensed it even as he stood at the entrance to the room, even as he watched the golden sunbeams streaming through the windows.

"It is a boil, my prince," the attendant whispered at the doorway. "Under his arm. He has ordered everyone to stay away, even Lady Hephzibah."

"Yes, yes, I know that. But he will see me," Isaiah responded. In a moment he stood at the king's bedside. Hezekiah's eyes moved only slightly, and his body stirred not at all. He was clad in a sleeveless gown of white linen, elaborately embroidered with a border of purple and red around the neck. Even in this time of trouble one of his attendants had bothered to try to make him look kingly. But his long, black hair was matted, his beard uncombed and disheveled. Worse yet, the odor of death hung ominously in the lovely, sunlit room.

Isaiah touched the king's forehead and felt the burning fever. A deep sense of helplessness suddenly overwhelmed him. He loved this man like one of his own sons, a bond that reached back across the long span of years to Hezekiah's troubled childhood, a love sorely tried but not destroyed by Hezekiah's many failures to fulfill Isaiah's hopes.

Yet, Isaiah thought, *there is so much good in him.*

Hezekiah's eyes reflected his awareness of Isaiah's presence. His lips moved weakly, yet no words would come. Isaiah grasped his hand, vaguely aware of the danger of the plague, yet more aware that his friend, his son-in-law, his king, was dying alone.

"I am here," he said. "Hezekiah . . . Hezey . . . I am with you."

"Where is Hephzibah?" the king mumbled. "She must not see me like this. Isaiah, don't let her come."

Great tears welled up in Isaiah's eyes, and he did not try to answer at once. He held Hezekiah's hand tightly in both his own and prayed silently that in this hour of darkest shadows the king would know that he was not alone, that he was loved.

"There is a boil," Hezekiah said. He was more coherent now. "In my armpit." He nodded slightly toward his right side. Isaiah gently lifted the king's arm, pulled open the gown, and exposed the ugly sore, dark and swollen, the unquestionable sign of the plague. *Why?* he thought. *Lord Yahweh, why this?*

"Is there no hope?" Hezekiah asked suddenly, tears streaming from his eyes. The king had seen the look of despair in Isaiah's face. The reality he had refused to accept suddenly became very clear to him, and he was frightened.

"Hezekiah, my son, my child, you must set your house in order, for you will not recover." The words came hard to Isaiah, but as Yahweh's prophet he could not speak cheerful falsehoods even in the face of inevitable tragedy. "Yes, you must surely die," he added. But as he spoke, he again grasped the king's hand to convey through touch what no words could say.

"Pray for me, Isaiah. I am too young to die. Please go and pray for me. You must not stay here. You are my heir, you know. You must protect yourself."

Isaiah sighed deeply. He did not want the kingship. He had never wanted it. "I will go," he said softly, but he would not go far. Through the open windows of the king's bedchamber, the royal garden beckoned. Beyond the far edge of the garden, in an open space unobstructed by trees and shadows, stood the sun-clock of King Ahaz, the one great monument for good that served to remind all of Jerusalem of Hezekiah's father. Almost without thinking, Isaiah directed his path toward the open court near the curious structure. There he sat on the lower steps of the sun-clock, praying for the life of King Hezekiah, while the clouds grew heavy and dark above him and the autumn afternoon turned from gold to the deepest gray.

Inside the palace Hezekiah lay still in the ivory bed. Fevered bits of poetry raced through his mind, fragments of old songs but mostly words of his own.

> In the noontide of my days
>   I must depart;
> I am consigned to Sheol for
>   the rest of my years.
> I will not see the Lord
>   in the land of the living.
> I will look upon man no more
>   among the inhabitants of the world.
> My eyes are weary

with looking upward.
O Lord, I am oppressed;
    be my security!
All my sleep has fled
    because of the bitterness of my soul.

Fitfully, he shifted about in the ivory bed, turning his face to the wall. This was a sign of deepest grief, and he wanted Lord Yahwah to comprehend his agony, his longing to live, his fear of death. "Remember, Lord, how I have walked before you in faithfulness and with a whole heart!" he cried. The pain of the boil wracked his whole body. He could not remain on his side. With intense difficulty, he moved himself again to lie on his back. "Lord!" he moaned. "Deliver me!" And he wept the more because he could feel no awareness that Yahweh had heard him.

Painful memories of happier times flooded through his mind. How long ago they seemed now! He remembered his coronation and the wonderful reforms at the start of his reign, the promises of a bright and glorious future. There was much he had wanted to do, and so much he would never accomplish now.

"Isaiah!" he whispered. "Isaiah, come back! Help me to die in peace!"

Outside, thunder rolled, but no rain fell. Isaiah, still seated on the steps of the sun-clock in the open court, watched as a pale glimmer of sun broke through the heavy clouds. He watched where the shadow of the time-marking gnomon fell on the sun-clock. Somehow it was farther up than it should be, about ten degrees higher than expected. It was as if time itself had turned backward.

The prophet knew something of the mysteries of weather. Through his long years of studying the wonders of Yahweh's creation, he had learned that the sages of old had sometimes observed how light rays seem to be bent by their passing through heavy clouds, though he could not recall ever observing such a sight himself. However it happened, Lord Yahweh made it happen.

Hezekiah will live. The words, spoken inside his consciousness, were as real as the seemingly misplaced shadow on the sun-clock. *He will live fifteen more years and have a son of his own to succeed him.* Something beyond human description had happened. Yahweh, in his great love, had for reasons known to him alone reached down to save Hezekiah ben-Ahaz from certain death.

Isaiah reentered Hezekiah's sickroom and found the king just as he had left him, lying still as death with his eyes focused on the beamed ceiling above him. Hezekiah's hands, long and thin, lay clasped tightly on the coverlet, clenched in pain and fear.

"My king," Isaiah said gently. Hezekiah did not move, but the prophet saw his son-in-law's eyelids flutter slightly. "Hezekiah, listen to me. Yahweh has sent us a sign. You will recover. You will not die, not now!" Isaiah bent over him and watched as a sparkle of hope came into Hezekiah's dark eyes.

"What are you saying, Isaiah?" The king sounded confused but hopeful. With energy he thought was beyond him, he sat up in bed. "I will live?" It was a question but also an affirmation. "I will live!" he exclaimed again. "Oh Isaiah! How do you know?"

"The shadow on the steps of King Ahaz's sun-clock— it seems to have receded. Lord Yahweh has sent us a signal—his guarantee—that he is giving you extra time and will let you live fifteen more years."

The tears that ran down Hezekiah's cheeks were tears of pure joy and hope. The boil was still there under his arm as big as ever. He could feel it. And with it the dizziness, the fever, the anguish of his illness was still there. He struggled to rise to his feet but fell back, moaning upon his pillows.

"Not today, Hezey, but in three days you will be well, and you will go up to the temple to praise Yahweh. For now, we must attend to this boil." Isaiah beckoned to the guard who hovered at the doorway. "Have the king's servants prepare a poultice of figs and spread it over the boil," he said. It was one of the time-tested remedies for lumps and swellings. *After all*, he reasoned, *Lord Yahweh expects us to use the skills we have in dealing with illness and not simply to count on miracles alone.*

Isaiah was still sitting by the king's bed when the poultice was brought in. With his own hands he applied it to the king's boil. The storm clouds of the afternoon grew thicker. *There would be no shadow at all on the clock now,* Isaiah thought. As the rain began to fall heavily, the darkness of early twilight filled the room.

When Hezekiah lapsed into sleep, Isaiah remained at his vigil, deep in continuing prayer, confident of the miracle of Yahweh's healing power at work in the king's body.

The room grew dark. A servant, the same man who had brought the poultice, remained vigilant at the doorway. "Prince Isaiah, should I come in and light the lamps?" he asked tentatively.

"Yes," Isaiah said nodding, "the danger is past."

The man went about his business, and the light of several oil lamps filled the shadowy room.

"And now would you go to my house," Isaiah requested, "and tell my family that I will stay here this night? Lady Hephzibah, my daughter, is there also. Tell her, tell them all, that Lord Yahweh has healed our king." Never in his life had Isaiah felt so certain of Yahweh's power.

Isaiah knew he would never have to fear the burden of kingship for himself now. Rather, he would remain as Hezekiah's advisor, more trusted than before, more to be relied upon in the difficult years that lay ahead. The responsibility of this might indeed interfere with Isaiah's plans for rebuilding his house and gathering a new group of disciples. But if so, was that not also part of Lord Yahweh's great plan?

In the flickering lamplight, Isaiah reached out and touched Hezekiah's hand. The fever was gone. The king's hand lay cool and relaxed on the coverlet.

Vast uncertainties lay ahead. When Hezekiah recovered, he would have to face the difficulties of collecting heavier tribute for Assyria from a kingdom much reduced in size and strength. The extension of the king's life did not guarantee that his remaining years would be happy. But because he had passed through this deep valley of darkness, Hezekiah would be a better, wiser king, and would find the ability to face his burdens more competently than he had ever done before.

With his wife hovering beside him, attentive and concerned, Hezekiah's spirits lifted considerably. She was the one person to whom he could unburden his deepest secrets without fear of betrayal or a spate of unwanted advice in return.

"I sent a message many weeks ago to the king of Babylon," he said to her one morning. He was sitting up in bed, sipping a cupful of warm broth and generally looking better.

"Merodach-baladan?" Hephzibah was unsure how to pronounce the Babylonian king's name, but she had certainly heard of him. Like Hezekiah, he was a vassal of Assyria, a tribute-payer, but then so was every other king Hephzibah had heard of, except the famous Black Pharaoh, Shabako.

The Assyrian Empire encompassed hundreds of small states and some formerly great ones, like faraway Babylon in the fertile valley of the great Tigris and Euphrates rivers. Babylon was one of the garden spots of the world and only a thousand years earlier had been the superpower that Assyria was now.

Merodach-baladan was eager to rebuild his kingdom

to what it had been in those vanished centuries of glory. Just as Hezekiah dreamed of the splendors of King David, so Merodach-baladan recalled his ancient predecessor, Hammurabi the lawgiver, who ruled in the time of Babylon's greatness.

"Any day now his couriers should come," Hezekiah continued. "If ever there were two states destined for alliance, they are Judah and Babylon. We face the same problems."

"The tribute, you mean?"

"Yes, of course, the tribute. And if only enough of the tributary states would rebel at the same time, Assyria could not stop us all. But the plan needs coordination. It needs to be done on a scale more vast than has ever been attempted before. When Pekah and Rezin tried it just before I was born, they lacked a widespread network of alliances. But with Merodach-baladan in the east and myself in the west, working together . . . Isaiah will not like this, Hephzibah. He doesn't understand how important it is for Judah to be really free again."

Hephzibah didn't understand either. She felt very confused, torn with conflict. When she listened to her father preach on the value of peace, she believed him wholeheartedly. But now Hezekiah was speaking of a vast international scheme to destroy Assyria and restore freedom to the tributary peoples, a plan that sounded very enticing indeed. What was really Lord Yahweh's will? Hephzibah knew how sincerely both her husband and her father sought to follow the ways of the God of Judah. How could they reach such different conclusions?

Hezekiah had finished his meal, and a servant cleared away the tray. "Have you talked to Papa about any of this?" she asked.

"No, because I know what he'll say, and I don't want to hear it. He doesn't realize that times are changing."

Hephzibah sat down on the edge of Hezekiah's bed. "I guess young men have said that about the older generation ever since time began," she said. "But I do think Papa undertands more than you give him credit for."

"You won't tell him about the Babylonians, will you?" Hezekiah sounded nervous again. Then a sudden coughing spasm sent Hephzibah scurrying to pour a cup of water. Hezekiah drank gratefully, then lay back on his pillow. "When the Babylonian envoys do come," he said, "one thing I won't do is take them on a tour of that confounded tunnel!"

Hephzibah's hand caressed his. She longed to hold him in her arms, to kiss him. "Those other girls." Hezekiah's mind seemed suddenly far from Babylon. "The three you sent me . . . My darling, I want you to know they mean nothing to me. You know how much I have wanted an heir, but none of these girls has been able to conceive by me. Yet two of them are young widows with children. So I have determined, my beloved, that I am at fault."

"Don't say that! There's nothing at all wrong with you!" Hezekiah was, in her opinion, a perfect lover. She had missed him greatly during the nights he had spent with one or another of her handpicked maidservants, and it was immensely gratifying to hear him say they meant nothing to him. Yet wasn't the inability to conceive always the woman's fault? Hephzibah had heard as much from her mother, and Naamah generally knew all there was to know on such matters.

"What I wanted to tell you is that I have decided to send the three of them as gifts to Merodach-baladan. They are lovely girls, all three of them, and they deserve something better than what I can give them here. And, of course, the ones with children may take them along." Hezekiah gazed into his wife's questioning eyes. "If there is to be a miracle, it will be *our* miracle, my Hephzibah. I want only you," he said and squeezed her hand.

"Oh, my darling, I love you so!" Hephzibah whispered.

Hezekiah pulled her down beside him and took her in his arms.

The Babylonian envoys arrived in Jerusalem a few days later, an impressive delegation of imposing, well-dressed, dark-haired men. Like Assyrians, they spoke Aramaic as their native tongue, and Hezekiah was delighted to show them that he could speak their language. His pronunciation was quite good, thanks to several years of study in his adolescence with a competent tutor, and if he occasionally made grammatical errors, the men of Babylon were too polite to say so.

Hezekiah, having finally recovered, was his usual ebullient self. He treated the Babylonians to a round of banquets, a tour of the courtyards of Lord Yahweh's temple, and a horseback ride around the whole circuit of the city walls to observe the recent construction under Maher's supervision. The king even showed them the inside entrance of the tunnel, giving them a vivid verbal account of its wonders.

But most of all, Hezekiah thought, in his calculated show of strength were the glimpses he gave them into the secret palace storechambers, where the weaponry recently taken from Gaza was stashed, along with Ahaz's long-hoarded treasures: precious metal and countless jars of oil and spices.

Things went remarkably well. The Babylonian king had sent Hezekiah a large and beautiful golden plate, "to celebrate your recovery from your recent illness," the envoys had said, though with the time and distance involved, Merodach-baladan could not possibly have known about it. Such was the game of diplomacy. Hezekiah responded with rich gifts for the envoys themselves and even richer treasurers for their master, including the three servant girls. After a farewell banquet that lasted long into the night, the Babylonian delegation departed the following morning on their long journey homeward.

Now all Hezekiah could do was hope they would give Merodach-baladan a glowing report of the greatness of Judah, and recommend joining the effort for all-out resistance to Assyria. It took so long to accomplish things of this sort.

It did not take long at all, however, for Isaiah to get to the king's palace on the morning of the Babylonians' departure. Maher had attended all the festivities. Isaiah had also been invited, but since he had declined to go his son had kept him posted on everything.

Hezekiah was glad to see his father-in-law and welcomed him cheerfully into his private suite. He was unprepared, however, for the look of sternness in Isaiah's eyes.

"What did you show those men from Babylon?" the prophet asked. "All of the secret storechambers?"

"Why yes, everything! There is nothing among my treasures that I have not showed them. They were most impressed!"

"Hezekiah!" Isaiah exclaimed. "Babylon is no friend to us! The time is coming, says Lord Yahweh, when the treasures of Judah will be taken as spoil to Babylon. Nothing will be left! Even some of your own descendants will be slaves in the palace of the Babylonian king!"

Hezekiah sat stunned for a moment, pondering Isaiah's words. This was not the sort of thing the prophet usually said. It was a specific threat rather than a general warning, and it dealt with the distant future rather than the present. Yet he had mentioned *descendants*. Whatever doom might come to Judah from Babylon in some later era, the very promise of descendants was a predication of hope.

"So long as it doesn't happen in my time!" Hezekiah responded at last. "The word of Lord Yahweh which you have spoken is good. For does it not mean there will be peace and security in my days?"

The word *peace* produced an immediate softening of Isaiah's reproving gaze. "Oh, Hezekiah, pray it will be so! And then do everything in your power, each day of your life, to make Lord Yahweh's peace prevail."

ELEVEN

The Assyrian Came Down

Merodach-baladan of Babylon did not fare well under Sennacherib. The Babylonian king was too important. Without waiting for Hezekiah to build a coalition against Assyria in the Westlands, he withheld his tribute payments to Sennacherib's treasury. Sennacherib set up a puppet king in Babylon and Merodach-baladan fled the country. So much for the king of Babylon!

Then Sennacherib marched down the Phoenician coast, capturing Sidon, Acco, and other cities. He pushed his campaign to the south, conquering Jaffa, Beth Dagon, and other cities in northern Philistia. Then, concentrating his efforts against Ekron, he defeated a coalition of Philistine and Egyptian forces. So much for Pharaoh Shabako and all the hopes that lay with Egypt! Isaiah had been right all along.

Sennacherib's troops invaded from the north, countless hordes of them, with all the vast arsenal of Assyrian weaponry, horses, chariots, and siege equipment. From one village to the next they swept southward. Entire towns with defenses far too inadequate to withstand siege surrendered, hoping for mercy, only to be put to the torches of the relentless Assyrians. The roads were full of refugees, fleeing southward, burdened with the meager possessions they could carry with them. The ruined towns and villages were full of corpses. Sennacherib's campaign would teach the rebels a lesson that would never be forgotten, and the path he left behind him was a desert of desolation.

On into Judah they came, closer and closer to Jerusalem. The Assyrians plundered practically everything north of the city walls. Judah's armed forces, concentrated in the capital city, anticipated the role of defending Jerusalem under siege, but they had not anticipated that Sennacherib would destroy almost everything in his path before he reached there.

Pharaoh Shabako, true to his promise, sent relief troops, but far too few. Surprised by the Assyrians in open country, the Egyptian and Ethiopian forces were cut to pieces. Only a handful of survivors lived to carry the bad news back to Pharaoh's court. Assyria was invincible. The Black Pharaoh was advised to desist from any further meddling in the Westlands.

Strangers thronged the streets of Jerusalem, and Isaiah, who had moved with Naamah back into the city house, eyed them warily. There was a preponderance of women, for the vast majority of able-bodied, fighting men in the villages had been slain attempting to defend their homes. More appalling was the fact that so many of the young widows—and some not so young—were going about dressed in their finest clothes and bangles, avidly husband-hunting in their desperate need for protection.

"The day is soon coming," Isaiah proclaimed one afternoon to a crowd who had gathered to hear him speak, "when seven women will take hold of one man, saying, 'We will eat our own bread and wear our own clothes, only let us be called by your name! Take away our reproach!'"

Some of the women in Isaiah's audience giggled, openly derisive of the fate that hung over them. Angrily, Isaiah went on.

"The days are coming soon when Lord Yahweh
      will take away all your fine things, your ankle
      bells, headbands, crescents, pendants, and
      bracelets!
Your scarves and hats and sashes!
Your perfume boxes, amulets, signet rings and
      nose jewels!
Festive dresses, cloaks, and handbags!
All the gauzy garments, the linen garments, the
      turbans, the veils!"

He looked out to the crowd and saw some of the women nervously fingering their jewels and finery. Dauntless, he continued:

"Instead of perfume there will be rottenness,
      and instead of a belt, a rope!
Instead of curled hair—baldness!
Instead of a rich robe—sackcloth!
Instead of beauty—shame!"

His eyes circled his audience, and suddenly he spotted Naamah among the crowd of women. She looked very upset and unhappy. Naamah was not sumptuously dressed, for she had never cared much for jewelry or elaborate clothes, but she wore an attractive bright blue linen dress with a handsome wide belt of darker blue. A light, gauze veil floated about her shoulders, and her handbag hung from a cord at her waist. Though she was not easily moved to tears, she now looked about ready to cry.

As the crowd began to disperse, Naamah made her way to Isaiah's side. "Why did you have to say all those terrible things?" she whispered. "Is it really as bad as you make us think?"

Isaiah nodded sadly, putting his hand on her arm in a gesture of comfort and support. "Yes," he said. "It really is as bad as I've said, and soon it will be worse, unless Hezekiah can be made to see reason."

"What do you mean?" Naamah asked.

"If he will go on and pay the tribute, I believe even now there is hope for Yahweh's mercy," Isaiah answered. "Oh, but what a terrible price this land has paid already!"

"Yahweh's mercy, yes. But what about Sennacherib's mercy?" Naamah's practicality prevailed.

"Yes, that too," Isaiah answered. "For after all, remember Sennacherib is only a tool in the hands of the Holy One of Israel."

It was several weeks before Hezekiah was convinced that the only option for Judah's survival would be the sending of belated tribute to Sennacherib, a tribute which he decided might be more palatable to the Judeans if described as a "peace gift." By this time, almost all the outlying towns and villages of the kingdom had fallen into Assyrian hands. Then, to everyone's surprise, instead of attacking Jerusalem, Sennacherib concentrated the full strength of his forces on Lachish, the "second city" of Judah. Strongly walled and well-defended, Lachish might hold out for several weeks. Yet without more help from Pharaoh, which seemed unlikely, the city would ultimately fall. Then only Jerusalem would remain. Even Hezekiah realized the time had come to try to salvage what was left.

"I have called you together to hear my plan," the king announced to his closest advisors gathered in the royal council room. "I have decided that we must send gifts and spokesmen to Sennacherib at Lachish to try and persuade him to come to terms with the Kingdom of Judah so that peace will be restored. Eliakim has been appointed to determine what gifts we will send. I believe you have the list prepared, have you not?"

"Yes, my king." Eliakim nervously twisted the small

scroll he held in his hands. It had been a most unhappy assignment, and he did not look forward to presenting his list to the king.

"Very well. We will review your recommendations in a moment," Hezekiah replied. "Before we do, we must determine who will go to Lachish to negotiate. I have already asked Isaiah if he will lead the delegation, and he has agreed to do so."

There were gasps of surprise from several of the men at the king's table. "Where is Prince Isaiah?" Shebna asked. "Why is he not here this afternoon?" The chief secretary glared at Maher as if he held him personally responsible for Isaiah's absence.

Eliakim, who knew all too well where Isaiah was, looked pleadingly at the king, hoping that Hezekiah would explain the prophet's whereabouts.

"We sent him to the temple," Hezekiah said with obvious reluctance, "to check on the treasures there and determine if we can spare the items Eliakim has listed for our peace gift to Sennacherib."

"Peace gift! It's tribute, that's what it is!" Shebna exclaimed. "And from the temple! From Lord Yahweh's own house!"

"Better from Lord Yahweh's house than from the houses of Yahweh's people," Hezekiah answered. "Yes, Shebna, it is tribute. I admit it. We have learned painful lessons this summer. Judah is too weak to stand alone, and Pharaoh Shabako has failed us. We must not risk further losses, further destruction. Isaiah has been right all along. We have disobeyed Lord Yahweh here and the kingdom has already borne heavy punishment."

"But to surrender now . . ." Shebna began to protest.

"Shebna, I want you to go with the delegation to Lachish. I am giving you the personal responsibility of protecting the peace gifts. Eliakim will go with you. And Maher, you also."

It was an assignment no one relished. Even Isaiah had

felt dismay at the king's appointment. Yet disobedience to royal authority was an alternative that none of the chosen men would have dared to consider. Each in his own way was genuinely committed to the monarchy and to Hezekiah's role as Yahweh's anointed one.

Maher, who was rather surprised at being selected, resolved quickly that the journey might in fact turn out to be a grand adventure. In any case it could not possibly be as bad as waiting in Jerusalem day after day for more dismal news.

Eliakim felt a certain satisfaction that Shebna, rather than himself, had been given the unenviable task of personally guarding the tribute treasures.

Shebna, staunch royalist though he was, felt overwhelming waves of resentment. Unguarded anger swept through him. "My king," he began politely, but with even less restraint than usual, "do you really think Prince Isaiah will be a suitable envoy?" Shebna, who could not forget the prophet's dire predictions that day outside his mausoleum, hated the very idea of a role that made him subservient to Isaiah. Jealousy and anger mixed with genuine patriotic pride as he went on. "Look at him, my king. He is your kinsman, true enough, but does he look like a prince? What will the Assyrians think of us if we send a prophet of Yahweh as the leader of our delegation? What will they think if the king's father-in-law comes in looking like some rustic! You know how Isaiah loves demonstrations. He might even decide to go in sackcloth and ashes or in his famous loincloth. What would Sennacherib say to that?"

When Shebna concluded his brief tirade, the room became strangely still.

"We shall see to it that Prince Isaiah has appropriate clothes for his mission," Hezekiah pronounced rather sharply. Yet Hezekiah knew there was a certain measure of truth in what Shebna had said. The Judean embassy did need to make an impressive appearance.

That evening during a private supper with his wife, Hezekiah mentioned the problem. Hephzibah seemed to know instinctively what to do. "You know the new robe I've been making for you . . . we'll give it to him. I'll tell him *I* want him to wear it, to look as splendid as possible on the embassy. And don't you say one word about it. He'll do it for me."

"Yes, I believe he will," Hezekiah responded.

Isaiah's summons to the palace the next morning plainly specified it was to be a private meeting in Lady Hephzibah's suite. As they waited for his arrival, Hezekiah and Hephzibah scrutinized the fine, dark red linen robe that Hephzibah had made. It was lavishly embroidered with gold and silver threads around the neck, cuffs, and hem—the product of weeks of patient labor. "It would have looked so handsome on you," Hephzibah remarked, "and dear Papa has never cared for anything like this. I only hope I can convince him to wear it."

"If you can't persuade him gently, I'll issue a royal command," Hezekiah said lightly, suppressing the worries he felt about issues far more serious than Isaiah's wardrobe.

Yet oddly enough, the concern about Isaiah's reaction to wearing the princely garb proved needless. The prophet examined the magnificent garment spread out on Hephzibah's couch, and listened patiently as she explained that she wanted him to wear it to Lachish to see the King of Assyria.

In the face of the difficult mission ahead, what Isaiah wore was of minimal concern to him, yet the fact that Hephzibah had made the robe herself seemed to please him greatly. It was a consolation, a little light in the gathering storm clouds. There was a hint of genuine pleasure in his eyes as he slipped the splendid garment over the coarse, plain brown linen robe that was his usual summer garb. Appreciatively, he fingered the bands of elaborate stitchery on the sleeves. "When I was a young man," he said, "I had something rather like this for my wedding. Not so fine, of course, but really quite handsome. It was something my mother had made." He smiled faintly. "Shebna will not know me in such fine feathers."

"Isaiah, I want you also to wear something else from me." Hezekiah unfastened from around his neck the silver chain on which hung the medallion of King David's star. It was his favorite ornament, one that he had worn for many years, not to be parted with lightly. Isaiah's first impulse was to refuse it. He cared nothing for such adornments. But he realized that in taking it, he would convey to Hezekiah the fact that they shared the same heavy burdens. Wordlessly, he nodded acceptance.

Hephzibah took the medallion from her husband and fastened the chain around her father's neck. "My dear, dear children," Isaiah said. There was so much more he wanted to say, but words seemed to elude him.

King Hezekiah, however, was never at a loss for words.

"Long ago," he remarked, "it was you, Isaiah, who taught me the meaning of King David's star—the symbol of the Lord Yahweh's promise that he will protect our family and that the Kingdom of Judah will endure forever."

As he spoke, Hezekiah looked pensively at the design tattooed on his wrist when he was a boy, remembering a time in his adolescence when he wept, desperately wishing it could be removed because he had wanted nothing to remind him of Ahaz. Isaiah had consoled him then, telling him wonderful things about Lord Yahweh's steadfast love for David and all his descendants who served him faithfully. That ongoing covenant was far more important, Isaiah had said, than the mistakes of one king like Ahaz.

Yet Isaiah had never declared that Judah would endure forever. The prophet was about to speak words of clarification, when he noticed the look in Hezekiah's eyes. There was unquestionably a light of optimism shining there. Hezekiah, ever resilient, had convinced himself that sending the peace gifts would save his kingdom.

"Yes, I know," Isaiah said simply. "Remember, I have the star on me, too." He turned back the elaborately embroidered sleeve band of his new robe and looked for a moment at the somewhat faded mark on his inner forearm. "I have always considered it a reminder of Lord Yahweh's love for Judah, and of hope for Judah's future.

Perhaps, Isaiah thought, *Hezekiah is right even though we have waited far too long. Perhaps the Assyrian king will accept the tribute and agree to leave Judah at peace in the future. We must always have hope, for after all, has not Lord Yahweh promised to protect Jerusalem and the Remnant of the faithful?*

The peace gifts were an impressive array. While Isaiah and the king went over final instructions for negotiation, Shebna and Eliakim supervised the packing of the treasures. Thirty talents of gold and eight hundred of silver, including vessels from the temple treasury, made up the principal offering. But along with this went boxes and jars full of precious spices, perfumes, and oils. Ivory-inlaid furniture and several couches and chairs from Hezekiah's palace, were an additional sacrifice the king made. Then, too, there were the human gifts—slaves from Hezekiah's palace staff, including a group of musicians whose services were not particularly essential, and the king's few concubines, who meant no more to him than the three servant girls he had sent home with the Babylonian delegation years before.

It was daybreak when Isaiah led the envoys out of

Jerusalem. The trip would be a slow one, for although the king and Shebna had supplied horses for the ambassadors and their attendants, the tribute treasures and baggage were packed in ox carts. The envoys, of necessity, slowed their pace to match that of the oxen. Thus encumbered, the journey to Lachish would take several days.

Each day, around noon, the group stopped to feed their animals, to take nourishment for themselves, and then to nap through the warmest hours of the afternoon, resuming their journey as the day grew cooler. Of course, not everyone slept at the same time. Some had to stay awake to guard the treasures. And Isaiah, who found sleep almost impossible, volunteered to do his share of guard duty.

Armed with a borrowed sword, which he strongly hoped he would never have to use, Isaiah paced restlessly before the baggage wagons. It was the third day since their departure from Jerusalem. All around them the countryside lay desolate and still. And Isaiah, who had traveled the road many times over the years on his visits to Jashub's family, felt stricken by the thoroughness of Sennacherib's devastion.

But soon it will be over, he told himself, trying to maintain an attitude of hope. *Sennacherib will accept the treasures and pull out. Lachish and Jerusalem will be safe.* Soon, Isaiah imagined, he would be visiting Jashub and Reba in Lachish. How fortunate that they lived in a strongly walled city rather than in one of the little villages that had been so thoroughly destroyed! He wondered if Jashub was even now taking part in the defense of the city. It was hard to picture his son as a soldier. Thank heavens Jashub's sons were still too young to serve! *Lord Yahweh protect them all,* he prayed, *till we arrive with the peace gifts and Lachish is safe.*

Suddenly the stillness of the sleeping camp was broken with the tinkle of tiny silver bells, those ridiculous anklets that so many women insisted on wearing. Out of the tent where the female slaves were resting had emerged a girl, lithe and shapely, with a long cascade of black, wavy hair floating about her shoulders. She was clad in a very wrinkled linen dress and, around both ankles, she wore strings of little bells. Warily she looked at Isaiah. "I could not sleep, my prince," she said in an apologetic tone. "It is too hot."

"Yes, yes, it is," Isaiah answered as the girl fell in step beside him.

"And I am too excited," she said. "I keep thinking about how wonderful it is to be going to a *better* place! It is more than I ever hoped for!"

"Better?" Isaiah was genuinely surprised. How could any daughter of Judah feel that service to Sennacherib was to be preferred over service to Hezekiah? "Are you one of the singing women?" he asked hesitantly.

"No, my prince. I am a concubine. I might turn out to be one of Sennacherib's favorites! King Hezekiah called for me only a few times. He is a good man, very kind, but his heart belongs to Lady Hephzibah. It's so terrible to feel unwanted. All of us girls are so glad to have another chance! Now we won't have to waste away in the harem any longer."

The frankness of the girl's revelations left Isaiah speechless for a moment. "Lord Yahweh sometimes works in strange ways," he said at last. "Since you feel he has delivered you, do not forget him when you go to the new land."

"Oh, I won't, my prince! I'll say a prayer of thankfulness every day!"

It was a promise that Isaiah doubted she would keep, yet oddly enough, his spirit felt lighter for having heard the girl express her feelings. In the distance, Eliakim was sounding the call for the sleepers to awaken. Soon the caravan of peaceseekers would be moving on. "They say we'll reach Lachish before this evening," the girl said excitedly. Then she turned and ran happily, lightly back to her tent.

If so, Isaiah thought, turning to the wagon where his baggage was stowed, *it is time to dress for our grand entry.* Back in his tent, he took off the travel-stained robe he had worn for the past three days and replaced it with the magnificent garment Hephzibah had made. He felt strangely happy, at peace with all the world, hopeful that the envoys soon would achieve their mission.

The party rode on for several hours. Then, toward late afternoon, a mile or two outside of Lachish, they were suddenly surrounded by a troop of Sennacherib's horsemen. "All that you have is ours!" The Assyrian captain shouted. "The Great King has sent us to collect your tribute now before you approach any further!"

This dire pronouncement threw the envoys into a state of complete confusion. "But we are ordered by King Hezekiah to present our gifts to the Great King Sennacherib in person," Shebna stormed.

"King Sennacherib chooses otherwise," the Assyrian officer replied, motioning for the Judeans to dismount. Even their horses, which were certainly not part of the tribute gift, were being seized.

Isaiah knew it was useless to protest as he watched the Assyrians swoop down on the ox carts and all their contents. There was excited chatter from the slaves as they were led away along with the baggage wagons. Confusion reigned.

Somehow Eliakim and Shebna managed to grab their own personal baggage, but everything else was whisked away before the envoys' eyes. And except for two attendants who were allowed to remain with the four chief negotiators, the entire Judean contingent was rapidly hustled off along with the confiscated treasures.

The prospects for a negotiated peace, which had seemed so good just hours before, were rapidly crumbling away.

TWELVE
At the Walls of Lachish

Distressed, humiliated, and surrounded by heavily armed guards, the men of King Hezekiah's embassy arrived at the Assyrian camp on foot about an hour later. There, it appeared, the envoys were to be housed in two small tents, closely guarded and well within the labyrinthine interior of the camp. Shebna and Eliakim and the two attendants would sleep on pallets in the larger tent. The smaller, a slightly better-provisioned tent featuring two cots and a scattering of other furniture, was for the two princes, King Hezekiah's kinsmen. A young Assyrian soldier, a boy of no more than fourteen or fifteen, conducted them to their accommodations. He spoke Hebrew haltingly, but he was obviously proud of himself. "I tell the Rabshakeh you come," he said smiling, full of his own importance. "If he negotiates, I call you."

A few moments later, after the young Assyrian had left, the Judean delegation gathered inside the larger tent to plan their next move. Shebna, frantic over the abrupt separation from their tribute treasures, cast his eyes about the tent and paced nervously. Eliakim, calmer, ordered the attendants to spread pallets on the ground and to unpack the bundle of food they had been allowed to bring into the camp with them.

"What did that youth mean—if he negotiates?" Shebna asked. "And why the Rabshakeh? He's one of Sennacherib's chief henchmen, but we were sent to speak with the Great King himself."

"It is altogether possible," Isaiah answered, "that none of the Assyrian leaders will talk to us at all. They have seized our tribute already. That may be the end of it." His voice was somber.

"Is that the word of the Lord Yahweh?" Shebna retorted. As always when he spoke with Isaiah there was an edge of mockery in his voice, even now when the two of them were partners in difficulty.

"No. It is simply my guess," the prophet replied. "I hope I am wrong."

"I cannot see what possible good it does to have a prophet of Yahweh on this embassy if you can't predict what is going to happen!" Fear made Shebna even more outspoken than usual, and long-suppressed hatred, normally held in check, suddenly surfaced.

"Oh, my friends," Isaiah pronounced sadly, "you have known me so long and understand so little! I cannot foresee the future at will, any more than other men can. On occasion Lord Yahweh has given me a glimpse of the judgment that will come if our people continue to not heed his commands. Sometimes he has given me dreams of what this world could be if we would only walk in his ways. Those things I know in the depths of my heart. But I have no idea at all what will happen tonight . . . or tomorrow."

"My father was appointed to this embassy because he is a prince of Judah," Maher put in, "not because he is a prophet of Yahweh."

Isaiah knew Maher's words were well meant, yet even this son of his did not really understand. The role of Yahweh's prophet, spokesman, servant was not something that could be turned off and on at will. He looked at the brand of Yahweh's service on his hand. Even though there were times when he had regretted the youthful impulsiveness that led him to have the mark imprinted on himself, he was now glad it was there, a visible token of a deep inner commitment.

As Isaiah was thinking on these things, he was startled by Eliakim's voice speaking in a very matter-of-fact manner. "I expect the Assyrian official, the Rabshakeh or whoever it might be, will see us in the morning. It is growing late now, and we must eat and then rest from our long journey."

"I am not hungry," Isaiah said. "Maher, you stay and dine with our friends. I am going to go to bed early."

Withdrawing with a dignity entirely suitable to a prince, Isaiah left the young envoys to their own devices. Yet sleep, as desirable as it might be, would be long in coming. In the stillness of his own tent he paced restlessly. Never in his long life had he felt such complete despair and uncertainty. If only he might be allowed to speak to King Sennacherib—or even to the Rabshakeh or any of the high-ranking Assyrian officials! Yet he deeply feared it was not to be, and one could not hope to negotiate peace terms if he were not allowed to negotiate at all!

"All my life, O Lord," he prayed, "I have preached your warnings of doom and destruction, yet I have always felt that if the worst came, it would be no more than this land deserved. Lord, you know how I have tried to keep Hezekiah on the path of peace for so long—and now this! He has made this terrible mistake. But he is not an evil man, Lord! And the people—the ordinary people—they have committed many wrongs but have not wanted war!"

Isaiah wept. In the silence he listened for Yahweh's voice and heard only the sounds of the camp outside—ugly military sounds, the clanking of armor and swords as somewhere nearby men cleaned their weapons for to-morrow's battles.

I am probably going to be killed, Isaiah thought. *I will not leave here alive.* He did not feel especially brave. He wanted to live. There was so much to do. He wanted to organize his writings, to write more, and most of all, to find more students who would carry on his work. He thought about his boxful of potsherds with the fragments of all his writings. At least the box was carefully en-sconced in the city house, but what did that matter if the Assyrians took Jerusalem?

Isaiah, who had enjoyed good health throughout most of his life, suddenly became aware of pains that wracked his whole body. Carefully he took off the fine robe that Hephzibah had made, folded it neatly, and placed it on a stool beside his cot. Thoughts of his daughter, of the love and hope in her eyes when she had presented him with the gift, comforted him.

Clad only in his undertunic, he lay down on the narrow cot, only to discover it was too short for his tall frame. As his feet hung uncomfortably over the end of the bed, he realized the air in the tent had grown much colder. There was a little coverlet folded on the bed, and he sat up to spread it out. But it was only a throw, not a full-sized blanket.

Ordinarily, he would have had no qualms about sleep-ing in his clothes, but he would not think of mussing the fine robe Hephzibah had made. His baggage contained a cloak, but that had been confiscated. Shivering now, he tried to lie very still. Almost unconsciously he fingered the silver medallion of King David's star that hung at his throat.

As he thought of how Hezekiah had given it to him with such confidence and pride, tears coursed down his cheeks. "Lord Yahweh, I don't understand what is hap-pening to us!" he whispered. "Help me! And help your people out of this wretched trap!"

He half expected to hear an immediate answer to his prayer, but only a single quiet thought entered his consciousness. *Lord Yahweh is in control, whatever happens.* That assurance gave him confidence, but it seemed faint consolation. Whatever happened would likely be disastrous.

Sleep came at last. Then the sound of someone entering the tent awakened him. It was Maher, singing loudly and thumping about in the darkness, obviously sodden with too much wine. Drunkenness was not usually one of Maher's vices. The terrible frustration of their embassy had apparently taken its toll on him, though where he had found an opportunity to become so thoroughly besotted in Sennacherib's camp Isaiah could scarcely imagine. The envoys had brought only a limited supply of wine, and most of it remained with their confiscated baggage.

"Maher," he whispered sternly, "where have you been? What have you been doing?"

"Negotiating, Papa." Maher's speech was slurred. "Negotiating with S'nacherib's big gen'ral." Noisily, the young man collapsed on his cot and in a moment was snoring loudly.

"Maher! Wake up! Tell me about it!" Isaiah demanded, but to no avail. Whatever he had to report would have to wait until morning, and then Isaiah could only hope his son would be able to remember what had been going on. It was not an encouraging situation, but at least Maher had said he'd been negotiating. *Perhaps Lord Yahweh is working in some mysterious way of his own,* Isaiah thought. With a small glimmer of renewed hope Isaiah fell back to sleep.

Maher faced the light of morning with the worst headache he could ever remember, while Isaiah, for no apparent reason, continued to feel less than fit himself. The little stabs of internal pain that had assailed him the night before returned when he awakened, and the disgust he

147

might otherwise have felt about Maher's hangover was mitigated somewhat by his own misery.

"Tell me what happened. Who did you get to see?" Isaiah had risen from his cot at the sound of Maher's groans and hovered now at his son's bedside.

Maher uttered something incoherent.

"You have to talk to me, son. Did you negotiate?" Isaiah touched his shoulder.

Maher nodded. "I guess I did. But they really wanted to see you. That boy that brought us here yesterday came back to Shebna's tent after you left. He said the Rabshakeh wanted to speak to the prince, and I told them I was the one." Maher groaned. "Oh, my head. Oh, Papa, I'm so sick!"

"He wanted me?" Isaiah asked. "Why did you lie to them? Whatever made you do such a thing?"

"I'm a prince of Judah, too," Maher muttered petulantly. Then, rising suddenly, he ran from the tent. Isaiah heard him coughing and retching outside.

Though now an adult, Maher was still in many ways an irresponsible boy. Isaiah's heart ached for his son, his sadness stronger than his anger. What he did not know, because Maher in his stupor could not find the words, was the fact that when the Assyrian summoned the prince, Maher had gone fully believing he was going to be killed. He was willing to die in his father's place.

The Rabshekeh, however, who was one of Sennacherib's most trusted officers, had merely plied Maher with wine and questioned him about the defenses of Jerusalem.

"I didn't tell him anything that could hurt us," Maher explained, reentering the tent. "I told him they'd never be able to take Jerusalem. I told him Hezey had built a tunnel, and we'd never run out of water."

"Maher!" Isaiah gasped and sat down on his cot, feeling slightly dizzy. Possibly the Assyrians already knew about the Siloam Tunnel, but for Maher to have boasted about it showed no common sense whatsoever.

"I also told him that Pharaoh Shabako is going to send us more troops."

"Oh, Maher!" Isaiah groaned. "That was a blatant lie, and it can't possibly do Judah any good."

"He was very interested in *that*," Maher went on. "I told him that Hezekiah preferred to end the struggle and make peace before the Egyptians come."

"You realize, don't you," Isaiah remarked, "that all of what you've said was very unwise?"

It was at this crucial moment that the young Assyrian soldier they had met the day before appeared at the entry to Isaiah and Maher's tent.

"The Rabshekeh is wanting to see the old prince," he announced solemnly. "He say the wrong one come before. The old one, the one who is the prophet of the God Yahweh—he want him."

"I am the prophet Isaiah. Give me a few moments to prepare myself."

"Hurry," said the youthful messenger, entirely unimpressed by Judean aristocracy. "The Rabshakeh is not liking to wait."

Quickly, Isaiah readied himself, combing his hair and beard, pulling on his splendid robe that Hephzibah had made, and slipping into his sandals. Apprehensive in spirit and not well physically, he still looked a nobleman to his core, this princely aura not entirely the result of Hephzibah's fine stitchery. There was an indefinable majesty in Isaiah's being, an inner radiance that came from Lord Yahweh.

Maher looked at his father with deep admiration, longing to be more like him, yet knowing he could never be. "God go with you," he said, softly.

Silently, Isaiah followed the young Assyrian through the winding paths of the camp toward the Rabshakeh's tent. Only a few men were in evidence, guarding the encampment. The vast majority of Sennacherib's troops were even now battering away at the walls of Lachish, plainly evident in the distance.

Isaiah thought of Jashub and his family inside Lachish. What might be their fate if the city fell? It was one thing to stand in Jerusalem and preach that the Assyrian invasion, the death and destruction all around, was no more than Judah deserved for plunging so senselessly into war. It was another thing to think in these terms when his own son and little grandchildren might be included among the Assyrians' victims.

The Rabshakeh's tent was of bright scarlet woolen fabric, regal yet substantial. Two armed guards with heavy wicker shields stood at the entrance. Beside one of them was a small, neatly stacked pyramid of human skulls. "Men of Judah we Assyrians killed already," the messenger boy boasted. "Just a few. There are many hundreds more."

Isaiah saw no need to comment. The young messenger entered the tent and motioned for him to follow. "Great Rabshakeh," the boy exclaimed in Aramaic, bowing to the ground , "I bring you Prince Isaiah."

The Rabshakeh, seated on an elaborate ivory chair, nodded. He was a tall man, thin and spare, with the bushy black hair and elaborately waxed little beard found so often among the Assyrians. His robe was blue linen, heavily decked with silver fringe. A wide belt of silver links circled his waist.

"Prince Isaiah," he repeated, but rather than the expected Aramaic, he spoke flawless Hebrew. His voice was unnaturally loud. "Sit down, Prince Isaiah, and we shall speak of your country while we have some refreshment."

As signaled, a serving maid drifted from behind curtains at the rear of the tent with two brimming goblets of wine. Isaiah accepted his and took only the smallest sip. The Rabshakeh enjoyed a deep draught.

"Your son says the Pharaoh's troops are on their way

to rescue Lachish—or Jerusalem. He was a bit hazy about the details." A loud laugh of derision accompanied the Rabshakeh's remark. "Seriously, you don't expect us to believe that, do you?"

Beneath the Assyrian's sneer, Isaiah sensed worry and confusion. "How should I know what you choose to believe?" he answered.

"Lachish will fall—today, tomorrow, or the next day. The defenders on the walls are growing fewer. Our men have the earthwork built almost to the top of the wall. It is only a matter of time."

"May I ask," Isaiah ventured, setting his goblet on the table, "why the Great King continues to make war on us after receiving our peace gifts?"

"Why?" the Rabshakeh shouted. "Why? Because that idiotic king of yours—Hezekiah—defied us! The peace gifts, as you call them, are no more than he owed us *before* he rebelled. The Great King has no use for rebels who try to come cringing back into his good graces. Lachish will fall, and then Jerusalem, and the land of Judah will perish. Your king, your foolish Hezekiah, cannot save you. Believe me, Prince Isaiah. Go back to Jerusalem and tell your king if he is wise he will surrender his capital city without fighting, and then Assyria will be merciful to the people."

Isaiah was trembling, struggling for composure, silently reaching out to Lord Yahweh for strength and courage.

"Your son told me about your king's wonderful tunnel," the Rabshakeh went on. "Don't rely on it. So Jerusalem has a fine water supply. It will only prolong the agonies of the siege for your people. Sooner or later we Assyrians will find the outside entrance to the tunnel and come in that way. It will be so much easier than building earthworks and scaling walls."

"The autumn rains are coming," Isaiah remarked calmly. "Last night's rain was just a foretaste. No commander wants to keep his troops in the field through the rainy season. Now is the perfect time to make peace if the Great King would only see fit to accept our gifts as the sign of our submission."

"There will be no peace!" The Rabshakeh pounded the table. His dark face reddened with anger. "Now, go! You are worse than your stupid son and worse than your warmongering king! Only a fool speaks of peace to Assyria!"

"Only a fool," Isaiah retorted, "desires war when peace is within his reach."

"Go!" shouted the Rabshakeh.

Isaiah rose and, conducted by the messenger who had brought him, returned to his own tent.

It was a somber party of Judeans who traveled out of the Assyrian camp that afternoon, headed toward Jerusalem. To Isaiah's surprise, the Rabshakeh had ordered their horses returned. Perhaps he reasoned that the sooner they reached Jerusalem with the Assyrian terms of unconditional surrender, the better.

None of the men felt much like talking. Even Shebna rode along silent and sullen after a few tentative remarks on how Jerusalem would surely continue resistance regardless of all Assyrian threats. Isaiah's grief as they passed through the desolate countryside lay too deep for words. Far more than on the previous day's journey to Lachish, he was struck by the fact that there were few signs of life, no travelers on the road except the envoys themselves. Their route led through deserted villages, past burned-out fields. Autumn, the time of fall planting, was coming, yet the hope that the new year should bring, the hope that he himself felt on this journey to Lachish a few days ago, was entirely gone.

The envoys of peace weep bitterly, he said to himself as he surveyed the area through which they rode. *The highways lie in waste, the wayfaring man ceases. Covenants are broken, cities are despised. There is no regard for man. The land mourns and languishes.*

In his mind Isaiah could see far beyond the road from Lachish to Jerusalem, beyond the little Kingdom of Judah, into the lands to the north, which had already felt the heavy hand of Assyrian vengeance.

He knew he must try and gather his thoughts and write them down when he returned home. He must try to make some sense out of what was happening. Trying to understand Lord Yahweh's purpose had never seemed more difficult. *Yahweh wanted peace, and our nation scorned peace, so we were visited by this. But what about the Remnant of Yahweh's faithful ones? Why must the innocent suffer along with the guilty? And why, when the peace gifts had been given to the Assyrians, did they persist in their hostility?* These were questions for which there were no simple answers.

The Judean envoys were about halfway to Jerusalem when a small troop of Assyrian horsemen galloped up behind them. Instinctively, Shebna reached for his sword, only to remember that their weapons had all be confiscated.

"Lachish has fallen!" the Assyrian captain called out. "Go on to Jerusalem and give the news to King Hezekiah!" With that announcement the officer wheeled about sharply, his men following.

"Wait!" Isaiah called. "The people of Lachish—what will become of them?"

The Assyrian did not see fit to reply, but Isaiah knew the usual policy was to carry off the women and children as prisoners of war while most of the men would be killed. *Only sometimes they spare the craftmen,* he thought. *Jashub, Jashub, my son!* In the depths of his heart Isaiah longed to turn back to Lachish, to discover what had happened to his son and his family, yet he knew he could not.

Similar thought must have stirred within Maher, untempered by any of Isaiah's caution. Without warning, without so much as a word to Isaiah, he turned his horse about and galloped after the Assyrians.

"Maher! Come back!" Isaiah cried. "It's no use!"

"I must find them!" Maher called.

Sadly, Isaiah watched him go. From there until the envoys reached Jerusalem, he rode on in silence, deep in contemplation and prayer. As they entered the city, the walls and housetops were full of excited people. Somehow the news of the fall of Lachish had preceded the envoys' arrival, but now the crowds shouted down to them for more information, a request which the envoys did not oblige.

The prophet felt weak and dizzy. The internal pains of the previous night assailed him anew, along with the discomfort of his long ride across the countryside. In a state of wonder, he observed the festive atmosphere of Jerusalem's streets. Crowds swarmed about the market stalls, eagerly purchasing food and drink, carrying home large baskets and jars with the air of celebrants preparing for a holiday, chattering and laughing.

"Don't they understand what is happening?" he muttered to himself, scarcely realizing that he spoke aloud.

"Of course they do, Isaiah. Better than you do," replied Shebna, riding at his side. "As soon as we've reported to the king, I plan to go home and do some celebrating myself. Tonight let us eat and drink and be merry, for tomorrow we may die."

Isaiah did not answer. Trembling, he slowed his horse to a halt, dismounted, and signaled to one of the attendants with the envoys' party. "Will you take my horse back to the royal stables, my lad?" They were approaching the palace, and Isaiah's own house was close by, just up the narrow street. "I cannot see the king this evening," he went on. "Eliakim, you can tell him all that has happened. Tell him I have gone home to pray for Yahweh's guidance for us all."

"Certainly." Eliakim looked worried. He had never

seen the prophet look so pale, so obviously ill as he did now. "Do you need help getting home?" he asked, his voice filled with concern.

"No, no. It's only a few more steps," Isaiah responded.

Eliakim and Shebna watched him walk away, then eyed each other warily.

"So much for our prophet," Shebna remarked with contempt. "The leader of our noble delegation."

Eliakim shot him a look of cold reproof. "Remember, Shebna, whatever else he is, Isaiah is also a father, and both of his sons are in mortal danger. Allow him to be human."

As the envoys turned to ride up the great ramp to the palace, and Isaiah returned home to grieve for his sons and to seek Yahweh's guidance, the horrors of war drew nearer to Yahweh's chosen city.

THIRTEEN
Avital

The second day after Isaiah's return to Jerusalem from
Lachish, Naamah sat sadly peering out the window.
"The streets are full of refugees," she said. "Mostly
women and children. I wonder if any of the Lachish
people escaped?" Her voice broke off. It simply wouldn't
do to verbalize what she and Isaiah both wondered. *Had
any of Jashub's family escaped?*

Isaiah, sitting at his table, writing—or rather, trying
to write—looked up. Physically, he felt considerably
better than on the evening of his return, but his spirit
was as troubled as ever. Scattered on the table before
him lay several inscribed potsherds on which he had tried
to come to terms with the nearing horrors of war, to
understand them all in the light of Yahweh's ongoing plan
and his stern demands for righteousness and justice.
One by one, he lifted them and reread his recent
thoughts:

What do you mean that you have gone up,
   all of you, to the housetops,
you who are full of shoutings,

tumultous city, exultant town?
Behold, you laugh and celebrate,
   you slay oxen and kill sheep;
   you eat meat and drink wine.
You say, "Let us eat and drink
   for tomorrow we may die."
But I said, "Look away from me,
   let me weep bitter tears,
Do not labor to comfort me
   for the destruction of my people."
For Lord Yahweh of hosts has a day
   of tumult and trampling and confusion,
battering down of walls
   and a shouting to the mountains.
He has taken away the covering of Judah.

Though these little fragments captured much of his mood, Naamah's comments brought Isaiah back to the present. Had he lost both of his sons? He thought of his oration a few weeks earlier, warning how the town would be overflowing with widows, desperate frightened women without anyone to protect them. The prediction was obviously coming to pass, even beyond his direst expectations.

"I ought to go out," Naamah added. "I ought to see if there's anything we can do, but I keep thinking of Jashub and Reba and the children. If they come, any of them, we must have a place for them—and for Maher, whenever he comes home. This is such an inconvenient house! If it weren't for the rain, we could let some of the refugees sleep on the roof, but this time of year it rains most of the time."

"It's not raining right now," Isaiah answered. "I'll go out and see if I can hear any news." He rose from his table with a sense of relief at having decided on one small constructive action.

A woman was waiting near the house as Isaiah emerged

into the street. She unashamedly approached him and clutched his arm. "Help me!" she pleaded.

A little boy, unkempt and bewildered, clung to her skirts, coughing and sniffling, but the woman ignored him completely. In contrast to the child, the woman was expensively dressed in soft pink linen and had obviously devoted considerable attention to her appearance. Although she was pregnant, she was graceful, slender of face and limbs. Her dark hair, barely covered by a filmy veil, was crimped in careful curls. Large bangle earrings hung from her ears, and a discreet nose jewel adorned her left nostril. Her eyelids were covered with a dark, thick paste of antimony, and her cheeks were a bit too rosy.

"Help me!" she repeated. "Prince Isaiah, the Assyrians are about to attack us, and I have nowhere to stay. I need a place for my son here, and the one about to be born. I must protect them. Please, my prince! You have a big house! I can contribute—see, I have silver." She patted a large, heavy handbag that hung from a cord over her arm.

Isaiah was momentarily stunned. The woman seemed so plainly the embodiment of his own recent dire predictions.

"Have you heard anything about escapes from Lachish, woman?" he asked.

"No, no! I'm from Anathoth."

The town was full of women whose husbands had been slain in recent weeks, homeless refugees from the nearby villages desperately seeking protection.

Revulsion and pity struggled within him as the woman stared at him with bold, desperate eyes.

"You *could* marry me. No bride price—I'll pay you. And once my child is born, which should be any day now, I promise I'll earn my keep." Her tone was so provocative that her meaning was obvious. "I know all about you, my prince—that you have a wife already, but now she's

getting old. And you are Lord Yahweh's prophet."
Boldly, she grasped Isaiah's right hand and stared intently at the brand of Yahweh's service imprinted there. "But in spite of this, I'll wager you're a man like any other."

Isaiah pulled his hand from her grasp. "Really, woman . . . ," he began in a stern voice. But his attention was suddenly drawn to her little boy, who was about three years old. He had wandered away and was sitting dejectedly on the steps of Isaiah's house, watching his mother with big, frightened eyes. Isaiah started in the direction of the steps, but the woman stopped him.

"Don't you understand that I'm willing to give myself to you?" she said in a tone of desperation mingled with passion. "Somewhere I have to find a man to take me. I know who you are, Prince Isaiah, and I want it to be you."

Rarely if ever in his life had Isaiah felt himself at such a loss for words as he was now. Though he had tried to ignore it, there was an earthy attractiveness in the woman. She was right in her remark that he was a man like other men. Though he had never sought another wife, there was no law against it, and in times like these, when the women so outnumbered the men . . .

"Your husband, the child's father," he began uncertainly, "was he killed? Had he no family to help you?"

"Husband!" she laughed. "I've had no husband. Not yet!"

Isaiah felt a wave of disgust sweep through him. "Don't look at me like that," the young woman went on. "I've lived as I can, though it was not really by choice. I don't want to be what I am. I heard you speak once. You said, 'Though your sins be as scarlet, they can be white as snow.' I liked that. It gave me hope. Didn't you mean it?"

Isaiah's momentary temptation had dissolved. A sense of loathing, more intense than any transient desire for her, swept over him; yet he found it equally disquieting. She was desperate, she needed protection, and she claimed to be repentant. Her little child and the other yet unborn did need protection. Perhaps he and Naamah could give her refuge. But to take in a harlot! *Lord Yahweh, what am I to do!* he prayed. To have her in the house, to have her as a constant source of temptation, trouble, and discord between himself and Naamah would surely be unwise, yet to turn her away would show a lack of mercy.

The woman saw Maher approaching before Isaiah did. Along the street the prophet's son came striding, head bowed, deep in thought. "It's Maher! They told me he'd gone off to Lachish and gotten killed!" she exclaimed joyously to Isaiah. "Maher! Dear Maher! You're alive!" she cried as she ran to him. "You've come back!" Unashamedly, she threw her arms around him, and the young man, painfully aware of his father's stare of disapproval and amazement, looked at her with disdain.

"Avital!" he exclaimed. "What are you doing here?"

"I had to come into town. The Assyrians are coming— you must know that! I didn't know what to do. I never thought I'd see you again."

"I see you have met my father." Maher had grasped Avital's hand and was walking with her toward Isaiah, who stood still, watching them as waves of anger rose within him.

"You know this woman, Maher?" Isaiah spoke coldly, dreading what he was about to hear.

"Yes, my father. This is Avital from Anathoth."

She was silent, her eyes downcast for a moment. "My lord Isaiah, I did not realize that Maher was your son," she said weakly. No longer was she the seductress. She seemed rather a frightened, confused little girl.

"But, Avital," Maher began, "I told you of my father many times." It was true. No matter how far he had departed from the ways of his upbringing, Maher was proud of the fact that he was the son of Prince Isaiah. Far from concealing it, he had boasted about it to this woman, this harlot he had visited in Anathoth more times than he cared to remember.

How many months had it been since that last visit? Maher counted back frantically—eight, perhaps, or nine? Never, never had he dreamed in those blissful days before the Assyrian invasion that he would find Avital in Jerusalem, pregnant, standing before his house, talking to his father! Maher wondered if she had been plying Isaiah for help, telling him that his son was the father of her child to be. What else could they have possibly been talking about? Maher's mind raced on. His father would never under any circumstance be found conversing with a woman like Avital.

Maher was so caught up in his immediate problem that the coming Assyrian attack seemed inconsequential beside it. He nervously grasped Avital's hands. He definitely did not love her; he certainly did not want to marry her; and while he might be the father of the child she carried, there was also a very good chance he was not. But he was trapped, and the only decent thing to do was to make the best of a bad situation. "Papa," he began hesitantly, "Avital and I had hoped to be married months ago. I did wrong not to seek your consent, but I surely intended to. If it had not been for the invasion," he stammered "and then our embassy to Lachish—"

"Maher! Are you the father of this woman's baby?" Isaiah's voice was as stern as when he was proclaiming Yahweh's most devastating warning to the citizenry of Judah. It was not the gentle voice of a loving parent.

Maher nodded miserably.

"Can you swear before Lord Yahweh that you are the infant's father?" Isaiah demanded, obviously unconvinced.

"Don't, Maher!" Avital interrupted. Then turning to

Isaiah, she said, "He might be. We can't know for sure." Her eyes blazed. She was suddenly more frightened of Yahweh and his prophet than she was of losing her chance at a good marriage. Isaiah knew well enough what she, and Lord Yahweh must know, too.

"What about the other one?" The prophet glanced at the small boy on the doorstep.

"Ethan?" Avital laughed nervously. "No. He came along before I ever met Maher."

To her relief, Isaiah did not question her further on the matter. His next words in fact, addressed to Maher, took the woman quite by surprise.

"I had hoped for better things for you, my son," he said forthrightly. "But since you have spoken for Avital and are willing to take her and claim her child as yours, I will give you my blessing." He turned to the woman. "Have you any kinsman to draw up the contract?"

"No, my prince. There is no one."

"Very well. I'll take care of it myself then. I suppose we should all go inside the house." Isaiah's voice was weary. His grief surpassed words. Perhaps he should have sent the woman away. In their brief acquaintance, he had already clearly seen that she was not a person of integrity. Yet here he was arranging to make her his daughter-in-law.

The little boy whom Avital had called Ethan suddenly ran to his mother's side as the group walked up the steps to the house. "Which one is my new papa?" he asked.

"Hush!" Avital replied with a disapproving look.

Isaiah bent and patted the child's shoulder. "Are you going to be my papa?" Ethan asked gleefully.

"I think we'd better say I am going to be your grandfather," Isaiah replied.

A few hours later, as darkness descended on the old house, Isaiah sat exhausted on the side of his bed, stunned by the events of the afternoon. Not only had he acquired a most unlikely new daughter-in-law, there was also news—bad news—about his other daughter-in-law, Reba, and her children.

"I saw them being herded with hundreds of other women and children," Maher had explained. "All I could discover is that they are to be taken somewhere east of the Euphrates." Maher had tried to negotiate release of Reba and the five children, but the Assyrians were not interested in offers of ransom. Concerning Jashub, he had been able to discover nothing at all, only that there were many rumors that the craftsmen were to be spared. It was a small hope for Isaiah and his family to cling to.

Isaiah sat very still, praying silently, seeking the Lord Yahweh's guidance, trying to understand what was happening and why such things must be. One thing was clear to him: He must go to the palace in the morning. He could not postpone his meeting with Hezekiah any longer.

Around the bed that Isaiah shared with Naamah hung an improvised curtain. He and Maher had strung it up that afternoon to give at least an illusion of privacy. Through the thin drape, Isaiah could see Naamah still stirring about. The small oil lamp buring on the center table illuminated the room as Naamah bent protectively to cover Ethan, who was sleeping on a bench in the corner. A moment later, she extinguished the lamp and slipped through the curtain to sit down close to Isaiah. "We only have the present, the now," she said in a soft whisper. "Lord Yahweh expects us to do the best we can just now. We've got a very frightened and pregnant young woman to take care of, and a little boy who needs all the love and good food we can give him. Right now, that is my assignment. Of course, I'm worried about Jashub and Reba and the children—and about us and Jerusalem. But all we can do is take things as they come."

Isaiah held her close. "Tomorrow my assignment is to talk to Hezekiah," he said. "Lord Yahweh will surely send me the words, but he hasn't yet."

The room was not cold, but Naamah could feel Isaiah shivering. Her cheek nestled against his shoulder. "Oh, my dear one," she whispered. "We have only the now, not even the morning yet."

Her words were good, and her presence beside him was like a healing balm. Without further talk, both of them slipped beneath the covers and lay quietly in each other's arms. It was a time not of passion, but of tenderness, of caring, and of drawing strength from each other.

In the morning, Isaiah went to see the king.

Garbed in a robe of sackcloth, he walked slowly toward the palace. A feeling of hopelessness had engulfed him the moment he awakened. "Lord Yahweh, help us!" Isaiah had prayed. "Tell me what to say to Hezekiah! Help us all to face whatever must be!"

Isaiah found it hard to come to accept the fact that he himself was likely to be killed by the Assyrians if Jerusalem fell. He had always believed that he and Naamah and their children were a part of the Remnant of the faithful, for whose sake Yahweh had spared Judah more than once before. But now Jashub was missing. Reba and their children carried off as prisoners of war. Jerusalem would most likely fall as Lachish had fallen, and what then?

He feared for himself, and even more he feared for Naamah. Would she, too, become a prisoner of war? No longer young and never beautiful, she could expect no preferential treatment, nor would she have wanted it if it meant being another man's concubine. If fortunate, she might survive as a slave to some Assyrian noblewoman. *Naamah, my prophetess! My lady, my only love!* Isaiah found himself weeping as he approached the palace.

He felt no certain answer at all from Yahweh, only the

terrible disquieting sense that these trials should be borne with courage. *When Jerusalem falls and I am taken prisoner and sentenced to die, I must still believe that Yahweh is with me.*

And what of Hezekiah? Was Yahweh with him? Sadly enough, it certainly did not seem so.

Isaiah entered the presence of the king most reluctantly. Their meeting was in Hezekiah's private suite. Hephzibah was there, too, tight-lipped and somber, appearing much older than Isaiah remembered her. She was dressed in a gown of rough brown sackcloth and her face was very pale and tear-streaked. "It is so terrible," she said to her father as he entered, "not knowing what to expect, not knowing if we will live or die. And if we live, will it be worse than death?" Isaiah longed to comfort her, but what was there to say?

The king, who never lacked for words, spoke not at all but motioned for Isaiah to be seated. Isaiah sat down on the couch beside his daughter, reached out, and grasped her hand. What would become of her? Would she become part of Sennacherib's harem? The Assyrian prided himself on his collection of wives of fallen kings, and Hephzibah was still a beautiful woman, one who might be highly prized because of her uncommonly fair skin. Isaiah remembered the girls who had been part of the tribute gift. He could hear again the soft voice of the one who had confided to him that she felt lucky indeed to be going to Sennacherib's court. Hephzibah would never share such sentiments.

Hezekiah spoke at last. "They took our peace gifts, but then they also took Lachish," he said. "I simply don't know what to expect next. Have you any word from Lord Yahweh?" he pleaded. He looked panicky. Though he had not put on sackcloth, he was dressed in a plain robe of dark blue linen. He looked more the ordinary citizen than the king. His eyes were heavy from lack of sleep, his long hair uncombed and disheveled. Something about him reminded Isaiah of Ahaz. It was the look of complete confusion, so unlike Hezekiah's usual confidence and determination.

"The Assyrians will attack Jerusalem," Isaiah responded. "You know that as well as I do, Hezekiah. It takes no mysterious insight into the future to predict it. We have a strong city. We may resist the siege for months, but ultimately Jerusalem will fall."

"I have done this to my people!" Hezekiah moaned.

Isaiah stood up, "Too late you see your folly!" All the pent-up anger and disappointment of months of unheeded warnings came bursting out. "Oh yes, you looked to your weapons in the house of the forest. You repaired the breaches of the city walls. You collected the waters of the lower pools and built your wonderful tunnel! You made a reservoir for the water of the old pool! But you did not look to Yahweh or have regard for him who planned it long ago!"

"I have looked to Lord Yahweh all my life long," Hezekiah countered, more in desperation than anger. "I wanted my people to be free of the yoke of Assyria, *really* free! I still believe it was a righteous goal! I do not understand why Yahweh has made our enemies triumph. Of course, our people have been guilty of many transgressions in God's eyes, but the Assyrians are so much worse than we are. How can he let them conquer us? Oh, Isaiah, is there no hope at all?"

Isaiah moved toward the doorway. "I suppose there is always hope," he said without much conviction. "But this time, it will take a miracle."

"Wait, Isaiah!" Hezekiah implored. The prophet turned again to face his son-in-law. His brief storm of anger was over, and what remained was his undeniable, indestructable devotion to his king.

"Forgive me, Isaiah," the king went on. "I did what I thought was right."

"Ask Lord Yahweh for forgiveness. It is not mine to

give. I only know you have broken my heart, and yet I care for you still!" It was a cry from the depths of Isaiah's spirit, and he walked away, not comprehending the magnitude of the words he had spoken.

FOURTEEN

The Rabshakeh's Oration

Although it had been an exhausting morning, Isaiah felt no real desire to return home to the city house, where serenity now seemed impossible. He dreaded the presence of the strangers they had taken in the day before, and he thought of Avital with particular loathing.

Naamah read the look of weariness in her husband's eyes as soon as he entered. "Something to eat?" she suggested.

Isaiah shook his head. "Where's Maher?" he asked half heartedly.

"He went down to the market to get us more provisions. The girl—Avital—had a purse full of silver and she gave it to him. I must say, it will help us."

Provisions really didn't matter, Isaiah thought. Nothing really mattered any more. He sat down on the stone bench near the door, closed his eyes and breathed deeply, longing with all his heart for guidance from Lord Yahweh, yet resigned to the fearful awareness that he and his family would not be exempt from the general woes of Judah.

Naamah sat beside him, grasped his hands as she

often did in their most serious moments together. "You should try to sleep," she said. "You were wakeful all through the night last night. Avital and Ethan are out in the courtyard. I'll keep them out there so you can have some quiet."

Isaiah rose, walked slowly to his bed, and pushed back the thin curtains that hung around it.

To lie down, to rest peacefully, wrapped in the gentle warmth of autumn sunshine, to feel the soft wind from the open windows as it stirred the curtains beside his bed—small, mundane blessings, perhaps to be savored for the last time.

Isaiah lay very still, his eyes closed. From the courtyard behind the house he could hear a faint echo of Avital's voice and that of little Ethan. He felt the breeze through the open windows.

"Hezey," he whispered, still feeling the grief of the morning's interview. "Oh my child, my dear child. I would have given my own life to make you what I hoped you would be!" In his mind's eye he saw himself as a young man with the frightened child Hezekiah in his arms, a fleeting glimpse of the past and of the reality of protective love.

He was not asleep, but nearly so, as another sudden memory swept over him, this time of himself as a very small child, scarcely older than little Ethan was now, safe in his mother's lap after some little upset now long forgotten. He felt strangely at peace. Lord Yahweh's love surrounded him like the love of a devoted parent. A sudden awareness seized him: *The worst is over now. Lord Yahweh has reached out his hands to rescue us. Jerusalem will not fall: Sennacherib will not take the Holy City.* Unlikely as it seemed, he felt the reality of it clearly. Yahweh was sending him a message of truth, love, and protection. There was something else also, something not so clear. *But it will come,* Isaiah thought. *It will all come clear, and soon, if not just now.* And with these thoughts, Isaiah sank into a sleep of wonderful serenity.

When Maher came home he had a large armload of supplies from the marketplace. "The Assyrians are gathering outside the Siloam Gate," he announced, setting the provisions on the table. "There is going to be some kind of conference. Papa will want to be there."

"No," Naamah whispered, with a glance toward the bed where Isaiah lay still as death. "Don't wake him! Go, find out all you can, but let your father rest."

Maher nodded. It seemed unfortunate that Isaiah should miss the excitement, but at a time like this, when their very moments were numbered, sleep was a precious gift from Yahweh, not to be disturbed.

While Isaiah slept through the beautiful clear autumn afternoon, Shebna and Eliakim, along with Joah, the king's recording secretary, went to the old conduit from the pool of Siloam, just outside the wall, to tell the Rabshekah that Jerusalem would not yield. On the wall clustered hundreds of citizens, a confused, jumbled mass of humanity, pressing close to the ramparts to see and hear the activity below. Among them was Maher, the son of Isaiah.

This time the Rabshakeh was attended by two high-ranking officers and a large troop of armed bodyguards. Not far away, more Assyrian troops scurried about setting up a base camp. They were obviously only a small part of Sennacherib's entire army. If Jerusalem attempted to hold out, within a day or two there would be thousands more men with their horses, chariots, and heavy equipment, and the siege would begin in earnest.

Silently, the crowd watched as the Assyrian envoys exchanged formalities with the Judean deputation. There were whispers among the onlookers, nothing more, for the word had been spread that Hezekiah expected them to remain perfectly silent in the face of the enemy. What better way to show their loyalty to all they believed in and their utter contempt for the invader!

Eliakim spoke in hushed tones as he delivered Hezekiah's refusal of surrender. "We will not give up our city," he told the Assyrians firmly. "We gave you our peace gifts and were willing to cease hostilities. We have done all we can. Our people are resolved to fight and to die for Jerusalem, for our King Hezekiah, and for Yahweh, our God."

The Rabshakeh listened impatiently, as if he had already known this would be the answer. Then in his loud, resonant voice, he called out. "Thus says Sennacherib, the Great King, the Mighty King, the King of Assyria, the King of the World! Do not let Hezekiah deceive you! Your city cannot stand!" The thunderous words could clearly be heard by the multitude on the wall above. Obviously, the Rabshakeh did not intend this to be a private conference, but rather the beginning of a public oration.

"My lord Rabshakeh," Eliakim spoke politely in Aramaic, "please let us speak in your language for we understand it. Don't speak to us in Hebrew, for the people on the wall will hear."

The Rabshakeh laughed loudly and replied, "My master wants everyone in Jerusalem to hear this." Then he shouted in Hebrew to the men listening on the wall. "On whom do you depend for help? Surely not Pharaoh!" he shouted. "Egypt is like a broken reed, a staff which will pierce the hand of any man who leans upon it! Where now are those pitiful forces he sent to help you? Dead! Crushed beneath the might of Assyria! Only a fool would believe Pharaoh will send you more aid now! And would you rely upon yourselves? You haven't two thousand troops left to man your defenses! Would you rely on your King Hezekiah and his wonderful tunnel? We will find the entrance to the tunnel!"

The stunning silence of the masses on the wall was disconcerting. Beneath his high cylindrical hat, the Rabshakeh's forehead dripped with perspiration, his dark cheeks reddened, his voice still resonant, turned to gentle pleading. "People of Judah, surrender!" he cried. "Thus says Sennacherib: Make your peace with me; open the gates and come out, and we shall take you to a land very similar to your own—a pleasant land, good and fruitful, a land of grain and wine, of bread and vineyards, where every man may sit in the shade of his own vine and fig tree."

Along with the others, Maher listened with a great lump in his throat and tears in his eyes. Would his brother Jashub perhaps be taken to such a land? Or had Reba and the children been spared only to become the slaves of some Assyrian noble who would use them as he pleased? Was it perhaps not better to do as Hezekiah had decided—to fight and die bravely for Jerusalem?

"But beware," the Rabshakeh thundered on. "Don't let Hezekiah deceive you. Don't let him persuade you to trust in Lord Yahweh by telling you 'Yahweh will surely deliver us.' Has the god of any nation ever been able to stop the might of Assyria? Where are they now, those gods of Hamath and Arpad and Samaria? Fallen! Trampled to dust! Why should Yahweh be any different? So you think this God of yours can deliver Jerusalem from my hand?"

The envoys said not a word, because Hezekiah had commanded them to say nothing in reply. It was obvious the interview was over. The hopelessness of the situation was real to them all now, even to Shebna, who was the first to begin rending his clothes as they returned to King Hezekiah's palace. Before they entered the king's presence, all three men, Eliakim, Shebna, and Joah, tore their cloaks into tatters, a visible sign of the bad news they carried.

Hezekiah listened to their report without comment, then tore off the blue linen robe he wore, ripped it almost to shreds, and put it on again. Then he picked up a bolt of sackcloth, lying ready on a nearby bench, and tore off a piece in which he wrapped himself as if it were a cloak. "Here, all of you," he said, "take some of this and wrap yourselves in it, and go to Isaiah. Ask him to plead with Lord Yahweh for the deliverance of Judah. As for me, I am going to the temple."

Obediently, Eliakim tore off pieces of sackcloth for himself and the others to wrap about themselves over their torn garments. Hezekiah watched them in silence. He seemed confused, unable even to act upon his announced decision to go to the temple.

"My lord king," Eliakim said gently, "the people on the wall heard everything, and they were silent, as you commanded them. Their hearts are with you."

Tears streamed from Hezekiah's eyes. "May God have mercy on us all," he whispered. "Now go to Isaiah. Perhaps Lord Yahweh will listen to him."

Even as he wept, there was in Hezekiah that glimmer of hope that refused to die.

The loud knocking on Isaiah's front door roused him from slumber. Naamah escorted in the envoys: Eliakim, Shebna, and Joah in their wraps of sackcloth. "The king has sent us," said Eliakim, who had assumed the role of spokesman for the group. "It is a mournful day, a day of great distress. There is no strength left in us. Only if the Lord will arise to strike down the presumptuous pride of the Assyrians, is there any hope."

Shebna and Joah merely nodded assent. All three men were very frightened, unable to believe in the hope they voiced. They had, after all, heard the Rabshakeh with their own ears. They saw the seriousness of the crisis, and they prepared to hear Isaiah urging unconditional surrender, a course that offered for the nobles, even for Isaiah himself, no hope at all.

Isaiah listened patiently. The wonderful sense of peace that he felt when he slept was still with him. He had seen no visions, but he knew that Lord Yahweh had taken charge, that the worst was over.

"Go back to King Hezekiah," he said, "and tell him this is the word from Yahweh: 'Do not be afraid because of the Rabshakeh's words.' Because the Assyrians have reviled the Lord, the Lord will deal with Sennacherib. He will make him hear a rumor that will cause him to return to his own land." Isaiah was not sure what the rumor would be, but he recalled vividly how worried the Rabshakeh had seemed by Maher's suggestion that further Egyptian aid was on the way to Judah. There was also the political reality that a great king like Sennacherib dared not stay away too long from his home base. In his absence, there were no doubt rumblings of discontent at home, perhaps even active plotting against his government. And the rainy season was beginning. The long, cold gray months of winter would soon be here when kings, as a rule, tried to avoid keeping their armies in the field. Besides, Sennacherib could already claim victory. He had taken Lachish and countless other smaller places, and he had seized the rich peace gifts.

"Go and tell Hezekiah that Jerusalem will not fall," Isaiah reiterated.

The men listened, almost incredulous, yet moved by the fire in the prophet's eyes. "You have changed your mind, Isaiah?" Shebna asked. "This is not what you were saying even this morning. The king told us that you said Jerusalem would fall."

"Yes, I did," Isaiah responded. "But this morning I spoke only what I knew as a man. Now I give you the words that Yahweh himself has put in my heart."

Even while Isaiah was speaking to the king's men, the Rabshakeh, along with a troop of attendants and bodyguards, left Jerusalem to report back to Sennacherib. The Assyrian king had set up camp outside Libnah, a small walled town not far away that still held out for Hezekiah.

The conference between the Great King and his chief officer was held in strict privacy. Sennacherib was obviously panicky. In the Rabshakeh's brief absence, more disturbing rumors had reached him. Pharaoh was sending a force of Egyptians and Ethiopians to the aid of Judah.

"We must press Hezekiah to surrender now," Sennacherib bellowed. "You failed me! You and your fine oratory! Why were you not able to frighten those people on the wall of Jerusalem into opening up the gates? Just a few traitors—just one—and our troops could have taken the city easily."

"I think they realize that full well, my lord king," the Rabshakeh answered humbly. "And they are determined not to let it happen. They say their God will save them."

Sennacherib frowned. He was angry and frustrated. He was also extremely worried, eager to get out of Judah before he lost all he had gained. "I will send Hezekiah a letter," he said. Calling for a scribe, he dictated:

Sennacherib, the Great King, the King of the World, to Hezekiah of Jerusalem: Do not let your God on whom you are relying deceive you! Do not believe his promise that Jerusalem will not come into my hands. Certainly you have heard what the kings of Assyria have done to all the lands who rebelled against us. We have destroyed them utterly. Why should you be delivered? Has the god of any nation delivered them? Where are the nations of Gozan and Haran, Rezeph and Tel Assar? Where are the kings of Hamath and Arpad, Sepharvaim, Hena, and Ivvah?

These questions needed no answer. Hezekiah would reconsider and surrender rather than let Jerusalem be destroyed and Judah be crushed by the might of Assyria. Hurriedly, Sennacherib scanned the papyrus the scribe had prepared. Hurriedly he sealed it with his royal seal and turned again to the Rabshakeh, who stood nervous and fearful at the king's side. "Go back to Jerusalem," Sennacherib ordered. "Ride all night if you must, and take him this. He *will* surrender!"

It was early morning when the exhausted Assyrians arrived again outside Jerusalem. The Rabshakeh's men handed the letter to Eliakim, who took it straightway to the king's palace. Hezekiah was still in bed, but wakeful. He had spent a long sleepless night in prayer. If Yahweh intended to save Jerusalem, there must soon come a sign to that effect. Was it in the letter Eliakim brought? Hezekiah grasped the papyrus scroll eagerly, broke the seal, and read the words in stunned horror.

Nothing had changed. Sennacherib had not given up.

"I must go up to the temple," Hezekiah said, his heart thumping so fast he scarcely realized what he was doing. He was still clad in the torn shreds of yesterday's robe, and over it he tossed the sackcloth cloak that lay on his bed. Though his feet were bare and the floor was cold, he shunned sandals. His only concern was to get to the temple, to get closer to Lord Yahweh. Clutching Sennacherib's letter, Hezekiah moved as if in a daze.

Isaiah had promised Jerusalem would be safe, but Isaiah, it seemed, was wrong. Hezekiah did not remember the walk from the palace to the temple with Eliakim hovering beside him, but somehow he was there, on his knees. He spread out Sennacherib's letter and began to pray, saying, "O Lord of Hosts, God of Israel, you alone are God over all the kingdoms of the earth. Listen, O Lord, and hear! Open your eyes, O Lord, and see! Hear the words of Sennacherib, which he has sent to mock the living God! It is true, O Lord, that the kings of Assyria have laid waste the other nations and lands and have cast their gods into the fire. But they were not really gods. They were idols of stone and wood, man-made things! Now, O Lord Yahweh, save us so that all the kingdoms of the earth will know that you are God, and you alone!"

Hezekiah wept.

At Isaiah's home, the household gathered around the breakfast table. No one spoke much. Ethan was wheezing and coughing, and Naamah held him in her lap and coaxed him to drink a little broth. Maher and Avital regarded each other warily with none of the joy of newlyweds. Avital toyed with a piece of bread. She was not really hungry, but food was precious, and she forced herself to eat a little.

Isaiah was not eating. There was a faraway look in his eyes as if he were completely unaware of those around him. He knew Hezekiah was in the temple, praying even more desperately than he had prayed the day before.

"I must go to the king," Isaiah said suddenly. "Where is my good robe, the one Hephzibah made?"

Naamah handed little Ethan to Avital, rose, and extracted Isaiah's beautiful robe from the chest on which she was sitting.

Then Isaiah, the prophet-prince, dressed as if for a great festival, went to the temple to seek the king.

FIFTEEN

Waiting

Hezekiah was still kneeling when Isaiah entered the temple. The great room was deathly quiet, for the king had turned from weeping to silent prayer. Isaiah watched him for a moment. Then in a calm, resounding voice he said, "Thus says Yahweh, the Lord God of Judah, 'I have heard your prayer to me about Sennacherib, the king of Assyria.'"

Hezekiah rose and turned to face Isaiah. He said nothing.

"This is the word that Yahweh has spoken concerning him," Isaiah went on. His voice became rhythmical, deep and moving, as if it were not Isaiah but Yahweh himself speaking:

"Whom have you mocked and scorned,
 O Sennacherib?
Against whom have you raised your voice
 and lifted up your eyes in pride?
Against the Holy One of Israel!
By your servants you have mocked the Lord,
 and you have said, 'With my many chariots
I have gone up the heights of the mountains,

to the far recesses of Lebanon.
I have felled its tallest cedars,
    its choicest cypresses;
I have reached its remotest heights,
    its densest forests.
I have dug wells and drunk their waters;
    I have dried up with the sole of my foot
    all the streams of Egypt.'

Have you not heard
    that I determined it long ago?
I planned from days of old,
    what now I bring to pass,
that you should make fortified cities
    crash into heaps of ruins,
Their inhabitants, shorn of strength,
    are dismayed and confounded,
They have become like plants of the field,
    like tender green shoots,
like grass sprouting on the housetops,
    blighted before it is grown.

But I know your sitting down,
    your going out and coming in,
    and your raging against me.
Because you have raged against me
    and your arrogance has reached my ears,
I will put my hook in your nose
    and my bit in your mouth,
and I will make you return
    by the way you came."

"Isaiah," gasped Hezekiah, "is it true?"

"Yes," said Isaiah. "We are to be delivered. There are still hard times ahead of us, but our nation will recover. The Remnant of Judah will bear fruit again. And as for Sennacherib, he will not enter this city. He will not set up camp, nor shoot one arrow here, nor build a siege ramp against the walls. By the way that he came he will return. This is the word of Lord Yahweh."

"How do you know, Isaiah? I want to believe you, but can you be sure?"

"I don't know how I know," the prophet answered. "I did not expect it myself. I dared not even hope, but then Lord Yahweh whispered these words in my heart, and I *know*."

"Come back to the palace with me," Hezekiah requested. "We must give this message to everyone."

Like wildfire, the news of Isaiah's prediction spread through the streets of Jerusalem that day. Many greeted it with skepticism. Isaiah was not given to making specific predictions of immediate events except to issue warnings of doom to a people who attemped to cast off the Assyrian yoke.

"King Hezekiah has started this rumor just to give us hope," some said. "Prince Isaiah certainly wouldn't say such things."

At the palace, however, Isaiah was saying exactly such things to Hezekiah's perplexed counselors.

"This is the message from our God," Isaiah proclaimed. As he spoke, the recording secretary, Joah, frantically took notes.

"Lord Yahweh of hosts has sworn:
 'As I have planned,
 so shall it be,
 and as I have purposed,
 so shall it stand,
 that I will break the Assyrian in my land,
 and upon my mountains trample him under foot.'
Lord Yahweh of Hosts has purposed,
 and who will annul it?
His hand is stretched out,
 and who will turn it back?"

"Yesterday," Eliakim remarked when the prophet

paused, "I might have believed you, Isaiah. But since the new letter from Sennacherib arrived this morning, and it is so obvious that he does not intend to give up, how can you still have hope?"

"That letter," Isaiah replied, "is his last desperate attempt to frighten us into surrender. In the past Lord Yahweh has used Sennacherib as the rod of his anger, but no more. The power of the man who calls himself the King of the World is nothing at all compared to the greatness of Yahweh, yet he dares to compare Yahweh to those powerless fallen idols of the lands he has conquered. His pride will not go unpunished."

Seated in an elaborate wicker chair in the king's audience hall, Isaiah reiterated his message over and over as various men of the court came and listened and went excitedly on their way to spread the news.

"Ah, the thunder of many peoples!" Isaiah exclaimed suddenly. Once again Joah began taking rapid notes.

"They rage like the raging sea!
    They roar like the roaring of mighty waters!
The Assyrians, too, roar
    like the roaring of many waters;
but Yahweh will rebuke them,
    and they will flee far away,
chased like chaff on the mountains before the wind
    and whirling dust before a storm.
At evening time, behold their terror!
    Before morning they are no more.
This is the portion of those who despoil us,
    and the lot of those who plunder us."

Hezekiah had returned to the temple to pray while Isaiah was left to counsel and reassure a frightened and incredulous multitude. The thought occurred to Isaiah that he was himself acting the role of the king of Judah, and it was a rather disquieting feeling.

And what if I am wrong? Fleeting doubts crossed

Isaiah's mind. *What if I have misunderstood Lord Yahweh's message?* But, no, it could not be. Never in his life had Isaiah felt so certain of anything as he did of the Assyrians' imminent withdrawal.

Throughout the day news continued to arrive from watchmen on the city walls. The Rabshakeh's party had departed early, presumably to return again to Libnah. The small base camp set up by the Assyrians the previous day remained, but as the long hours wore on, there was no sign of additional Assyrian troop movement toward Jerusalem. Outside the city walls, as far as one could see in any direction, the countryside lay desolate and still. Whatever Sennacherib was doing, he was apparently not preparing to besiege Jerusalem.

At the prophet's city house, the young woman Avital was in the throes of labor. Sooner than calculated, the child, who might or might not be Maher's, was about to make its entry into the world. Avital amid screams had collapsed on her cot. She looked imploringly at her new mother-in-law. "Can you help me?" she gasped between moans.

Naamah, unlike many women, had never really studied the art of midwifery or even assisted at a birth. "I can try," she responded, somewhat panicky. "Maher, go quickly and get help! Just bang on doors till you find a woman who can help us. No, first try Beulah, three doors down. If she's not there, just keep looking! And take Ethan with you!"

Maher went out without a word. Ethan was crying loudly, frightened by his mother's screams, and Naamah felt relieved when Maher carried him off. "You'll be all right, my dear," she said soothingly. "You've been through this before."

The young woman continued to moan.

"Breathe deeply," Naamah counseled. The girl on the cot closed her eyes, and Naamah held her hand.

"You don't have a birthing stool," Avital mumbled.

"No, but don't worry, Maher will find someone who does. They'll bring it." She grasped the girl's hand tightly. For moments that seemed like hours they waited. Avital's contractions grew more frequent, her moans deeper.

Then when Maher returned with a midwife but without Ethan, Avital looked up, anxiety evident in her eyes, and asked, "Where is Ethan?"

"This woman's daughter is keeping him," Maher said. "He's fine. This is Beulah. She lives just down the street. Ethan is in good hands. Don't worry!" He watched the skilled woman assist Avital onto a small, three-legged birthing stool. With that, he went out into the courtyard, respectful of the custom that men should not be present in the birthing chamber.

Within moments the child was born. As Beulah severed the cord, Naamah brought a pan of warm water from the cauldron over the fireplace. "The baby is not breathing," Beulah whispered. "A beautiful little girl, but she is stillborn."

Avital heard and moaned again. What followed would always haunt Maher's memory. As he reentered the house, the women were working to stanch Avital's sudden hemorrhaging. It wasn't long before the girl from Anathouth, whom he hadn't really loved, went into shock and died. Maher felt immensely relieved but immeasurably guilty.

Beulah looked at Maher sadly, seeing him as a shocked and grieving young husband and father who had just lost his most beloved. "I will go home and tell my husband. He'll help with the burial," she said in a gentle voice. Over the years, she had seen so many women die that she was almost inured to it, but she had never grown hardened to the reactions of the survivors. Some wept wildly while others seemed too stunned to cry. Maher, the son of Isaiah, simply looked confused.

"Beulah, will you come back and help me prepare them?" Naaman asked.

"Yes, yes, of course."

The conversation continued in subdued whispers while Maher stood by feeling helpless. "Someone ought to go and find Papa," he remarked. "I'll go up to the palace and get him."

Almost blindly he turned toward the door, trying to comprehend the realities of the day's events--at home and on the larger scene of Judah. Just that morning, Isaiah had reiterated his belief that the worst was over, that Jerusalem was about to be delivered from the Assyrian threat. Was Avital's death a sign from Yahweh, and if so, what did it portend? And what of the orphaned child, Ethan? Who would assume responsibility for him? The thoughts that swept through Maher's mind were almost overpowering as he walked up the ramp to the palace.

Isaiah was not there. After many hours of sitting in the king's audience hall, delivering his predictions of Sennacherib's retreat, Isaiah had gone with King Hezekiah on a circuit of the city walls. Deeply discouraged, Maher trailed after them. He found them at the tower of one of the city gates, where a large crowd had gathered. Hezekiah was speaking.

"Be strong and of good courage, my people!" The king's voice rang out, clear and confident. "Deliverance is at hand! Jerusalem will not be attacked! We have received word that Sennacherib has left Libnah and his troops are moving northward. The men outside Jerusalem have broken camp, too. They are leaving Judah! Lord Yahweh has saved us!"

Making his way through the pressing crowd, Maher tried to catch his father's eye, but Isaiah, at the king's side, failed to look in Maher's direction. The crowd murmured excitedly.

"Lord Yahweh has made Sennacherib hear a rumor

that has caused him so much fear that he cannot get out of Judah quickly enough!" Hezekiah continued. He did not seem inclined to elaborate further on this point and explain the rumor. Maher wondered if perhaps his own suggestions to the Rabshakeh about aid from Pharaoh had contributed to the Assyrians' decision to withdraw. Perhaps, but then again, perhaps not.

"I hear there's trouble for Sennacherib back in Nineveh," someone in the crowd shouted.

Maher felt impatient. Jerusalem was to be spared. The throngs on the wall, pressing so eagerly to hear the king's words, had received a reprieve from condemnation. It was an event that would live in Judah's history forever. Yet in the face of the miracle, the ordinary business of living and dying was still going on—like Avital and her stillborn child.

After what seemed like endless hours, Maher saw Isaiah glancing in his direction. The younger man waved frantically and watched Isaiah respond with a reproving frown. The king had finished speaking and was moving on, apparently to continue the circuit of the walls, to deliver the same speech to another crowd at another tower. His subjects cleared a path for him, shouting gleefully, "Blessed be Yahweh! Long live the king!"

Isaiah, dignified but glowing with happiness, followed close beside Hezekiah, and Maher realized it was no time to intrude upon them with the news of the death of the harlot of Anathoth.

It was late that afternoon before Isaiah returned home, and by then the bodies of Avital and her stillborn infant had been prepared for burial and discreetly removed from the house. Maher slumped disconsolately on a bench by the fireplace while Naamah sat on her bed, holding little Ethan in her lap. The boy was sleeping peacefully. After a tentative question of "Where's my mama?" he had seemed satisfied by Naamah's answer: "She's gone away." Perhaps because Avital had neglected him shamefully for most of his short life, the boy did not seem unduly distressed by his mother's absence.

With Isaiah's return, Naamah gently laid the sleeping child on the bed and rose to greet her husband. In the moments that followed, they apprised each other of the day's news. The wonderful, joyous fulfillment of Isaiah's predictions was a strange contrast to the unexpected death of the young woman who had found refuge in his house.

There was so much to talk over. Isaiah, Naamah, and Maher sat up far later than was customary by the shadowy light of the fireplace.

"We must take care of Ethan," Naamah pronounced. "The child has no one but us."

Isaiah nodded. He had every intention of keeping the child, of raising the boy as his son, an ironic gift from Yahweh. Ethan might—just might—prove to be the disciple that neither of his own sons had been.

"As for me," Maher said suddenly, "I am going to go east and look for Jashub and Reba. I'll find them somewhere. Now that the Assyrians are withdrawing, I expect they'll be perfectly willing to listen to offers of ransom. I am leaving tomorrow morning if Hezekiah will open the gates."

Maher's parents were unprepared for this announcement. Mixed emotions tore at both Isaiah and his wife. The hope that Maher's quest would be successful clashed with the fear that he, too, would be lost. But Isaiah, who had seen so many reasons to have hope in the days just past, allowed his optimism to triumph. "If the gates are open in the morning," he said, "then that is a sign that you should go, and may the Holy One of Israel guide you wherever the road may lead you.

The gates were open in the morning, and even as Maher was leaving Jerusalem through one of them, an excited messenger came running in through another. "There's death in the Assyrian camp!" he shouted to all who would hear. "Out on the north road! Hundreds of men are dying or are dead already! Last night, they say, the death angel struck them! Lord Yahweh has delivered us in an even greater way then we hoped! The rest of them are retreating fast!"

"Isaiah said it would happen!" Excited voices spread the news through every street of the city, from the homes of the humblest citizens to the mansions of the rich. Isaiah was roused from a late breakfast by neighbors banging on his door with the joyful tidings. "It is as you said, my lord prince!"

As Isaiah walked to the palace, adoring throngs surrounded him, plucking at his robe, pressing their way into his path. "You said Lord Yahweh would strike down Sennacherib, and he's done it!"

The prophet felt vaguely uneasy. "Is Sennacherib dead?" he asked in some confusion.

No one in the crowd seemed to know if Sennacherib was dead or not, nor did they seem to care. Hundreds, perhaps thousands, of the enemy were dead, stricken down by the sword of Yahweh.

There was something sadly amiss, Isaiah thought, in such gleeful rejoicing in anyone's death. Yet they *were* the enemy, the destroyers now destroyed.

"The Assyrian shall fall by a sword, not of man," Isaiah exclaimed, "and a sword, not of man, shall devour him!" It was a sort of belated prediction, a summation of the news he had just heard. "He shall flee from the sword. His strength shall pass away in terror, and his officers desert the standard in panic."

Within hours, these words and others like them would be quoted all over the city as further evidence that Isaiah had predicted the plague.

At the moment, however, Isaiah simply wished he knew more precisely what was happening. Once he reached the palace, he found more detailed news. The

Assyrian king apparently was still very much alive, but many of his troops did indeed lie dead or dying in the place where they had made camp the night before. Moreover, Sennacherib had ordered his able-bodied men to hasten their retreat. On swift horses with only minimal baggage, the remainder of the Assyrian host was galloping northward as rapidly as possible, trying to outpace the death angel who, they feared, hovered close behind them.

King Hezekiah, like his humblest subjects, was gleeful over the news. "We must send inspectors out there soon," he reflected. "The Assyrians may have abandoned some valuable supplies."

"The place is overrun with rats," reported Shebna, who somehow seemed to have garnered considerable inside information. "It would probably be best to stay away from it for a while. The rats and the vultures will dispose of the corpses soon enough."

All morning Isaiah listened to talk of this sort, saying very little, feeling grateful that Maher had chosen a different route and would not likely be anywhere near the plague site. In the afternoon, he went home to attend Avital's simple burial.

"Nothing seems real," Naamah said as they walked back to their city house in the gathering twilight after the funeral. "Ever since the invasion started, I feel as if I am living in some sort of dream world—that sometime I will wake up and find that none of these things have really happened."

"Yes, I understand." They had stopped at Beulah's house once again to get Ethan from the woman who had kept him during the burial service. Isaiah gathered him up in his arms and was rewarded by a hug and a whispered response of "Papa" from the little boy.

"You mustn't let him call you that," Naamah said rather sharply.

Isaiah did not answer.

"This dreadful old house!" It was Naamah who broke the silence as they reached their own door. "I want to go home, Isaiah, *really* home."

"I know," he answered. It was something he too had thought much about. "We'll see about it soon," he promised. Great drops of rain began to fall as they entered, and the autumn wind howled mournfully through the narrow street. *How can I ever tell her?* Isaiah thought.

For as surely as he had known that Yahweh would spare Jerusalem, he knew that his country house was gone, the home where he had taken Naamah as a bride so many years before. Now there would be only a heap of stone and charred timber. In his mind he could see the ruins as clearly as if he stood among them. It was part of the chastisement that Sennecherib's ruthlessness had brought on the whole land.

Throughout the evening there were other things to occupy them—the routine of an evening meal and the presence of Ethan, lively and energetic, almost recovered now from the cough that had bothered him since his arrival. Isaiah played with the child while Naamah prepared supper, and Naamah's questions was pushed to the back of his mind.

A few hours later, however, Isaiah lay in bed sleepless. He thought about Jashub and Maher, about the hundreds of dead Assyrians in Sennacherib's camp, and the fact that the enemy withdrawal did not necessarily mean the end of Judah's tribute payments. The large room where Isaiah lay was dark and full of creaking sounds. He could hear little Ethan on his small bed across the room breathing heavily in a deep sleep. Naamah lay quietly at Isaiah's side perhaps sleeping, but he wasn't sure.

The loss of our house will be far harder on her than on me, Isaiah thought, his mind returning to the matter he hated to face. *I could be satisfied to stay here, so much closer to the king's palace.*

"Isaiah." He felt his wife touch his arm. Her voice was a soft whisper, but it spoke volumes. "When do you think we can go home?"

Turning, he pressed her close against him and felt the tears running down her cheeks. "Oh, my love," she said, "I am so tired, so very tired, but Lord Yahweh is giving us a new start. And we must go home."

Isaiah continued to hold her and to feel within himself the same longings, the same emotions she felt—the combination of deep grief and unutterable weariness. Yet along with these rose a new and indestructible hope for better times to come. That hope, so gravely shaken in the last few months, was, after all, what they had both lived for, and the Assyrian retreat was proof that it had not been in vain. "Tomorrow," he said at last, "I'll go out and see how things are—see what we have to do."

"Tomorrow," she whispered sleepily, pulling the bed covers closer about her. Isaiah could sense the peace sweeping over her. Moments passed, and Isaiah, wakeful, held her close while she slept. *There are so many times when Yahweh seems to be silent, hidden, beyond reach*, he thought, *but even now, through Naamah, he is sending me the courage to carry on.*

Long moments later, Isaiah's reverie was shattered when little Ethan awoke crying. His were the wails of a little child who had faced too many uncertainties for entirely too long and whose sleep was troubled by frightful nightmares.

Naamah sat up and sighed deeply, but Isaiah was out of bed before her. Across the room she could hear him, lifting Ethan from his bed, whispering soothing, loving words and pacing back and forth with the child in his arms. In a short time Ethan's cries subsided. Isaiah sat with him on the stone ledge that was his bed, holding the child in his lap and singing softly as he had sung to his own children long ago.

Snuggling beneath the bed covers, Naamah listened to

her husband's beautiful voice in the darkened room and felt a happiness of the sort she had feared had disappeared forever. Outside the autumn wind howled fiercely through the streets of the old city, but in the hearts of Naamah and Isaiah, spring had come again.

SIXTEEN
Out of the Rubble

True to his word, the following morning Isaiah prepared to go to the country place. Naamah, visibly revived, smiled as she prepared breakfast for the household. Ethan too seemed to have caught Naamah's spirit of cheerfulness. His eyes were brighter. He was not coughing much at all. Without protest, he gulped the broth Naamah fed him, then waved his arms and chattered happily when Isaiah picked him up.

What a joy that child is, Isaiah thought as he walked out of the city toward the country house. Any misgivings he had had about the child's mother had no effect on his feelings for Ethan. Of that Isaiah was certain. For some reason, Yahweh had entrusted this little life to his and Naamah's care, perhaps to replace the sons they had lost.

No, I mustn't think they're lost. Isaiah reproved himself silently. *Maher will certainly come back, and there's good reason to hope he'll find Jashub and bring him home—and Reba and the children, too.* Life would go on. Ethan was a sign from Yahweh of that very fact.

Yet as he walked through the autumn morning outside

Jerusalem's walls, Isaiah entered a world of death, desolate and stillness. It was even worse than he remembered on his recent trip home from Lachish. Then he rode swiftly with a party of envoys. Now he walked alone. There were no signs of human life or habitation. Familiar cottages that he had passed thousands of times lay in charred heaps.

Far more horrible were the bodies of dead animals and humans that he found lying along the roadside. Vultures clustered around some of them quickly devouring any fleshly remains. Other corpses lay as skeletons, the bones bleaching in the Judean sun. Isaiah dared not stop to examine any of them. Most were far beyond identification by now.

In the little homes along the roadside, whole families apparently died together under the Assyrians' attack. Jashub and Reba and their children were perhaps most fortunate to have been taken as prisoners of war instead. For them there was hope that life would go on. For these others, nearer Jerusalem but outside the protection of the walls, there was nothing.

How many of the capital city's refugees now faced returning to a home that no longer existed? Isaiah wondered. In some of the places he passed he caught sight of burned fragments of furniture, broken household utensils and dishes. Such terrible, senseless waste! *Men and women work hard to produce the little necessities of life, the nice things that lift humanity above the animals, and then other men come who delight only in destruction!*

Obviously, this year we will have to live off the land, Isaiah thought as he reached the border of his estate. At least most of his trees had been spared. There would be figs again next summer and olives in season. *If Naamah and I can get a cow, and a goat or two, and possibly a few sheep, we can begin again,* he thought. *We can lease the city house and start rebuilding out here.*

Because Isaiah's house lay in a little valley, it was not

until he reached the hilltop overlooking it that he could see the extent of the damage to his family homestead. There it stood, what was left of it, roofless, the walls battered down almost to their foundations. Broken pieces of furniture lay strewn about the grounds. Several stone benches too heavy to carry off were smashed to pieces, the broken fragments scattered about. Pottery dishes, many of them made by Jashub, and anything of value had all disappeared.

As Isaiah stood viewing the rubble, he suddenly heard a faint sound of crying amid the ruins of his house. It was a weak, frightened little whimper, like that of some small animal of the wild, and yet it was entirely too human. Isaiah quickly scrambled over the rubble in the direction of the sounds. There on the ground, in the corner of a ruined room, sat a little girl, surely not much more than two years old. Straight, stringy black hair hung over her face. Barefooted, she was dressed in a dirty, ragged linen tunic and nothing else. At a glance, Isaiah could see a deep gash, crusted with blood, on one of her spindly legs, but otherwise she appeared unhurt.

Stunned by the sight of Isaiah, but too afraid to cry and too weak to run, the little girl cowered against the wall.

"Little girl," Isaiah said gently, "what are you doing out here?"

Frightened, she hung her head as Isaiah approached. He knelt beside her and lifted her small chin. The little girl's eyes were lovely, a deep, radiant brown. "Are you all alone?" Isaiah asked her, smiling.

The child did not respond but smiled shyly. Isaiah scooped her up in his arms. She nuzzled against his shoulder, and he smoothed back the unkempt hair from her eyes. Then, like an enemy arrow, the thought pierced his consciousness: *She is a little Assyrian—one of theirs—the child of some camp-follower, abandoned, perhaps orphaned in the recent plague and hasty retreat. There is no way to know for sure.* As he held the little girl against his chest, he felt the beating of her heart. *They are so like us, really. She might have been one of my own little granddaughters. Where are Jashub's children now that they've been driven from the ruins of Lachish? Gone forever to be prisoners in a distant land?*

After a moment of speculation, Isaiah's thoughts returned to the present. "Child, you must be hungry," he said. Carefully, he set the little girl down on a heap of stones in what had once been the main room of his country house. Naamah had packed a lunch for him, and though he had felt no inclination to eat on his lonely walk through the countryside, he was now extremely glad for the neatly-wrapped packet she had insisted on his bringing. Isaiah unfolded the linen wrapping and spread it on the ground at the child's side. Kneeling beside her, he unwrapped several dried figs.

"Here, child." He held one of the figs out to her. She grabbed it and gobbled it up, then another and another. There was also a bit of bread and some cheese. These the hungry child snatched from the napkin and consumed eagerly. It was likely the first meal she had had in several days.

"Do you have a mother?" Isaiah asked. The small refugee, still eating, looked at him uncomprehendingly. He tried again, this time in halting Aramaic, but her response was just as blank.

The wind was getting colder. The food was all gone, and Isaiah lifted the little girl in his arms, rearranging his cloak to shelter her in its warmth. As she snuggled against him, Isaiah could feel the chill in the child's thin limbs. It would be a long walk back to the city, and though the girl was not really heavy, neither was Isaiah young anymore. At several points along the way, the burden seemed almost too much to bear. But thoughts of home, a warm fire and food, and Naamah urged him on. And there was a calm awareness that Yahweh was giving him new strength.

Look upon Zion, he thought as he glimpsed the temple mount in the distance.

> Your eyes will see Jerusalem,
> a quiet habitation, an immovable tent,
> whose stakes will never be plucked up,
> nor will any of its cords be broken.

Suddenly he recalled one of his old tunes and thought of some new words.

> There Lord Yahweh in majesty will be for us,
> A place of broad rivers and streams.
> For Yahweh is our judge; Yahweh is our ruler;
> Yahweh is our king. He will save us.

The gray shadows of autumn twilight hung heavily over Jerusalem before Isaiah reached home that afternoon. During the long walk through the desolate countryside the certainty of Yahweh's nearness continued to grow within him, certainty that the new era was beginning. In spite of everything, there was much to live and hope for.

And then at last, Isaiah was back at the city house, standing before Naamah with the bundle he had brought home with him. "Lord Yahweh has given us another one." From the folds of his cloak, he unwrapped the sleeping child and place her in Naamah's waiting arms.

"This one," he said, "is a girl."

Naamah was undaunted by any of the difficulties that accompanied the new situation. She immediately stripped off the little girl's ragged dress and began preparing a bath. Dragging a large basin to a spot near the fireplace, she poured into it cold water from a jar and hot water from a pot over the fire.

"Why is she so dirty?" asked Ethan.

Without answering, Naamah seated the little refugee in the basin and began to wash her from head to toe.

"Is she going to live with us? Where did you get her, Papa? Why is her leg all hurt like that?" Ethan's questions continued to flow.

The little girl, whimpering a bit under Naamah's vigorous scrubbing, still showed no inclination to say anything at all.

"There, child, it's all right," Naamah soothed. "We'll have you all clean and pretty. Can you tell me your name?" The girl merely hung her head.

As Isaiah gathered Ethan into his lap and related simply the story of the day's strange events, Naamah lifted the little girl from the tub and dried her. Wrapping her in one of her own long scarves, she said, "I'll find some fabric to make her a dress tomorrow. Right now, it's getting time for supper."

The girl, clean and seemingly delighted with her new garb, climbed upon one of the stone ledges in the corner and sat down proudly, taking in the whole scene in silent wonder.

"What's her name, Papa?" Without waiting for an answer, Ethan slipped out of Isaiah's lap, approached his new-found friend, and began bombarding the quiet little stranger with a flow of questions.

Naamah paused from stirring the large cauldron of stew over the fireplace and looked at her husband. "Isaiah . . . " Her voice was apprehensive. "I don't think that child understands a word we've said. I think she's one of *theirs*—an Assyrian."

"Yes, I believe she is," he replied. "I feel quite sure of it."

"But, Isaiah. . . ."

Whatever Naamah was about to say was lost, however, as Ethan's voice rang out triumphantly from the corner of the room. "Her name is Zina!" he exclaimed. "She told me!"

"Zina?" Naamah said uncertainly.

Isaiah quickly got up and went over to the bench

where the children were sitting. "She told you?" he asked, kneeling down beside them.

Ethan, glowing with satisfaction, repeated his performance. "Say 'Zina'!" he commanded.

"Zina." Her voice was clear and confident.

"That's her name," Ethan added as if to wipe away any doubts.

"Zina," repeated Naamah. "Could be Assyrian, but it could be one of ours, too, I suppose."

"Whatever she is," Isaiah replied, "she is one of us now."

One morning at his regular council meeting, King Hezekiah announced his intention to visit Sennacherib's abandoned camp.

The news that morning had not been encouraging. A letter had arrived from Sennacherib stating that since he had received the peace gifts, and since winter was coming on, he had decided on temporary withdrawal from Judah. However, Hezekiah and his kingdom could expect the Assyrians to return again in the spring unless, of course, Hezekiah would care to avoid future hostilities by keeping up the annual tribute payments.

"We have no real choice but to pay," Isaiah said without being asked. The scenes of his recent trip to the ruins of his country home were vivid before his eyes. "It will be harder now than before, since so many of our people have fallen. But Lord Yahweh *did* spare Jerusalem, and that in itself is a great miracle. We must be grateful for it, not throw it away."

"I don't understand what you mean by that," Shebna interrupted. "Give us a few months to recoup our losses and to get back in touch with Pharaoh. We can be ready if Sennacherib comes back next spring, which is actually quite unlikely. You notice he mentioned nothing in his letter about the plague or about rumors of trouble elsewhere."

"Certainly not!" Isaiah exclaimed angrily. "What king of Assyria has ever admitted to any kind of setback? Especially to a subjected enemy? Shebna, sometimes you do not use even the little wisdom that Lord Yahweh gave you!"

"I only meant he's suffered terrible losses, yet he still thinks he can frighten us!" Shebna countered.

Hezekiah and the chief minister, Eliakim, listened to this heated exchange without comment. Eliakim was inclined to agree with Isaiah, but years of experience as a statesman had taught him to shape his opinions to match those of the king.

Hezekiah's impassive expression betrayed no hint of where he stood on the matter. "It is time we went out to inspect Sennacherib's camp," he pronounced, rising. "Surely the danger of plague has passed by now." He looked directly at the skeptical prophet. "Isaiah, you are welcome to come along if you wish."

"No, my king. Not unless you really need me. I have seen enough of ruin in the past few days to last a lifetime."

"Very well." Hezekiah dismissed him graciously, though puzzled by Isaiah's response. But then, safe inside the walls of Jerusalem ever since the Assyrian invasion began, Hezekiah had yet to see any real devastation.

The desolation scenes that greeted Hezekiah and his men as they rode along through the countryside to Sennacherib's abandoned campsite equalled those Isaiah had observed a few days earlier on a different road. Slowly, almost imperceptibly, Hezekiah began to understand exactly what the prophet had meant. Yet to Hezekiah, the reality was even more grim, for in the dark recesses of his mind pulsed the awareness that none of this would have come about had he remained Sennacherib's faithful vassal as Isaiah had constantly advised. What was it the prophet had threatened long ago when Hezekiah had come so close to rebellion against Sennacherib's father, Sargon?

> If you are willing and obedient,
>> you shall eat the good of the land.
> But if you refuse and rebel,
>> you shall be devoured by the sword,
>> for the mouth of Yahweh has spoken!

It was a warning that was still valid, and Hezekiah was determined that, in spite of Shebna's continuing militaristic stance, he would himself from now on walk in the ways of peace.

The Assyrian camp was a shambles, and the king's men rode warily through heaps of decomposing bodies. Even the anticipated vultures were missing, except for some dead ones that lay among their intended prey, huge heaps of black feathers, devourers stricken down by the more potent angel of death. Rats scurried everywhere. The few pieces of leather equipment, quivers, shield straps, and bowstrings that lay about, were gnawed to uselessness.

"Put it all to the torch!" Hezekiah shouted to some of his bodyguards who followed at a discreet distance. One man had brought along a fire pot, and in a few moments some of the others had gathered enough brush to kindle a strong blaze.

"Now, let's get out of here!" the king ordered. "I wonder how many men they lost here?" Eliakim asked.

"Thousands!" Shebna exulted. The sight of the enemy's disaster thoroughly delighted him. "I'd estimate a hundred thousand—no, closer to two hundred thousand. For the record let's say a hundred and eighty-five thousand—a good, uneven number."

Hezekiah and Eliakim both felt the figure was exaggerated, but the severity of the loss was real enough. Perhaps Shebna was right. Perhaps it would be safe to withhold further tribute. Sennacherib would never dare to set foot in Judah again!

Why was Isaiah so stubbornly cautious? After all, the prophet had said that Lord Yahweh would protect Jerusalem, that the Remnant of Judah would again flourish. How much easier it would be to rebuild the broken kingdom without the terrible tax burden for the tribute payments. And how much more secure would be Hezekiah's own position if, in the eyes of his people, he could remain forever the hero who had saved them from Sennacherib—with considerable help from Lord Yahweh of course!

Torn with indecision, Hezekiah returned to his palace. He would have to speak more about it with Shebna in the morning. But not just at present. He felt uncommonly tired, feverish, almost trembly. *What I need now is simply a good rest,* he told himself, dismissing his followers and going straight to his own suite. *A long, long rest.*

The next morning Isaiah awoke as the light of dawn cast a pale glow through the shutters of the city house. He had always loved the stillness of these very early hours when Lord Yahweh's beneficent presence seemed to hover so close.

As Naamah and the children slept, Isaiah looked at them all with a feeling of love and hope. Very soon he would begin the rebuilding he had promised. The new beginning, the new era was dawning, and the latter part of his own life would be better than the years gone by. Surely he could persuade Hezekiah to submit to the Assyrian tribute and then at last he, Isaiah, would be able to do what he was really born to do—gather a new group of students and prepare a collection of his writings.

SEVENTEEN

Henceforth, I Shall Walk Softly

A crowd had assembled in the courtyard of the temple. Hezekiah heard the choir singing his Song of Recovery, a song that seemed to apply to his own illness and to the deliverance of Jerusalem as well. He had written down the words the day before, and Isaiah had supplied a tune.

> "Surely it was for my benefit
> that I had great bitterness.
> In your love, O Lord, you kept me
> from the pit of destruction.
> You have cast all my sins
> behind your back.
> Sheol cannot thank you,
> death cannot praise you.
> The living, the living—they praise you,
> as I am doing today."

As the concluding stanza of the song ended, the eager multitudes before the temple waited for the priestly ritual of thank offerings to Lord Yahweh, which would mean feasting and celebrating afterward. The people, who had endured for so long the hardships of the

Assyrian invasion, were eager to enjoy the king's bounty. But first, the king must make his speech.

The heralds sounded their trumpets as slowly, almost reluctantly, Hezekiah mounted the steps of the bronze platform between the two great bronze columns of the temple. The crowd chanted approval. *Strange*, Hezekiah thought, *that any of them should love me after what I have done to them.*

But the sound of their cheering suggested that the dynastic loyalty of the Judeans was at an all-time high. Hezekiah leaned heavily on his gilded wooden staff. It was not a mere power symbol, a scepter of authority, but a very real support for his still weak body. The lingering effects of his illness still hung heavily upon him along with the realization that the wonderful deliverance from Sennacherib was not all it seemed to be. Judah was not really free. Unless he wished to subject his land to another invasion and inevitable defeat, tribute would have to be paid just as before. By now he was certain that he would have to pay the tribute for the rest of his life. Yet explaining the reality of it to his subjects seemed an ordeal comparable to the agonies of the plague.

"My people," Hezekiah began slowly, "hear me! As we have seen in recent days, Lord Yahweh has saved Jerusalem, his chosen city, from the hand of the enemy. He has struck down the Assyrians and made Sennacherib turn back to the land from which he came. Moreover, when I myself lay at the brink of death, he delivered me from the gates of Sheol that I might live and reign over this land of Judah for a longer time. Through all of these trials, Lord Yahweh has taught me that from this day forward I must seek the ways of peace and not of war, of submission and not rebellion." The king paused for a moment, watching his audience, wondering if they really understood what he was telling them. Then in an awesome voice, he added a final sentence. "Henceforth," he said, "I shall walk softly all my days."

It was his acknowledgment of defeat along with his gratitude to be alive. It was a tacit admission that his militant schemes were a thing of the past. The autumn wind whipped at the king's cloak and tossed his long black hair. Slowly he stepped down from the royal platform.

There were murmurs among the crowd, yet Hezekiah only half-heard them. He had come through his ordeal, and soon the feasting and celebrating would begin. Forgetfulness would come.

"Isaiah!" someone shouted. It was Shebna the warmonger, angered by the apparent collapse of all his plans, enraged that his adversary's ideals seemed to have won out after all. "Let's hear from our prophet!" Shebna's voice grew even harsher and he launched into an angry tirade. "Tell us about this peace that we're to have, Isaiah! The peace of servitude and tribute and degradation! I ask you, is this any cause to celebrate? Is this really peace at all?"

The murmuring among the people grew louder. Hezekiah, confused and frightened, looked at his father-in-law searchingly. "They want you to speak," he said. "Go up on the platform."

The dreadful, depressing cold wind blew harder now than before. Isaiah looked quickly into his son-in-law's eyes and saw mirrored there the younger man's deep anguish.

A few seconds later, the prophet stood alone on the bronze platform. Even as he had climbed the steps, the crowd continued shouting. Shebna obviously had many friends. "Do we really have peace?" someone called. "Did our sons die that we might go on paying tribute?"

Isaiah wanted to weep—for Jashub and Maher, his own missing sons, for all of Judah's slain, for those who remained in the land and knew too well the elusiveness of peace, but most of all, for Hezekiah the king, who at last, but perhaps too late, understood. However, this was no time for weeping. "We have only a foretaste of true peace," Isaiah said, "but it is Yahweh's sign for us in this present age of the better time to come." As he spoke, he felt Yahweh's wonderful power surging through him, almost comparable to the rapturous exultation he had felt when he heard Lord Yahweh calling him in the temple so many years ago. In a strong, clear voice that reached to every corner of the courtyard, he proclaimed:

"In the last days
the mountain of the Lord's temple
    will be established
as chief among the mountains.
It will be raised above the hills,
    and all nations will stream to it.
Many peoples will come and say,
'Come, let us go up to the
mountain of Yahweh,
    to the house of the God of Jacob.
He will teach us his ways,
    so that we may walk in his paths.'
The law will go out from Zion,
    the word of Yahweh from Jerusalem.
He will judge between the nations
    and will settle disputes for many peoples.
They will beat their swords
    into plowshares,
    and their spears into pruning hooks.
Nation will not take up sword against nation,
    nor will they train for war any more."

For a moment the crowd was marvelously still. Then a voice shattered the silence, a stranger's voice, perhaps one of Shebna's friends.

"When, Isaiah, when?"

Isaiah's transport of ecstasy had passed, but the hope was still strong in him. "I do not know *when*," he said, "but this much I do know. Lord Yahweh has put in our hearts the dream of universal peace, and he plants no dream within us unless that dream can someday become a reality."

Among the crowd, Isaiah noticed his old friend, the prophet Micah of Moresheth, with a little wax tablet and stylus in hand, taking notes. He was grateful someone was writing down what he had spoken.

"To study war no more. . . ." Was that what he had said? All his previous efforts to describe the coming of the kingdom of peace paled beside this one. Now, if ever, Lord Yahweh had spoken through his prophet. By nightfall, someone would make a tune for those closing lines, and the people, happy with the immediate gifts of the king's bounty, would be singing them in the streets of Jerusalem for a long time to come. *A seed has been planted*, Isaiah thought, and he was happy.

But, meanwhile, in the royal ladies' chamber, where Naamah and Hephzibah and the wives of some of the nobles sat listening to the ceremonies, a sudden sob broke the stillness. It was Naamah, weeping for only a moment before she reverted to her usual serene self. The court ladies unquestionably thought she grieved for her missing sons, but Hephzibah bent close to her mother, and she alone heard Naamah's whisper. "True peace may come in the latter days, but our Isaiah will not be here to see it."

Hephzibah did not ask the meaning of her mother's words.

Through the long winter that followed, Isaiah and his family remained at the city house. It was too cold and too rainy to think of rebuilding. Besides, labor was in very short supply, and there was far more important work to be done in restoring Judah. Isaiah spent many hours daily at the palace with Hezekiah, going over recent census figures compiled since the invasion, and listening to disputes between litigants with rival claims to the same plots of land. Among other devastation, Sennacherib's men had dislocated numerous property line markers, while written documentation in many cases had disappeared as well. Isaiah's inclination, whenever proof was lacking, was to award disputed properties to those who seemed most in need. He worked quickly, carefully, and with as much justice as humanly possible.

Hezekiah, when left on his own, pondered too long before making any decisions whatsoever. He had made far too many bad choices in the past.

However, with no prompting from Isaiah, Hezekiah had demanded Shebna's resignation. To everyone's surprise, the king's old friend withdrew from court life graciously. Shebna had a new young wife, and somehow, through all the difficulties of the invasion, he had managed to hang on to most of his vast properties within Jerusalem. His life would continue quite pleasantly, he hoped, though he still shivered whenever he recalled Isaiah's dire prediction about him.

Weeks turned to months. Hezekiah searched the palace chambers for potential tribute gifts. It was plainly understood that even some offerings brought to the temple would have to be diverted to the annual tribute fund. Life became barer and simpler for everyone, not just for the poor of the land but for the royal household as well.

And because Hezekiah helped to bear the burden along with his subjects, the people still loved him. He was Yahweh's chosen one, rescued by God himself from the gates of Sheol. If he was not really the Prince of the Promise, and obviously he wasn't, he was still their valiant, well-intentioned Hezekiah, the good king.

No one spoke openly about what would happen should the king die. Isaiah was his closest heir, but Isaiah was some twenty years Hezekiah's senior, and Isaiah's own sons were missing. Of course, there were other relatives. Isaiah had brothers and nephews aplenty. Among them someone, sooner or later, would have to be designated as next in line after Isaiah.

Unless Hezekiah himself might beget a son. "Remember Abraham and Sarah," the king would say whenever the subject was mentioned. "I and Lady Hephzibah are not nearly as old as *they* were when Isaac was born. Nothing is impossible for Lord Yahweh!"

EIGHTEEN
Another Miracle

In the spring of the year, about six months after Hezekiah's remarkable recovery, Hephzibah began to notice changes in her body—changes she knew signaled the end to her hopes of bearing an heir. Then she began to experience unusual symptoms—discomforting nausea when she awakened in the morning and waves of queasiness that assailed her throughout the day. As weeks passed, her abdomen almost imperceptibly began to swell.

"I can't understand why I feel so bad," she said to her mother one afternoon. "I know I am not as young as I was, but I never expected the change would be so hard."

It was a beautiful, clear spring afternoon, warm but not uncomfortably so, after a morning of light rain. The palace garden was full of flowers that grew so profusely at this time of year, and the whole world seemed washed in the light of hope and healing. The children, Ethan and Zina, were running around the benches, hiding under the stone tables, squealing with childish happiness while the two women, mother and daughter, talked.

Nervously, Hephzibah continued to describe her

symptoms as Naamah listened intently. Hephzibah, clad in a simple dress of light green linen, seemed still a young girl in her mother's eyes. In spite of her expressed fears of aging, in spite of the discomfort she described, she was still lovely to look at, but as fragile and delicate as the early spring flowers.

"Child," said Naamah at last, "have you considered that you might be pregnant?"

Hephzibah gasped. "Mama, I'm too old! It couldn't be. Oh, Mama, do you think it could be after so many, many years?"

"From what you've told me, I think it's entirely possible," Naamah answered.

A look of radiance crossed Hephzibah's face, and her green eyes sparkled. "We mustn't tell Hezekiah," she said, "until we're absolutely sure. I don't want him to be disappointed. Oh, Mama, I thought I was dying, and maybe, maybe this means I have just begun to live!" She wept, but her tears were joyful tears as Naamah held her close.

Within another week or two, Hephzibah felt confident enough of her mother's diagnosis to tell Hezekiah. The king, excited and delighted beyond measure, told everyone who would listen. Throughout Jerusalem the news of Lady Hephzibah's pregnancy was deemed the greatest miracle since the receding shadow on the sunclock.

And in spite of her continued bouts with morning sickness, Hephzibah seemed radiant, a joyous creature, glowing with the confidence of the life growing within her. "To look at her, one would think she was a young bride," her ladies remarked out of her hearing.

Although Hephzibah was still a woman of stunning beauty, it was true that she was no longer really young. She had been Hezekiah's wife for almost twenty years. As the weeks slipped by, Hephzibah's willowy, slender contours swelled to an alarming bigness even though the time of her delivery was still months away. She often felt excessively weary, and at times it seemed difficult to move at all.

Naamah was with her daughter often during those first months, but since she had borne three children with no difficulties at all, it was hard for her to understand Hephzibah's increasing apprehension. "You must not worry so much, child," she said soothingly. "Mother Sarah, the forebearer of us all, gave birth to Issac when she was ninety years old. Then there was Rachel, the mother of Joseph, and Hannah, who had Samuel, and Samson's mother, whatever her name was. Why, it seems to me that in many cases where a woman has had a child after years of barrenness he has been special in the sight of the Lord, one who grew up to do great things for Lord Yahweh."

"I hope you're right," Hephzibah answered. It was cheering to think about these famous mothers of history, to imagine what they must have thought and wondered through their long months of waiting.

Time dragged by interminably: Hephzibah kept herself occupied with needlework, making blankets and clothes for the baby while she and her mother talked for hours.

"The spring rains have ended," Naamah said one afternoon. Then after a brief silence she went on. "I know your father has been helping the king all these long months with all sorts of plans for meeting the tribute more justly and rebuilding the kingdom. I think it's time Hezekiah let us go to rebuild our own house."

Hephzibah looked surprised. "I thought you and Papa would stay in the city now. The country house is completely demolished. There is nothing to go back to. You have a good place here, close by. Oh, I know you've never liked that house. But if you really don't want to live there anymore, Hezekiah would be glad to provide you with a suite here at the palace. There's plenty of room."

"No," said Naamah. "Your father and I want to rebuild our home. He hasn't said anything about it recently, but I know it's what he wants most of all."

"But it's hard to find laborers," Hephzibah protested. "So many of our young men were killed, and those who remain are needed for other work."

"Isaiah is still strong," Naamah answered, "and so am I. I can help. Even the children can help carry stones. And if we need other helpers, they will come. We can live in a tent until the house is built. I've thought it out. I know we can do it."

Hephzibah, momentarily stunned, began to catch her mother's enthusiasm. "I believe you can!" she exlaimed. "You and Papa—you two together with Lord Yahweh's help—there is nothing that can stop you! I'll speak to Hezekiah about it." In her mind she could envision the home of her childhood rebuilt, a visible symbol of the renewal that was going on throughout Judah. "Oh, if only I were stronger," she added. "I'd go out there with you and help myself!"

Isaiah and Naamah often looked back to the summer of the rebuilding as perhaps the happiest time of their lives. From the outset, King Hezekiah did all he could to support the project. He located a few strong young men to help with the heavy labor and provided tents where Isaiah's family and their assistants might live while construction was underway.

Once they had made camp on Isaiah's estate, a daily routine was quickly established. Everyone was up and stirring before daybreak. Naamah prepared a light breakfast, and by the time dawn crept over the horizon the men were ready to begin work before the day grew too warm.

To Naamah's surprise, Isaiah thrived on physical labor. Clad only in a short linen kilt, sweaty and often grimy from the business of lifting and piling heavy stones, he seemed nonetheless to grow younger as the sun bronzed his skin.

True to her word, Naamah also worked on the building. Her hands grew rough from handling the coarse stones, yet being able to help rebuild the home she loved brought her happiness.

Ethan and Zina looked on the whole enterprise as a wonderful game. They learned to gather the small rocks that were much needed as filler between the larger stones, and they watched Isaiah with fascination as he fitted their rocks into the growing walls.

As the heat of the day grew more intense, work would cease, and after a hearty lunch, everyone retired for a long afternoon nap. As evening neared and it was again cool enough to work, the building process was resumed, only to stop when the sky grew dark. Then Isaiah and his family and the workers gathered around the campfire for their evening meal. Sometimes after supper, Isaiah would play his lyre and the whole company would join together in song.

In that time of miraculous newness, though he sometimes worried about his absent sons, Isaiah felt that somehow Maher and Jashub and Jashub's family were all safe. He was confident that soon he would receive news about them. It was only natural that Maher's search should be taking many months. Assyria was far away, and he might have to follow any number of false leads before actually locating his missing kinfolk. Yet news was bound to come eventually. Naamah shared her husband's optimism. "Any day now, they will come home," she often commented. "Or at least we'll get a message."

But the summer days passed, and there was still no word of their absent loved ones.

Isaiah and Naamah were taken completely by surprise when early one morning other visitors did arrive: Hezekiah and Hephzibah, traveling far more simply than would have been expected of the king and his lady.

Hezekiah rode on horseback, while Hephzibah sat in a litter chair carried by four sturdy bearers. Behind them came several other servants leading a train of donkeys laden with food, provisions, and tents for Hezekiah and Hephzibah and their party.

Isaiah ran to greet them. "I have come to help you rebuild your house," announced Hezekiah, dismounting from his horse and handing the reins to an attendant.

Isaiah embraced his son-in-law, whom he had not seen for several weeks, with the same joy that he might have greeted one of his own sons. Hezekiah still seemed frail and far too thin. His hairline had receded noticeably since his illness, and his beard was streaked with gray. Dressed far more simply than his usual style, he wore an unadorned robe of brown linen.

"I mean it. I am ready to work," he said with a smile. "But you will have to tell me what to do."

Hephzibah's bearers assisted her out of her litter, and Isaiah turned to embrace her. She looked very pale and there was a hint of malaise in her deep-set green eyes. She was delighted to see that the new house resembled the old one. Both the exterior and the floor plan were the same. It was wonderful to be home, to see the home of her childhood rising again from the rubble. Surely it was a sign of the promised renewal.

Work continued as usual during the few days Hezekiah and Hephzibah made camp on Isaiah's estate. In fact, it progressed much faster thanks to the extra laborers who had come with the royal party. Then construction began on the roof. Great cypress beams, supplied through the king's generosity, were now hauled up and laid in place.

Hezekiah, true to his promise, assisted with the actual work of rebuilding but had to stop often for brief rests because he had little stamina.

Hephzibah, meanwhile, spent many hours sitting in the shade, sewing, singing, entertaining Zina and Ethan, telling them stories, and making up little games. As she assisted her mother with the children and the preparation of meals, she found real contentment in the role of a country wife. How different from her life of pampered security inside the palace, and how wonderfully invigorating! To have Hezekiah beside her, and yet also to be able to enjoy the daily company of the parents whom she loved so dearly was for Hephzibah truly the best of both worlds.

The heat of the day subsided rapidly when evening came and the nights were cool and pleasant. In their tent, the night before their scheduled departure, Hezekiah and Hephzibah curled up under blankets.

"I believe I have never been so happy in my whole life as in these past few days," Hephzibah whispered. "Oh, Hezekiah, I wish we didn't have to go back! Not so soon!"

Hezekiah did not tell her that he was greatly looking forward to returning to routine life at the palace. While he, too, had found their country visit an idyllic interlude after all the stress of recent months, he was very tired and longed to exchange his pallet on the ground for the softness of his royal bed. "After the baby is born, we can come back here for a few days," he promised, "and stay *inside* the house. It will be all finished by then."

For a few moments Hephzibah lay very still, her head nestled upon her husband's shoulder. "I only wish we'd hear something about my brothers," she said at last. "I try not to worry, but it's been a long time now."

"Yes." Hezekiah understood her anxiety better than he wanted to admit. "Before we left Jerusalem, I sent out couriers to try to trace them. As soon as they find out anything, we'll know."

For Hephzibah, this assurance was encouraging. Like her parents, she still believed that sooner or later the lost ones would be home again. In her mind she could visualize the joyful reunion, the excitement and the happiness of her brothers' return mingled with her joy in the child she was soon to bear. And thinking of the future in rosiest terms, she fell asleep peacefully in Hezekiah's arms.

Not long after their return to the palace, summer became autumn. Then came the early rains, and as the skies remained gray for days at a time, Hephzibah grew more apprehensive and worried. The two couriers Hezekiah had sent out to search for Jashub and Maher had still not returned, and with every passing day the likelihood of good news decreased.

Still Hephzibah found joy in Hezekiah's elation over the imminent birth of his heir. She saw little of him through the day hours, but when evening came, he scorned the royal banquet hall and its host of hangers-on to dine privately with her in her suite and then to stay with her through the night. They found themselves bound to each other by deeper ties of devotion than ever before.

"When we were young," Hephzibah said once, "I used to worry that someday I would run out of things to talk to you about."

Hezekiah smiled. He *never* ran out of things to talk about. Most often, he entertained her with the daily happenings in the court, the hundreds of little incidents that demanded the king's attention. Sometimes he read to her from a scroll of newly collected proverbs and folk sayings he had asked his scribes to find and copy, and they would laugh with delight over some of them. Sometimes they talked about the years long vanished, the years of their childhood and early youth.

"When I think about those times," Hephzibah remarked one evening, "it seems like it was always summer. I know there were gray days, like there are now, but I scarcely remember them."

Hezekiah did not respond, for he remembered only too well many of the gray days of his youth. Yet for

Hephzibah's sake, he concentrated on happy memories. The fear and anger and hurt in his relationships with his father were suppressed, unspoken.

"Do you remember," Hephzibah went on dreamily, "those songs Papa made about the coming of the Peaceable Kingdom?"

Yes, Hezekiah remembered, though it had been years since he heard them. In his mind, he could see himself and Hephzibah as children, along with Jashub and Maher, listening enthralled as Isaiah sang the beautiful, haunting melodies foretelling the time of universal peace.

"I have copies of them all," Hephzibah said. "I found them recently, cleaning up, going through things." Awkwardly, she rose from her couch and opened a chest to extract several small scrolls. "There may be some here you've never seen. Papa wrote this one when you were born. Your mother had it, and she left it to me long ago."

Gently, Hephzibah unrolled the little sheet of papyrus, carefully copied in Abijah's most elegant handwriting. "I don't know if it's a song, or just a poem, but it's so beautiful," she said. "Listen."

"The people who walked in darkness
    have seen a great light.
Those who dwelt in a land of deep darkness,
    on them has a light shined.
For to us a child is born,
    to us a son is given,
and the government will be on his shoulders.
    And his name will be called
Wonderful Counselor, Mighty God,
    Everlasting Father, Prince of Peace.
Of the increase of his government and peace
    there will be no end.
He will reign on David's throne
    and over his kingdom
to establish and uphold it

with justice and with righteousness
from this time forth and forever.

The zeal of Lord of hosts will do this."

Tears coursed down Hezekiah's cheeks as Hephzibah read. Yes, he had heard the poem many years before, not from Isaiah, but from his own mother, who had read it to him several times, confident that he would grow up to fulfill the prophet's expectations. "I have failed so badly," he said. "I have failed everyone—but Isaiah most of all. And yet, he never turned against me."

Hephzibah was startled. It was a reaction she had not expected. "Hezekiah! Oh, my dearest, don't grieve so! I don't think Papa would ever say you failed. When a child is born, who knows what his life will bring? Who knew then that you would have to fight the Assyrians?"

Have to fight them? Hezekiah thought. *I didn't have to fight. In unheeding folly, I rebelled.* "I have been far from a prince of peace," he said aloud, "but Lord Yahweh knows I am trying now."

"Perhaps," said Hephzibah, "you are the forerunner, and our son will be the one who will bring the final consummation."

Our son. Hephzibah's thoughts soared. *The child of Hezekiah and Hephzibah.* This child would not only be the descendant of the long line of the kings of Judah but would also carry in him the heritage of his grandfather, Isaiah the prophet.

"Perhaps he will fulfill the promise," reflected Hezekiah. For his wife's sake, it was a hope to cherish, to dream about, to cling to in the midst of uncertainty, if only because it brought such a glow of happiness to Hephzibah's eyes.

"You look doubtful," Hephzibah commented. "I know that if the Peaceable Kingdom ever really comes, it will be the greatest miracle that Judah has ever seen.

But I believe in miracles, don't you?"

"Yes," replied Hezekiah. "Of course, I do." Yet because he had seen so many of them, he dared not hope too deeply for any more.

NINETEEN
Manasseh

A week later, on one of the coldest and grayest days of winter, Lady Hephzibah went into labor.

Outside the closed doors of Hephzibah's chamber, King Hezekiah and his father-in-law waited. Isaiah sat, calm and still, on a bench in the hall, while the king paced restlessly as expectant fathers have done since time began. They both prayed, silently, for the well-being of the woman behind the closed doors—gentle, lovely Hephzibah, who was older than most first-time mothers and far from strong. Neither man spoke, for their fears were very real. They both believed so strongly in Lord Yahweh's unquestioned power that to have uttered platitudes would have been meaningless.

Time dragged on. Hezekiah could see in his mind's eye the shadow declining on the steps of the sun-clock in the courtyard. Twilight came, and palace servants lighted the lamps in the hall. Outside, the winter wind howled mournfully. Isaiah pulled his cloak tighter around him. *Naamah's babies, my children, came so easily,* he thought.

"Is it always like this?" Hezekiah said.

"No." Isaiah sighed deeply. "No, it's not."

From beyond the doors came a sudden shriek, Hephzibah's voice lifted in unbearable agony. "I must go to her," Hezekiah said, starting for the door.

Isaiah leaped up from his bench and grasped his son-in-law's arm. "It isn't done," he said. *How foolish is custom,* he thought, *but men are not permitted in the birthing chamber. Not even a king—particulary a king—should dare defy the old, unwritten laws.* "Naamah is with her," he added.

Hephzibah's wailing continued in little spasms. "Hezekiah!" She cried out the name of the man she loved and needed.

Defiantly Hezekiah flung open the doors, and as the astonished women gasped, he rushed to his wife's side. Her face was contorted with pain. Naamah was holding her hand. Out of the bevy of women who surrounded Hephzibah, Naamah alone seemed calm.

Hezekiah pulled a little bench beside his wife and sat on it, grasping her free hand while Naamah continued to hold the other. Hephzibah's eyes reflected gratitude for his presence, but her agony was too great for words.

As two midwives hovered over her Hephzibah gave a final scream. Then came a baby's lusty cry. The skilled women knew exactly what to do and sprang into a flurry of activity. Mara, the elder of them looked up, smiling at Hezekiah. "It's a boy, my King. A fine, healthy boy."

Hepzibah heard, too. "Hezekiah, I have given you a son," she whispered weakly, squeezing her husband's hand.

Mara and her helper washed the infant. After wrapping him in swaddling bands, Mara placed the squirming bundle in Naamah's arms. The proud grandmother smiled, relieved and happy. For a moment or two she was entirely entranced by this small bit of humanity, this extension of herself that she held close against her breast. "Isaiah!" she gasped suddenly, remembering that he waited outside. She ran to where he stood in the open doorway, but Isaiah scarcely glanced at the infant Naamah held. The strange sense of imminent disaster that sometimes assailed Isaiah swept through him now. Suddenly he realized that the life of Hephzibah, his little girl, was in great danger.

His eyes surveyed the shadowy room. The midwives had assisted Hephzibah to her bed, and Hezekiah sat beside her, gently smoothing back her long hair, whispering words of love and joy and pride. It was a scene perhaps not to be interrupted, but Isaiah strode to his daughter's bedside anyway because of the deep fears within him.

Weakly, Hephzibah reached out to him, and he grasped her hand. "Papa!" she whispered. "Oh, Papa, I love you! Don't leave me!" Big tears streamed down her face. "The pain . . . ," she muttered. "Help me!"

"We're all here," Isaiah said. "Hezey and your mother and I. We won't leave you."

"Really now, Isaiah," Naamah spoke with authority. "You must leave. She is very weak. She needs to sleep. The birthing room is no place for menfolk. You, too, Hezey. You shouldn't stay."

Reluctantly they both obeyed. Without another word, Hezekiah withdrew to his own suite. He tossed fitfully in his bed, his worries over his wife clouding the joy he had expected to feel at the birth of his child.

Isaiah went only as far as the hall outside the birthing chamber. For long moments he paced back and forth before the door. He had just decided to reenter when a piercing cry rent the stillness, and Naamah opened the door and fell sobbing into his arms.

Hephzibah was dead!

Isaiah and Naamah, stunned and heartbroken, sat on the bench in the shadowy palace hall, holding each other and weeping for this terrible new loss and for all the uncertainties that surrounded them.

Meanwhile, inside the birthing room a lusty-lunged little prince nuzzled at his nurse's breast, blissfully unaware of the sorrow that his birth had brought—and would continue to bring those who could have loved him most.

"The child must have a name!" It was the eighth day, the day when the baby would be circumcised according to Lord Yahweh's ancient covenant with Abraham. It was the day also for announcing the infant's name.

Isaiah and Naamah, both clad in mourners' robes of sackcloth, had come to the king's private reception room. Isaiah had shaved off his beard, a sign of deepest grief, and there was a scarf tied tightly about Naamah's head, concealing the fact that she had chopped off her long hair as her token of mourning for her daughter.

Strange how grief and joy could be mixed. In Naamah's arms lay the infant, her grandson, sleeping peacefully. "You must decide on something, Hezey," she said. "Your son cannot go through life nameless." Only Naamah, whose own sorrow was deeper than words could express, could have spoken to the king in such a way.

Hezekiah looked at her but said nothing. In the few days since Hephzibah's death, Naamah seemed to have aged greatly. Hezekiah felt a strong affection for her. She was a kind woman, understanding and compassionate, and he wished he could tell her he was grateful to her, but he could not speak.

"Don't you want to hold him? You haven't, you know. He *is* your son."

Hezekiah reached out and took the infant from Naamah. "My son," he murmured. How often had he dreamed of the joy that such an event would bring, and instead there was no joy at all. The boy must have a name, and even that was a choice Hezekiah did not want to face. He had always liked his own name: *Hezekiah,*

"Yahweh is my strength." No boy was ever named for his own father, yet Hezekiah had planned for some name of the same type, something to express his confidence and trust in Lord Yahweh, his gratitude and happiness. But not now. Nothing of that sort would do.

"Manasseh," he said suddenly, looking at his son's tiny features. "I shall call him Manasseh."

It was a very old-fashioned name, not stylish at all, even though it had been the name of one of the tribes of Israel, those who claimed descent from the Patriarch Manasseh, son of Joseph, son of Jacob. But, more important, the name came from an old Hebrew word meaning "making to forget." Hezekiah knew that if he were ever to come to the point where he could love this child of his, he must forget that the boy's birth had cost Hephzibah her life.

Naamah understood, and she smiled faintly. Isaiah also understood. He had given his own sons unusual names and had always felt that a child's name was a matter of deep significance. "Manasseh," he repeated. "Yes, I like that. I like it very much." Isaiah saw in the name a glimmer of hope that joy in his son would enable Hezekiah to forget the pain of the loss of Hephzibah.

So it was that the crown prince of Judah was given the strange, unfashionable name from long ago.

But the forgetfulness Hezekiah sought came very slowly. Without Hephzibah, he was desolate, and though he wanted to seek Isaiah's help, it was many days before he was able to speak frankly with him.

It was still winter when Naamah and Isaiah invited the king to visit them at their home in the country to escape from the palace, the familiar surroundings that seemed to harbor his grief.

"Perhaps, if he were to come out here . . . ," Isaiah had suggested, and Naamah was completely agreeable. Their own heartache hung heavily upon them like the oppressive gray clouds that hung over the land of

Judah. Yet Isaiah grieved at least as much for Hezekiah, trying to face the future, as he did for the loss of Hephzibah.

And Hezekiah came to Isaiah's house as he had come when he was a little boy, seeking refuge from crushing sorrow. Without attendants and without any of his kingly ornaments, he came for a few days to be a simple countryman with his in-laws, the only family he had.

The prophet's household was full of activity. The children, especially little Zina, took a liking to King Hezekiah, and the king, so long childless, so unfamiliar with the ways of the very young, found his heart warming toward them. Zina, completely cured of her early difficulties in talking, chattered eagerly to the man she called "Uncle Hezey," not realizing that he was the king. From her, and from Ethan, the loving familiarity came naturally, and Hezekiah was pleased by it.

"I hope Manasseh will turn out as well as these two," he said to Isaiah. Then he said to the children, "I have a little boy at home, and when he's bigger, I'll bring him to see you."

"Are you my uncle?" Ethan asked, still vaguely remembering a whole succession of "uncles" in the house of his mother, Avital.

"Not really," Hezekiah answered, "but I guess we could pretend that I am." This seemed to satisfy Ethan. There would be time to straighten out the complicated relationships in later years.

But whatever diversion the children provided, whatever momentary escape from his grief, the loss of Hephzibah still weighed heavily upon Hezekiah. It was a reality that was always there, haunting his nights and filling his days with a thousand little stabs of pain.

Sooner or later, the subject was bound to arise with the children. "I remember when you were here before, a long time ago, when we built the house," Zina pronounced seriously one evening as the family ate supper.

"And there was the pretty lady who came with you. Where is she?"

Hezekiah could not answer. He looked down at his plate, his eyes misty with tears.

"She died." Ethan somehow had put together the pieces of Isaiah's and Naamah's recent mourning. "Like my first mother died. Yours, too, Zina. It just happens. But Lord Yahweh sent us a new mother and a papa, too."

"Maybe he'll send Hezey a new wife," Zina put in.

Hezekiah shook his head sadly. How easily these children accepted the reality of death! To be so young, so easily healed of loss!

"Let's not talk about sad things," Naamah said, sensing Hezekiah's despair. Soon the children were chattering happily about other matters.

Later that evening, while Naamah was putting Ethan and Zina to bed, the king and his father-in-law drew their benches close to the fireplace. At last Hezekiah knew he could no longer hold back the emotions stirring within him. The time had come for talking.

"Lord Yahweh healed me," Hezekiah said. "He held back my life from the pit of destruction. He gave me new hope, but then he took Hephzibah. I would have rather died myself than to have lost her!" Great tears poured from his eyes, the tears so long repressed, the tears that had to come. It was not unmanly to cry for personal loss, not even to let Isaiah see him cry, for Isaiah was his friend, his best friend, and the father of his beloved. And Isaiah was Lord Yahweh's prophet, closer to God than most men would ever be.

Yahweh has filled Isaiah's spirit with a special grace, Hezekiah thought, *a grace that I have never, never had, or even really understood.* And even now, though Isaiah was mourning too, he had borne Hephzibah's loss with more serenity than Hezekiah could comprehend.

He looked at Isaiah as if certain that consolation would come now, and he saw that Isaiah was weeping.

"The Lord does not give us all the answers," Isaiah said through his tears. "His ways are not our ways. As the heavens are high above the earth, so his ways are above ours. We do not know why he took her, but we may be sure he has his reasons." Isaiah's voice grew steadier. "And we know he can, and he will, give us strength to endure through all of life's troubles until our own time comes."

Yes, Hezekiah thought. *Yahweh is my strength, my source of courage.* It was what his own mother had taught him from his earliest childhood. It was what he had believed through all the terrors of Sennacherib's invasion and then his own terrible illness. It was the idea reflected in his own name, which he always felt suited him so well.

He felt sudden pangs of grief and loneliness for his mother, gone now these many years. He had loved her deeply, and cherished her memory, but usually when he thought of her it was without pain. She was a part of that lost world, that other world of happy memory where she lived still, lovely Lady Abijah, the guiding light of his childhood. Would there ever come a time when Hephzibah, too, would belong only to that memory world—a time when he could think of her with love without the crushing sorrow? Perhaps. It was the first hint of divinely sent strength beginning to course through him. With stumbling inadequacy of expression, he tried to explain it to Isaiah, who seemed to understand perfectly.

By the time Hezekiah returned to the palace and to the thousand routine matters of governing his little kingdom, a sense of peace and equanimity had descended upon him. If he continued to grieve for Hephzibah, he did so in private.

But when various courtiers suggested he take another wife, Hezekiah refused. While it would have been good to find someone he could love, someone to help him forget, the memory of Hephzibah was still too firmly fixed in his heart. As months passed even Isaiah and

Naamah urged him to marry again. "You should try to have more sons," Isaiah urged. "What if something should happen to Manasseh?"

Hezekiah shook his head sadly. Though he could not explain his fears, he knew that never again would he be willing to risk sending another woman to her death by planting his seed within her.

But if Hezekiah unconsciously blamed himself for Hephzibah's death, there were others who placed the burden elsewhere. Manasseh's nursemaids, who found him from infancy a difficult child, whispered superstitiously among themselves. "A babe who kills his mother grows up to no good!"

By the time little Manasseh was walking, he had become an expert at temper tantrums—kicking, screaming, and crying till he was red in the face. A mother might have disciplined him, but the nurses Hezekiah employed to tend the child were overawed by the fact that their charge was the king's son. It was hard indeed to discipline a prince. Better to let him have his own way, which seemed to keep him reasonably contented until the next upset came along. Manasseh was becoming outrageously spoiled and growing more and more unlovable with every passing day.

All too soon the time came when Manasseh began to comprehend his nursemaid's comments. It was simple enough. They talked as though he wasn't there. He was merely a thing to them, an object incapable of real understanding. "Killed his mother . . . that's why his father doesn't love him." It was a fragment overheard. "His grandparents don't either. Lady Hephzibah was their daughter."

Manasseh, too young to realize the women were wrong, locked these words in his heart. His father seemed distant and far away. His visits were brief, and he always seemed ill at ease. Grandfather Isaiah and

Grandmother Naamah were busy caring for their children—orphans whom they seemed to love more than their own grandchild.

Nobody would ever really love him. Manasseh was sure of it, and he told himself it didn't matter. He'd show them he could get along perfectly well without love!

TWENTY
Here a Little, There a Little

Isaiah and Naamah were indeed very busy through the years of Manasseh's early childhood. With their country house rebuilt, Isaiah let it be known that once again he was looking for disciples. Any young man who felt the call to Yahweh's service could pitch his tent near the prophet's home and stay as long as he wished. Life on Isaiah's estate was simple but good. While there were few of the luxuries one would have expected in a princely household, there was always sufficient food, thanks to the yields of the prophet's crops and livestock. Some of the students brought their families and settled as tenants.

Most of them, Isaiah realized, were far better suited for farming or herding sheep and goats than for studying. They were simple country folk, most of them sincerely devoted to Yahweh's service, but as far as Isaiah could tell, there was not one among them with the potential to become a truly great prophet.

"How are things going?" Naamah asked him one evening as they strolled together along a lane out toward one of the fields. They had so few moments when they were alone together that Naamah cherished each one of them.

"Slowly, slowly," Isaiah responded. "Here a little, there a little, precept upon precept, line upon line. But as long as they want to learn at all, I'll keep trying."

There was a hint of sadness in his voice. Just a few weeks earlier they had finally received word that Maher was dead, slain by an unknown assailant in a far eastern corner of Assyria. It had been three years since he had set out on his futile quest for his brother. A traveling companion who escaped unhurt managed to get the message to King Hezekiah. He had been in no hurry, since he really did not believe Maher's claims to be a prince of Judah.

Of Jashub and Reba and their children there was no word at all, ever.

The students, the would-be disciples, helped to fill some of the emptiness in Isaiah's heart. So did Ethan and Zina, the new family Lord Yahweh had bestowed upon the prophet and his wife. Life in any household with small children was full of numerous daily joys and sorrows, but for Isaiah, the joy outweighed the difficulties. While both of the children were devoted to Naamah, it was Isaiah they followed about at every opportunity. Isaiah was their "Papa." Naamah was "Lady," spoken with total love and affection by the two children who could never quite accept her as "Mother." Since both of the children were dark like Naamah, and Ethan particularly resembled his adopted mother, many of the students assumed that the children were somehow related to the prophet and his wife—grandchildren, perhaps. Naamah insisted on keeping the record straight. "We must always be honest about these things." She admonished Isaiah about it hundreds of times when he would have preferred to keep their origins secret.

"But, Naamah, you know as well as I do how some of our people—good, God-fearing, decent people— feel about illegitimate children. They'll turn them into outcasts as if it were the poor children's fault! We're going to have trouble getting them married off, just you wait and see."

"It's a bit too soon to worry about that," Naamah responded.

"Yes," Isaiah answered. "There are more immediate problems, like trying to teach Ethan to read! Zina is doing well enough, but Ethan is something else again." Though he didn't say so, Isaiah wished it might have been the other way around. With girls it really didn't matter, though he'd never deny Zina the chance to learn if she wanted to. With boys it *did* matter. Ethan, whom he had hoped would be interested in helping him get his writings together, was eight years old and still as blithely illiterate as he'd been months before when Isaiah's efforts began.

On a winter evening a few weeks later, Isaiah and his little protégé lingered at the supper table while Naamah and Zina cleared away the remains of the evening meal. It was time to launch a new program.

"Ethan, think with me now," Isaiah pleaded. "I'm going to read you the story of Joseph again, and you let your eyes follow along as I point to the words. It isn't hard. Just watch the shape of the letters." Isaiah lifted a scroll, recently borrowed from the king's palace, and spread it out on the table. Hezekiah said that a refugee from Israel had brought him the scroll some years earlier, and it was full of good stories of long ago, stories to captivate the imagination of any reader, child or adult. One of the best of them all was the long tale of Joseph and his brothers. Ethan and Zina—and Naamah—had listened spellbound when Isaiah read it to them. Perhaps it might hold the key for teaching the boy to read, a task that was proving far more difficult than Isaiah had expected.

"Listen now. Here we go. 'This is the history of the

family of Jacob. Joseph was seventeen years old and he was watching the flock with his brothers. . . .'" Isaiah's finger pointed to the words as he read, and Ethan watched intently. "Now, let's go back. You read that part to me."

Ethan pointed uncertainly to the word *this*. "Here," he began, "is the story of Joseph."

"No, no, Ethan, be careful. It doesn't say that."

"Well, it's something like that. I don't know."

"You're not thinking, Ethan." Isaiah sighed deeply. How many children had he taught to read? First, when he was still a lad, there had been his own younger brothers, and later Jashub and Maher and Hephzibah—and Hezekiah—and children of the students who lived on his estate. And then, of course, there was Naamah, not a child but a determined woman, who in spite of difficulties had learned to read quite adequately. She had been his most difficult pupil—until now.

"Look at the first word, Ethan. Now what does it say?"

"I don't know," the boy whispered. "I can't remember."

"Oh, child, you're just not trying!" There was anger in Isaiah's voice. As he rolled up the scroll on the table and walked away, anger mixed with deep disappointment. Ethan, at seven, was certainly old enough to be reading, yet Isaiah was making no progress at all with him. There did not seem to be anything wrong with the boy's eyesight, and when he talked he certainly seemed as bright as most children his age.

Isaiah knew what most schoolmasters would suggest: the boy who is slow to learn should be chastised. A little stern discipline with a light cane across his bottom would work wonders, they would say. Isaiah could not bring himself to strike Ethan. He was, in fact, immediately sorry that he had spoken so sharply, yet deep frustration still stirred within him. "Lord Yahweh," he muttered, "you sent me this child to be a helper to me in my old age, and yet he is a fool who cannot learn." Isaiah retired to his chamber, feeling very old and inexpressibly weary. Tears poured from his eyes. Then came deep sobs from the depths of his being as he wept for the lost years, for opportunities gone forever, and for the fearful uncertainties of the future. Alone on his bed he wept more deeply than he had done since the night of Hephzibah's death some years before.

The door stood open, and after a few moments Ethan tiptoed in. "Papa," he ventured hesitantly, "did I do something bad?"

Isaiah sat up and took the boy onto his lap. "Not really *bad*, son. It's just that I want so much to teach you, and you just don't seem to want to learn."

"I like the stories when you read them to me," Ethan remarked, as if that would solve everything.

"Child, I won't always be here to read to you," Isaiah answered. Never before had he said anything of this sort to either of the children. Though they realized that Isaiah and Naamah were older than the parents of their young friends, it had never been an issue that seemed to matter.

"I guess I'll just have to keep trying," Ethan said seriously. "But it's so hard. The words all look alike to me."

Isaiah hugged him close, this son who was not really his son at all, this gift from Lord Yahweh. "We'll keep trying together," Isaiah said.

Both the old man and the little boy knew the effort would continue, but they also knew it was never going to be easy.

In Hezekiah's palace in Jerusalem, another child was growing up, a child as different from the good-natured, plodding Ethan as two lads could possibly be. Manasseh, the king's son, was a wild boy, too often full of inexplicable anger, too often sullen. At his best he was high-spirited, running like a streak of wildfire through the palace halls, shouting at the top of his voice. There was fierce energy in him. He clambered up the stone pillars on the porches. He climbed trees and dangled precariously from fragile limbs. Climbing—always climbing upward. He loved King Ahaz's sun-clock with its great series of steps, and often he would spend hours there, seemingly lost in a world of his own, making up elaborate stories and acting out his fantasies.

There were rarely other children of his age to play with, for when any of the nobles brought their sons to visit the young prince, the results were inevitably disastrous. Manasseh could not understand friendship. When denied anything he wanted, he would strike out in fierce, unreasoned rage, hitting, clawing, even biting his young companions, and screaming like a wild beast. After one bad experience, Isaiah knew well enough to keep Zina and Ethan away, for Manasseh, who somehow knew all about their origins, taunted them and heaped verbal abuse upon their long-dead mothers.

Hezekiah found Manasseh entirely unlovable. *This is my only child,* the king often thought. *I must try to be a good father to him.*

He tried. He visited him, sometimes bringing him little surprise gifts, which Manasseh usually tossed on the floor in contempt. Once, feeling particularly hopeful of somehow reaching his strange, unappealing son, Hezekiah lifted five-year-old Manasseh on his shoulders to carry him up to the rooftop porch. With strong little fingers, Manasseh grasped a handful of the king's thinning hair and tugged hard. "You're getting bald!" he mocked.

"Manasseh! Let go!" Hezekiah commanded. "That hurts."

The boy giggled.

"Manasseh!" There was anger in the king's voice as he detached his son's fingers from his hair and set him squarely on the ground. "You mustn't hurt other people."

"Why?"

"It isn't good." Hezekiah wanted to be patient. "It's not the way Lord Yahweh wants us to act."

Manasseh made an ugly face, then turned and scurried away. "Come back here, son!" Hezekiah demanded. "I am your father and I am also the king. You do not walk away from me without my permission. Do you understand?"

Manasseh said nothing and sat down on the ground.

"Answer me, child!" Hezekiah grasped Manasseh's shoulders angrily. There was only a cold withering stare from those deep green eyes, so like Hephzibah's. *I should spank him*, Hezekiah thought. He must have discipline. But even in his anger, he was repelled at the thought of hurting Hephzibah's child.

"Don't you love me, Manasseh?" he asked. Releasing his hold on the boy's shoulders, he stooped down and looked him squarely in the face. "You know how much I care for you."

"I hate you! I hate you!" Manasseh screamed.

Hezekiah set the boy on his feet and without another word walked away before Manasseh could see the tears in his eyes.

"Lord Yahweh," he whispered, under his breath, "what kind of child have you given me?"

While there was something about Isaiah that seemed attuned to the heart of eternal childhood, a gift for communicating with the very young that made him a favorite of almost every child who had ever crossed his path, he found Manasseh utterly baffling and beyond reach. On visits to the palace, Isaiah often made an effort to see his grandson, only to be rebuffed time and again. The prophet's songs and stories, which had fascinated two generations of children, only seemed to bore Manasseh, nor would he ever share his own thoughts with his grandfather in spite of Isaiah's efforts to draw him out.

"The boy is like a fire burning in the pits below the earth," Hezekiah remarked to Isaiah.

The old prophet nodded. "I have always thought," Isaiah said, "that people who are the most bitter, the most difficult, most unlovely, become so because they are *unloved*. Usually that is how it is. But Manasseh! Lord Yahweh knows we *want* the child to feel loved! We are so willing to reach out to him, and yet he eludes us!"

"Perhaps he will improve with age," remarked Hezekiah.

It was a false hope. Manasseh definitely did not improve, if by improvement one meant development of a more winning disposition. Yet there was some cause for optimism. Manasseh early showed indications of being a good student. Once started, he learned to read and write with few of the agonies that most children suffered. He also had a distinct gift for languages, and Hezekiah was delighted when the boy expressed interest in studying Aramaic and Egyptian. Though he hated any corrections from his tutors, his desire to learn was even stronger than his resentments, and so he persisted and learned a great deal.

By this time, poor Ethan still could only identify about three or four words per sentence, and his writing and spelling skills were even worse.

Years passed. Though still strong and blessed with perfect health, Isaiah, to his dismay, found his eyesight fading. He could see perfectly well at a distance, but the letters inscribed on his potsherds and scrolls were rapidly becoming indecipherable blurs, even when he held them at arm's length.

"We are getting old, my dearest," Naamah commented one evening as she watched him struggling to read one of the precious fragments from his cypress box.

Naamah could still see the tiny writing perfectly, though she could not recognize objects halfway across the room.

Isaiah nodded. He was getting old, yet in recent years, far more than in the chaotic days of his youth, he felt young at heart.

"I had some pieces here somewhere," Isaiah said, "some potsherds where I'd written the history of Sennacherib's invasion and some of the other events of Hezey's reign. I wanted to get them together."

"More important to get your own sayings together," Naamah commented. She peered into the jumbled mass of potsherds in the cypress box and sighed deeply. "Oh, Isaiah, why did you ever let things get so disorderly? Why some of these sayings aren't even yours! Look, here's Hezekiah's Song of Recovery. Remember that? I expect it's the only poem poor Hezey ever wrote, and really it's not very good."

"Oh, but it's important. It's part of our history. Everything I've saved is important."

Naamah, seated beside the box, continued rifling through the pottery fragments. "All these about the Prince of Peace—perhaps we should destroy them. Hezekiah certainly never lived up to such extravagant hopes, and it's even more certain Manasseh never will."

"No, we must save them!" Isaiah declared firmly. "My mistake was in hoping to live to see the Peaceable Kingdom. But I still believe it will come someday, and we must keep this hope alive until it is fulfilled.

"When I was a boy," he went on, "my father said the greatest part of old King Uzziah's tragedy was that he had to live so long without hope of any kind. But Lord Yahweh has given us a hope that can never be destroyed, a dream to cling to no matter how dark the shadows around us. I know that someday there will be true peace on earth. And the whole world will be full of the knowledge of the one and only God."

Isaiah sighed, then continued. "In all of history no eye has seen nor ear heard of any god like Yahweh, who loves his people and acts on the behalf of those who wait for him."

"I wonder," said Naamah, "how long the world will have to wait for this wonderful kingdom of peace you keep talking about."

"That is exactly what I *don't* know," Isaiah replied.

Slowly he closed the lid of his box. "Hezey wants me to come into the city tomorrow. He says he has something important to talk about."

"I hope he hasn't come up with any more plots against Assyria," Naamah remarked. "That is certainly no way to bring about a more peaceful world."

"No," Isaiah answered. "That is one thing we needn't worry about. He has no strength for such things anymore." He paused. "Unless I am mistaken, and I pray Lord Yahweh that I am, our Hezekiah is getting ready to die."

TWENTY-ONE
Declining Shadows

"When I was ill," said King Hezekiah to the prophet the next day, "you told me I would live fifteen years longer. Isaiah, I have now lived more than thirteen of those years. My time is running out!" Hezekiah's distraught voice broke as he and his father-in-law sat talking in the king's private suite at the palace.

It was a cold day, and Hezekiah, who had noticeably aged in recent years, hovered uncomfortably over the little brazier beside his chair and warmed his hands. There was a look of sadness about him and also, though Isaiah tried to ignore it, a deathly pallor. Never really robust since his brush with death years before, Hezekiah had, in the last few months, grown increasingly frail. His steps were slow and uncertain, and though he never complained publicly of the pains that wracked his body, he had occasionally confided these worries to Isaiah, hoping the prophet might find him some herbs to ease his distress. Isaiah had tried, but with no success.

"Fifteen years," Hezekiah repeated somberly, "and less than two of them are left." It had taken great courage for him finally to unburden himself of the distinct worry that haunted him more and more, the certainty that his days were numbered. But once he had said it, he felt slightly better.

Isaiah looked genuinely stunned. "Have the years passed so quickly?"

"My time is almost gone," Hezekiah replied. "I was afraid to die back then, but now it will be a blessing." He sighed deeply. "Only there is so much I need to prepare. Manasseh is still a child, but in another month he will be twelve. At that time I want to have him anointed as my co-regent, and I want you to perform the ceremony."

"Hezey," Isaiah objected, "don't you think you could wait a while longer? Manasseh is so . . ." He paused for the right word. "So . . . *unsettled*."

"I am hoping that he will become more settled when he realizes the importance of what he is about to become. Lord Yahweh knows I am constantly disappointed with the boy, but he is my only son, and the house of David must go on. If I should die before he is anointed there could be trouble."

Isaiah knew that Hezekiah was indeed dying, yet unlike the short but almost fatal illness of years before, he now faced what would likely be a slow and painful decline. "Hezekiah, you know I would give you all the years that are left to me if I could," he said. He meant it truly. Why should Hezekiah be dying while Isaiah himself, so much older, continued to thrive and enjoy the best of health?

The king was visibly touched by Isaiah's statement but did not respond to it directly. "I only want you to help me secure Manasseh's succession," he said after a moment.

"Hezey, you know I will support Manasseh in every way, and, even though I am against it, I will even anoint him if that is what you really want."

"King David had his son Solomon anointed as co-regent before he died." Hezekiah appealed to historical precedent. "Only he was too sick to be there, to see it happen. I want to see Manasseh's coronation—to be present, to take part in it. I want it to be on his twelfth birthday."

"In the very worst time of the winter, when it's likely to be cold and raining?" Isaiah could not resist a further attempt at dissuasion.

"I was crowned in the winter," Hezekiah responded, "and the sun shone the whole day. Don't you remember?"

Isaiah nodded. He felt a deep sadness, a grief compounded by Hezekiah's illness and his own uncertainties about Manasseh's ability for kingship. Recent events boded ill for Judah, and much as Isaiah loved his homeland, he was entirely powerless to stop them.

It was Hezekiah who broke the silence with a touch of his inevitable optimism. "I believe that Lord Yahweh will make the sun shine on Manasseh, too." But there was a noticeable lack of confidence in his voice as he spoke.

The sun did not shine on Manasseh's twelfth birthday. There came instead a chilling rainstorm of such proportions that the anointing ceremony, traditionally held on the bronze platform outside King Solomon's temple, had to be moved indoors. Outside in the temple courtyard, disappointed crowds hovered under improvised awnings, waiting only for the distribution of royal bounty after the services. There was disgruntled talk among them. "Yahweh is letting us all see his disapproval of this business." "The king should have postponed it. He's not dead yet. It could wait."

But no one was more disappointed than Manasseh himself. Had he been given a choice in the matter, he would have opted for postponement since he was eager for the acclaim of the multitude. "When *he's* dead," the boy muttered, glancing at his father, "I'm going to have another coronation, a *real* one!"

Isaiah heard and laid a restraining hand on his grandson's arm. "This will be the real one," he whispered. "In a way it's even better because here we are *inside* the temple. This is the place where I had a vision of Lord Yahweh and heard him calling me when I was young."

"You don't think I believe that nonsense!" Manasseh responded sullenly.

The Levitical choir began chanting, and sweet, solemn music filled the air. King Hezekiah had been carried into the temple in a wicker litter chair, but now he stood, leaning heavily on his gilded wooden staff. "Lord Yahweh," he intoned solemnly as the music stopped, "I present to you Manasseh, my son, who is to be king with me and after me."

Manasseh moved forward to the open space before the altar of incense, the very spot where Isaiah had seen his vision more than half a century before, and the place where Hezekiah had once spread out Sennacherib's insulting letter and prayed for deliverance. For a moment the boy stood quietly, all eyes upon him. He was a handsome lad, tall, well-built, big for his age. He was clad in a sumptuous robe of white wool, bordered with bands of purple and red, elaborately decked with gold fringe. His brown hair cascaded about his shoulders, thick and luxuriant. Whatever else, he looked the part of a Davidic prince.

At a given signal Manasseh knelt, and Isaiah moved forward with the vial of anointing oil. Carefully, the prophet poured a few drops of the oil on his grandson's head and pronounced the ritual formula: "Lord Yahweh has anointed you, Manasseh ben-Hezekiah, to be king over his people. And you shall reign over the people of Yahweh, and you will save them from the hand of their enemies." These were ancient words, based, it was said, on the words of the prophet Samuel when he anointed the first king, Saul, more than three hundred years before. "Do you not see him whom Lord Yahweh has chosen?" Isaiah continued as Manasseh rose to face the assembled dignitaries. "There is none like him among all the people! Long live the king!"

"Long live King Manasseh!" said Hezekiah. On a sudden impulse, he handed his staff to Eliakim and moved unaided to embrace his son. For long moments he held him close. While tears streamed from the father's eyes, the son stood looking uncomfortable and sullen. "Lord Yahweh," Hezekiah said, regaining his composure, "bless this young man with long life and prosperity, with happiness and peace."

Carefully, reverently, the king removed the golden circlet crown he wore and placed it on Manasseh's head, where it slid insecurely to a lopsided angle. With a nonchalant gesture, the boy attempted to straighten it as Isaiah signaled to the choirmaster to resume the ritual chanting. Hezekiah, the only man in the sanctuary permitted to sit, returned to his chair. The ceremony was over. For good or ill, Manasseh was an anointed king.

During the next two years, King Hezekiah's health continued to decline. No longer did he keep secret the pains he felt. Much of his time he spent in bed, languid and weak, often unable to eat. Manasseh visited him daily because the king required it, but their visits were always strained. The boy eyed his father warily, watching for signs of imminent death, while Hezekiah, with wishful thinking, continued to believe that his relationship with his son was growing better.

Usually they talked very little. Manasseh would sit on his father's bed while the old king held his hand or patted it. Manasseh was always uncomfortable. He hated to feel his father's touch upon him. He hated the atmosphere of gathering shadows. Most of all, he deplored Hezekiah's frequent comments expressing his love, for no matter what was said, Manasseh could not really believe himself loved by his father or anyone else. His feelings for Hezekiah combined a small amount of pity with a large measure of disgust.

The king had lost the good looks of his youth. He was painfully thin, with deep hollow cheeks and pain-haunted eyes. The sparse fringe of hair around his nearly bald head matched the gray of his straggly beard. The skin of his arms and hands was blotchy and frequently bruised, his voice raspy and weak like that of an old man.

Manasseh felt no bond of kinship to him at all. He saw his father simply as an obstacle in his path and waited eagerly for Hezekiah to die, hoping he would not have to be present when it happened.

Isaiah was a frequent visitor, too, but unlike Manasseh, who came out of a sense of obligation, he came because he wanted to. Isaiah wanted Hezekiah to know how much he was still loved.

The king enjoyed Isaiah's visits. As long as he was able to get about at all, he would allow Isaiah to help him out of bed. Then, leaning heavily on the prophet's arm, Hezekiah would walk about with him in the enclosed courtyard beside the royal bedchamber. They talked of days long past, sometimes laughing about memories they shared.

It was on one of those afternoons in the king's garden, as they talked of Isaiah's family, that the prophet suddenly hit upon a splendid idea. "Hezey, let me send you my girl Zina to be your nurse. I know you have plenty of servants and attendants, but Zina would be special. She is very fond of you and always has been."

"You're not asking me to marry again at my age?" Hezekiah said with a smile. "I remember the story of old King David and Abishag the Shunammite. Would you have Zina be my Abishag?"

"No, but I did think perhaps you could help me find her a suitable husband. She is a lovely girl, like my own daughter, but she is an Assyrian, and we'll never know her origins. She may be illegitimate, and most people hold that against her. It's the same with my boy, Ethan. I haven't been able to find a wife for him either, but

248

he's still young. I worry more about Zina."

"I thought that Ethan was the older one," said Hezekiah.

"Oh, he is by a few months, I suppose, but girls mature so much faster. Most of Zina's friends have married now. I know it's hard on her, feeling unwanted, though she doesn't talk about it. Let her serve you, Hezey, and help her if you can."

"Certainly." The king smiled warmly. "In fact, I could arrange to give her to Manasseh eventually as a concubine. If he took a fancy to her, her future would be secure."

"Absolutely not!" Isaiah was stunned. "If you even contemplate such a thing, I'll never let her set foot in the palace! I want her to have a good, decent husband, someone who will love her and give her a chance for a happy life."

Hezekiah understood. "Let her come," he said. "I will do what I can for her."

So Zina came, and her presence in the king's chamber was like spring sunshine after the long winter rains. The girl was a born nurse, gentle yet strong. She gave the old king attentive care, and something more—the warmth of genuine concern. For Hezekiah she was like the daughter he had never had. He loved to hear her sing and play the lute. She had learned all of Isaiah's songs and many others, and often as he lay in bed, he listened to her music and drifted into a gentle dream world where once again he was young and happy and free from pain.

Once he dreamed the voice he heard was that of Lady Abijah, his mother. He awoke startled, unsure where he was. "Mother!" he gasped in his half-dazed sleep. "Mother!"

Zina rose and hovered over him, wiping away the tears from his eyes.

"Just a dream, Zina," he whispered. "Your voice is just like hers."

"It's all right to cry, my king." She sat on the bed beside him and grasped his hand gently while the old king wept for losses of long ago and for the grim realities of the present.

"You are a good woman, Zina," he said at last. "Lord Yahweh sent you to be the light of my old age. Don't let me lose you."

At the curtained doorway, unseen by either of them, Manasseh lurked, listening intently before stalking away in silent rage. Who was this Assyrian girl, this Zina, to have wormed her way into his father's heart? Something, he decided, would have to be done quickly before the old man made a total fool of himself.

"I want her, Father!" It was the next morning and Manasseh sat at the king's bedside, his pale eyes sparkling craftily. "Zina. Don't tell me I'm too young for a woman. I am almost fourteen."

"You're too young," said Hezekiah with disgust. "Another year or two, you can have all the girls you want, believe me. I will be dead by then, and you can have a whole harem full of them, though most will be more trouble than they're worth, I can assure you. But you cannot have Zina. Not now, not ever!" While Hezekiah's voice was weak, the force of conviction behind it was strong.

The subject of their conversation was nowhere about. She was off having a late breakfast with some of the other palace maidservants. Manasseh had observed her daily schedule carefully and chosen his time well. "Really, Father, I had hoped you'd understand. You always told me I had only to ask for anything in your power to give, and I'd have it. Isn't that what you said?" Manasseh's voice became light, teasing.

"*Things*, yes," Hezekiah sighed. "Zina is not a *thing*. She is a human being just as you are."

"She doesn't belong to anyone else," Manasseh argued. He had expected his father to refuse his request, and he was immediately ready with a more devastating piece of ammunition. "If I can't have her lawfully, I'll take her anyway, and you certainly won't be able to stop me." His smile was sinister. "Remember, I am king, too. You made me king."

"You are my son, and you will obey me."

Manasseh laughed. "If you want her to be safe, you'd better send her home. No more nursemaiding. You could marry her yourself, of course, but that would merely assure that I'll get her when you're gone. The king's property passes to his heir without question. I'm willing to wait. As you continue to remind us all, it won't be long."

"Leave me, Manasseh!" With difficulty Hezekiah sat up in bed, his face red with anger. "Go! If you ever speak to me like this again, I'll disinherit you."

"You can't disinherit me!" Manasseh rose and moved to the doorway. "You have no one else!" Delighted with his own cleverness, the young king turned abruptly and stalked away.

As soon as Manasseh was gone, Hezekiah struck the gong at his bedside. An attendant appeared rapidly. "Go find Zina and bring her here at once," he said. "And then get word to Isaiah that he is to come immediately."

"Yes, my king. Where shall I look for Prince Isaiah, my king?"

"I don't know where to look. Just get him as quickly as possible!"

The attendant nodded, bowed politely, and withdrew. Within moments, Zina was at the king's bedside. She sensed at once that something serious had upset him.

"Sit down, dear child," he whispered. "We have great troubles, you and I. I am going to have to send you home."

"No!" she gasped. Only yesterday he had said, "Don't let me lose you." Zina had long ago resolved to serve him until he died. He had made her feel needed, given her a purpose in life. In a way that she could not explain, she loved him, and the thought of having to leave him was devastating. "Whatever has happened, my king?" she asked.

In a few painful sentences, he explained to her about Manasseh.

"If I were to be married," Zina said, "I'd be safe."

Hezekiah sighed deeply. For weeks, ever since Zina had come, he had been putting out inquiries for a suitable husband for her, but no one among the men of the court would consider an Assyrian—particularly one of unknown parentage—as a prospective legal wife.

"If it would help, I'd marry you myself," Hezekiah said, "but that would only mean Manasseh could take you the moment I'm gone. You don't want that, and Isaiah certainly wouldn't allow it."

"I have an idea," Zina replied. Far from the dismay Hezekiah expected, the girl looked positively happy. "I could marry Ethan! Oh, I don't know why Papa never thought of it! I know Ethan and I grew up like brother and sister, but we're not really. We're not kin at all. And he's a good person, a kind, decent young man. And nobody wants him, either! I'd say we're perfect for each other. He could come live here at the palace as one of your bodyguards—and protect me at the same time!"

The arrangement sounded almost too good to be true. "Do you love him?" Hezekiah asked.

"Certainly, I love him—like a brother. But I can learn to love him as a husband, I know I can. Most marriages are arranged by the parents, and couples learn to love each other. How much easier with someone I already know!"

By the time Isaiah arrived at the palace a few hours later, Hezekiah was ready to present him with every imaginable reason why he should consent to the unlikely match of Ethan and Zina.

Isaiah, however, needed little persuasion, though the

idea took him by surprise. "He's so young," he ventured, only to be reminded that in all likelihood, Ethan was at least a few months older than Zina herself.

"And he's not a scholar. Never did learn to read much, that boy. He has always seemed bright enough otherwise," Isaiah could not forget his disappointment over Ethan's lack of literacy skills.

"Oh, Papa, do you think I care about that?" Zina exclaimed. "There are other things more important than reading!"

Isaiah nodded solemnly. "I should have thought of this idea myself long ago," he said.

The betrothal was formalized, the wedding celebrated, and within a few days, the newlyweds were assigned rooms adjoining King Hezekiah's suite in the palace. Zina continued her nursing duties as before, while Ethan proved most valuable in assisting with the more difficult matters of lifting the king out of bed when needed and helping him bathe.

Far from being rid of Zina, Manasseh had merely succeeded in bringing in another rival for Hezekiah's affections. The young king, frustrated and angry, swallowed his pride. *It can't be much longer*, he told himself continually. *His time is running out*. Like everyone else, Manasseh believed implicitly that death would come to Hezekiah when he reached the fifteenth year after his wonderful recovery.

The months passed slowly. From his bed the king continued to confer daily with his ministers of state, who helped to manage the daily business of government—Eliakim, and Joah, and sometimes Isaiah, too. Meanwhile Manasseh remained a decorative, powerless figurehead.

Then, with the approach of the New Year, almost two years after Manasseh's coronation, King Hezekiah seemed a bit stronger. Isaiah found him one afternoon sitting up in bed, his eyes sparkling with something of his youthful vigor. Zina sat on a bench beside his bed.

"I was just telling Zina how I am going to bring in the New Year one more time," he announced cheerfully. "They can carry me up on the platform. Manasseh can help me as he did last year, but he is not to proclaim the New Year by himself while I'm still alive."

Proclaiming the New Year was the king's most important ceremonial function. That was the day when he was most visible to the multitudes of his subjects, the day above all others when he might receive their acclamations and feel united with his people in the ancient Davidic covenant. When he was well, Hezekiah had always enjoyed the New Year immensely, and the fact that he was determined to celebrate it again seemed to Isaiah an encouraging sign.

Yet in planning this ceremony, as in everything else of any importance in his long reign, Hezekiah was determined to make his own rules. He would *not* have a new robe—a needless expense, he said, for one who was so soon to die. Manasseh could certainly have new clothes if he wished, but Hezekiah would be quite content with the robe he had.

A few days before the New Year, Zina found his coronation robe, long packed away in a storage chest, old but magnificent still. It was red, Hezekiah's favorite color, with elaborate embroidery and silver fringe.

"It's really very grand," Zina declared enthusiastically as she unfolded it and held it out to the king for his inspection. It had been so many months since he had worn anything but linen bed gowns. How good it would be to see him in something of his old splendor!

The king regarded the handsome garment with a rueful smile. "Much too grand for an old man like me," he said, "but it will serve the purpose."

The morning of New Year's day dawned, a wonderful golden autumn morning without a cloud in the sky.

Hezekiah awakened early. The internal pains that had become a part of his existence were sharper than usual, but he ignored them. Ethan would be in soon to help him out of bed and dress for the ceremony. In spite of his pain, he felt at peace with the world, even with Manasseh, who had been on his very best behavior ever since Zina's young husband had come to live at the palace. Although he was wide awake, eager for the New Year festival, a stronger feeling also tugged at Hezekiah's consciousness, a wish that he might simply forego the stress of the holiday completely.

He was lying very still when Ethan entered. The young man was strong and muscular, able to help the frail king out of bed without any real difficulty. Nor was the exertion of getting him into his festive garment as hard as either of them had feared. Once dressed, Hezekiah sat in the wicker chair beside his bed. Zina came in and combed his beard and his little fringe of hair. He could have done so himself, but it seemed to give her pleasure to serve him.

"My king, you are truly magnificent," she said.

"When you were a child, you called me 'Uncle Hezey.' You and Ethan both did." Zina thought it odd that he should mention it now. For months he had been perfectly satisfied with the polite courtly address, 'my king.'

"Dear, dear Uncle Hezey," Zina patted his hand lovingly. "Hezekiah, my king."

Ethan, looking embarrassed, said nothing, but there was devoted concern in his eyes, just as in Zina's.

"You two must get yourselves ready for the festival." Hezekiah went on. "It's still quite early. As for me, I think . . ." He clutched his abdomen, and a grimace of deep pain crossed his face. "I think I should lie down and rest a while." Without help he rose from his chair, moved a few steps, and collapsed upon his bed. "I am all right. I just need to lie down. Now go on and get yourselves ready. When Isaiah comes, send him in."

Ethan and Zina returned to their suite, and in the morning stillness the king lay quietly upon his bed. Waves of deep peace enfolded him. The pains he had known so long seemed to disappear. Alone but unafraid, he was sinking deeper toward the edge of death.

I shall see the Lord no more in the land of the living, he thought. It was a line from the song of his long-ago recovery. *No more in the land of the living.* There was no terror in it now, only the perfect, perfect peace that hovered just beyond his grasp.

And then, with the rays of the early morning sun streaming through the windows of his room, King Hezekiah, clad in the finery of a happier time long ago, gently and serenely died.

"We left him to die alone!" Zina said, sobbing.

Isaiah had come, discovered the king's lifeless body, then hurried to call his attendants. Now a crowd of them gathered around the king's bedside, all dressed in festival garb, incongruous in a room of mourning. Many of them wept loudly, even Ethan, but Zina was the most distressed of them all. Isaiah put his arm around her and patted her shoulder.

Isaiah found he could not really grieve as the others for Hezekiah, whose death was a blessed release. Of course, he had loved him and would miss him forever, but the years had taught him to deal better with love and loss than these younger ones could hope to understand.

Suddenly a messenger burst in, one of the circle of Manasseh's young flatterers. "King Manasseh has decreed the New Year festivities will go on as planned. Do not mourn! There will be feasting tonight! The old king is dead! Long live his son!"

Stunned silence fell over the mourners. It was then that bitter tears poured from Isaiah's eyes. He was weeping after all.

TWENTY-TWO

The Grass Withers, the Flower Fades

Manasseh was king on his own now. For a few weeks, it seemed that the land of Judah would undergo no radical changes. Eliakim and Joah, the old king's counselors, continued to guide affairs of state. Young King Manasseh was entirely too busy having a good time to concern himself about politics.

He was greatly concerned, however, about the matter of the many gods. Very soon it became common knowledge that the old Canaanite fertility gods, Baal and Ashteroth, had Manasseh's approval. As much as Hezekiah had tried to suppress it, throughout his long reign, the worship of these gods had always continued in secret. And now, suddenly, it was very much out in the open again. At fourteen, Manasseh felt entirely ready to be led into the secrets of the fertility cult by eager volunteer priestesses only a year or two older than he.

In addition to his fascination with the sexual aspects of the two fertility gods, Manasseh also possessed an intense interest in the many gods worshiped by the Egyptians and all the occult rituals that went along with them. Before he had reigned on his own more than a few months, the palace was full of magicians and diviners, striving to win Manasseh's favor and impress him with their mystical arts.

Manasseh was having a glorious time doing everything he had been told he must never do. Faithful Yahweh worshipers shook their heads sadly. "He's very young," some said. "He'll settle down in time."

Time passed, and although the prophets of the Lord continued in outspoken denunciation of what was happening, the Judean people rapidly adjusted to their new king, paying little attention to the prophets. Baal, Ashteroth, and a whole host of Egyptian gods offered them something much more exciting and far less demanding.

Isaiah, in his seventies, saw his life's work falling into ruin before his eyes. All his previous fears about Manasseh's suitability for kingship paled before the reality of it. Worst of all, his grandson refused to see him. Isaiah's repeated requests for an audience with the king were flatly denied with no explanation given.

There was nothing to do but to attempt to reach the masses. Surely there would remain a remnant of the faithful! Surely some of them could be made to see the error of the new king's ideas, the utter folly of his idolatry and immorality.

Almost daily the aged Isaiah preached at the gates of Jerusalem or in the surrounding cities of Judah. Often he led a group of his student prophets into the hills around Jerusalem where they would take turns preaching. But in the scorching heat of one particular afternoon, Isaiah himself proclaimed his burning message from the Holy One of Israel.

"Behold your God!" he shouted at the top of his voice. "All flesh is grass, and its beauty is like the flower of the field. The grass withers, the flower fades. But the word of our God, Yahweh, will stand forever."

Isaiah never had trouble drawing a crowd. The problem

was getting them to pay attention to what he was saying. "Listen to what Lord Yahweh says to you," the impassioned prophet cried. "'You have burdened me with your sins, you have wearied me with you iniquities. Return to me, for I have redeemed you. I, Lord Yahweh, am he who blots out your transgressions for my own sake, and I will not remember your sins.'"

The crowd around the prophet grew, the faces mirroring both curiosity and inner turmoil. There was no lasting happiness in their debauchery. Whether they would admit it or not, their souls hungered for peace. Even the young among them seemed tired and old.

As Isaiah surveyed his audience, a white-haired man with a scraggly beard bent over his walking staff, straining to hear the prophet's words. A swaggering young man beside him, possibly not more that twenty, squinted into the sun, his arms folded across his chest, his face taut as if daring the prophet to say anything that would make him change his way of living. A pale, pregnant woman, apparently near her time of delivery, wiped the perspiration from her brow and leaned against her thin, worried-looking husband. An infant in his mother's arms began to cry lustily, and the embarrassed mother snuggled the child to her breast to quiet him. Isaiah's heart was moved with compassion for all these people whom the Lord Almighty, the Creator, loved so dearly.

The prophet's voice softened as he continued. "Lord Yahweh will feed his flock like a shepherd. He will gather the lambs in his arms, and carry them in his bosom. He will gently lead those that are with young."

The people stared at Isaiah, evidently not understanding what he was trying to say. *They must be made to see the foolishness of worshiping their idols*, Isaiah thought. *Their idols don't love them like Yahweh does*. Again, he raised his voice in strong, rebuking tones.

"How do *you* envision God?" Isaiah asked. "Is he some idol before whom you must bow? How can you even think about making idols to worship? Your images are cold, hard, and hideous. They have no feelings, no compassion. They can't see, or hear, or move! How can you worship something which you yourselves have made of gold, or silver, or wood?"

At the mention of their precious idols, many of the people began to leave, some in disgust, some in shame, some threatening Isaiah for speaking against the practices established by the new king.

Frustration and rage boiled within the prophet. "Lift up your eyes on high, my people, and see who created the very substances from which you have fashioned your gods. Lord Yahweh is the everlasting God, the Creator of all things."

With most of the crowd gone, Isaiah shook his head and headed back toward Jerusalem, surrounded by his awed and frightened students. A few of the people followed, plying Isaiah with questions about how they might know that Yahweh is the only true God.

It had been a hot day of traveling and preaching, and some of the students, partly out of concern for their elderly teacher and partly out of their own discomfort, asked to stop and rest.

Isaiah, himself feeling the effects of the long day, found a place in the shade of an acacia tree and beckoned for his students and inquirers to sit down around him. There were not questions for several moments as a sudden cool breeze refreshed them. Isaiah looked up into the sky. *Lord Yahweh, with what words shall I convince these people?* he prayed in silence. The cool breeze changed direction, and high in the sky Isaiah noticed a mightly eagle in flight. Feeble as his eyesight was for close work, he could still see reasonably well at a distance. He drew strength as he watched the bird soar gracefully for several moments.

At last he spoke. "Again, let me say that Yahweh *is* the everlasting God, the Creator of us all. He doesn't faint or become weary. His understanding is unsearchable. Even young men faint and become weary, falling exhausted by the way." Isaiah looked at the young student prophets sprawled on the ground around him and smiled. "But they who wait upon Lord Yahweh shall renew their strength."

The prophet gazed up into the sky again and pointed to the eagle gliding overhead. "They shall mount up with wings like eagles. They shall run and not be weary; they will walk and not faint."

Again, Isaiah saw awe in the faces of his students, admiration for their teacher's ability to draw spiritual truth from everyday events and creatures around him. Yet beneath that awe surely lay the fear of what would happen if Manasseh heard Isaiah preaching this way, fear of what would happen to *them* if they preached that Yahweh alone should be worshiped.

Isaiah knew each of his students well. He knew which ones would turn in fear if persecution came. He knew which ones would risk their lives to proclaim the truth of Yahweh. And persecution was sure to come.

Manasseh was rapidly becoming far worse that Ahaz had ever been. Ahaz had been willing to let the prophets speak even though he ignored them most of the time. Manasseh wanted to silence them altogether.

Conformation of Manasseh's plan surfaced in a brief interview with Isaiah several months after Hezekiah's death. Manasseh finally consented to see his grandfather. Seated in splendor in the official audience hall, the young king kept Isaiah standing before him, a deplorable breach of etiquette in view of the prophet's age and kinship to the king.

"I have only one thing to say to you. Go back to your country place and stay there!" Manasseh proclaimed in his high-pitched voice.

"How can I be silent when Lord Yahweh compels me to speak?" Isaiah asked. "You know the laws of Judah and

Israel, my king. From ancient days it was decreed that no ruler shall dare to silence Yahweh's prophets. And none ever tried, except Queen Jezebel in Israel long ago."

"She was a great ruler," Manasseh interrupted. "Not afraid of a little provincial god and a swarm of obnoxious holy men. Our kings would have been well-advised to learn from her."

"She fell to her death, son, and was devoured by the dogs of the street."

"I don't need history lessons!" Manasseh stormed. "Isaiah, I want you out of my way, out of my life, and out of my city! Get back to your farm and stay there if you value your life. And do not let me see your face again!"

The interview was over. Manasseh signaled to two of his guards, who hustled Isaiah out of the room.

The miles to his country house had never seemed longer, but once at home he found Naamah waiting as always, with sensible advice.

"He says stay away from Jerusalem. So, you stay away. Just wait. It is a little storm that will soon blow over, I expect." She patted his arm gently. "Ethan can check on news when he goes into the city. Manasseh certainly can't really intend to silence Lord Yahweh's prophets. Such things just do not happen in Judah."

So Isaiah waited, but the news was always bad. Several young prophets had been arrested and cruelly executed, their bodies sawn asunder at the waist. Others had disappeared, perhaps confined in the king's prison.

Isaiah, increasingly stunned, stayed close to home. Sometimes he opened his cypress box and looked at the years of labor reflected on the potsherds there. But his eyesight was worse than ever, and the lines upon the pieces of pottery were blurred. Sometimes when he tried to spend long periods of time writing, his head would ache so badly that he surrendered to Naamah's pleas to let her write as he dictated Yahweh's words.

There was so much Lord Yahweh wanted him to say. If he could not preach it, he must write it, record it for generations to come. The Almighty God had indeed warned of coming destruction. On one of the potsherds Isaiah wrote:

> Zion had become a wilderness,
>> Jerusalem a desolation.
> Our holy and beautiful house,
>> where our fathers praised Yahweh,
> has been burned by fire,
>> and all our pleasant places
>> have become ruins.

But the words Isaiah now had from the Lord promised a better day.

> In overflowing wrath for a moment
>> I hid my face from you,
> but with everlasting love
>> I will have compassion on you.
> For this is like the days of Noah to me:
>> as I swore that the waters of Noah
>> should no more go over the earth,
> so I have sworn that I will not be
>> angry with you and will not rebuke you.
> For the mountains may depart
>> and the hills be removed,
> but my steadfast love will not
>> depart from you.

Isaiah had positive words of encouragement for the future, but it seemed so far off. And the present realities of Manasseh's cruelty often overshadowed the bright hope for a better day coming.

As the months slipped on and his few remaining students left, he had little heart for the task of writing.

Manasseh had, in effect, silenced Lord Yahweh's prophets. There was simply no more teaching or preaching in public because any man who disobeyed the king's decree could expect to die.

Then as young King Manasseh became more confident of his own strength, he dismissed Hezekiah's old counselors and replaced them with a circle of his young friends.

The whole business of listening to legal disputes and pronouncing judgments appealed to him. He vastly enjoyed sovereign power. Unfortunately, his arbitrary whims seemed his only guide in what he called justice. The litigant who could offer him a suitable reward was pratically assured of a favorable verdict, while the poor who came to the king without resources could hope for few if any favors.

Manasseh was rapidly growing older, but he most definitely was not growing wiser.

The voice of the Lord was silent in the kingdom of Judah, and Isaiah, grieved beyond words, pondered the situation, praying for guidance. He spent much of his time outdoors, working as the seasons permitted among his grapevines, fig trees, and olive trees. In physical labor he found some release from his agonizing inability to fulfill his calling. He found a closeness to Yahweh in being close to Yahweh's creation. Continually he prayed that things might change, that Manasseh would realize the folly of his ways and begin anew.

Yet how was he to change if there was no one to instruct him? The longer Isaiah pondered, the more he realized that he simply could not ignore his grandson's existence nor could he live out his remaining years in the silence that Manasseh had imposed on Yahweh's prophets.

One sunny summer morning when Manasseh was sixteen, his grandfather the prophet-prince of Judah, set out for Jerusalem, dressed in a fine brown linen robe that Zina had made for him. His steps were quick with determination as he walked through the beautiful countryside in the cool of the morning, enjoying the sparrows twittering in the trees by the side of the road. But, nearing the city, he slowed his pace as he contemplated the task before him.

Leaning seductively against the gates of Jerusalem soliciting worshipers, were several of the priestesses of the fertility gods, Baal and Ashteroth. Nausea and anger swept over Isaiah as he walked past them into the city. He knew that his attempt to reason with Manasseh would likely assure his own execution. But Manasseh could do nothing worse to him for speaking one last time to the people.

Carefully stepping up onto a low wall beside a pool of water, Isaiah raised his voice and pleaded for the people to listen to the words of Lord Yahweh. "Ho, everyone who is thirsty!" the prophet cried. "Come to the waters, and whoever has no money, come, buy and eat."

The children in the streets ran to Isaiah and tried to climb up on the wall with him, clinging to the hem of his robe. All the children loved Isaiah, and now they supposed him to be offering them something to eat or drink. Isaiah's heart ached for them, for they must endure the sad consequences of their parents' sins before the glory of the Holy One of Israel would be revealed.

Patting the children lovingly, Isaiah looked out over their heads and continued speaking to the gathering crowd. "Why do you spend your money for things that aren't bread? Why do you labor for things that don't satisfy? Listen carefully to me, and eat what is good. Open your ears. Come, listen, so that your soul may live."

Whispers and murmurs rippled through the crowd. People looked at each other in horror. Didn't he know what would happen to him for speaking out? Why had he returned to preaching after so long a silence?

"Seek the Lord while he may be found," Isaiah continued, his voice strong and resolute. "Call upon him while he is near. Let the wicked forsake his way, and the unrighteous man his thoughts. Return to Yahweh, and he will have mercy on you. Return to Almighty God, for he will abundantly pardon."

A tall, robust-looking, white-haired man took a step forward, his face drawn in a worried frown. Isaiah took a deep breath. He knew this man, a farmer named Heber, and had had many deep discussions with him over the years.

Heber cleared his throat loudly. "My esteemed prophet," he began, "we would like to believe what you have said, but we have fallen. We have allowed our lives and our nation to crumble into ruins. How can Yahweh forgive us?"

A younger man gave Heber a shove. "Shut up, old man," he said angrily. "Speak for yourself if you think you need Yahweh or his forgiveness. I have no need for Yahweh. I have all I need right here." Grinning, he grabbed a scantily clad priestess of Ashtoreth who stood nearby and wrapped his arms around her.

Heber ignored the rude man and looked earnestly to Isaiah again. "How can Lord Yahweh possibly pardon our sins against him?"

"This is what Yahweh, your God, the Holy One of Israel says," Isaiah replied. "My thoughts are not your thoughts, neither are your ways my ways. Just as the heavens are higher than the earth, so are my ways higher than your ways and my thoughts than your thoughts. You are precious in my sight, and honored, and I love you."

Again the people stirred, whispering one to another in amazement. Isaiah noticed the rude young man striding off toward the king's palace, and he knew there would be trouble.

Isaiah spoke again. "The word that goes forth from my mouth will not return to me empty, but it will accomplish my purpose."

As the crowd began to disperse, Isaiah himself walked

straightway to the palace. Moments later he stood, unbowed by age, tall and erect and very much still the aristocrat, before Hezekiah and Hephzibah's son. There he waited, as etiquette demanded, for the king to speak first. The royal audience hall, where Manasseh had agreed to see him, was full of a great crowd of attendants and courtiers. As before, Isaiah was not invited to sit.

Although it was early in the day, Manasseh's eyes were heavy. He was obviously feeling the effects of whatever celebrating he had enjoyed the night before. He scowled angrily at his grandfather.

"Well, what is it now?" he asked at last. "I hear you have been preaching again, rebuking the people for their appreciation of the finer gods and telling them to seek the God Yahweh while he is near. How can you blaspheme like that?"

Isaiah looked at his grandson in disbelief, unable to comprehend or respond.

"Yes, I said *blaspheme*," Manasseh hissed. "You said, 'Seek Yahweh while he is near,' but you know well that Moses said, 'Who will make the Lord so near that we can call to him?' You are so fond of telling us all about your experience of seeing the Holy One of Israel 'upon a throne, high and lifted up,' yet according to Moses, Yahweh said, 'No man shall see me and live.' And most repugnant of all," he sneered, "when Moses told us that Yahweh will fulfill the number of our days, you said to my father, 'I will add fifteen years to your life.'"

Isaiah was too stunned by his grandson's ignorant rebuke to tell him that the words that he spoke to Hezekiah were from the mouth of the Lord or to remind him that if Lord Yaahweh had not extended the king's life that Manasseh would never have been born. He stood silent before the preposterous accusations.

Manasseh, irritated by the silence, continued. "What are you doing here now, anyway? I told you to stay out in the country!"

"Yes, you did, my king, and I have stayed away for more than two years, but Lord Yahweh tells me I may stay away no longer. I am old. I have little time left, but I must use it well. I cannot serve God if I cannot speak for him! Manasseh, I want you to listen to me!"

Manasseh rose angrily. "No, you hypocrite!" he shouted, his voice betraying deep fear and uncertainty. "I'll have none of this!"

At a signal from the king, two armed guards seized Isaiah.

"Lock him up!" Manasseh shouted.

So it was that Isaiah was escorted to prison while a crowd of spectators watched helplessly, no one daring to raise a hand in his behalf.

Later that day the guard, Hanun, unaware of the new prisoner's identity, came to place the manacles on his wrists, lingered to talk, and agreed to carry the news to Naamah.

Naamah came, visited her husband, and was required to leave. Yet with the hope that somehow she might succeed in touching Manasseh's conscience, she returned the next morning.

It was encouraging that Manasseh was willing to see her. But his greeting was scarcely what a grandmother expected from her grandson.

"I knew you would come," he said coldly. "Perhaps you should know I have been considering putting you under restraint too."

"Manasseh!" Naamah exclaimed, ignoring his threat. "Just listen to me!"

"Sit down," he said, motioning to a little stool at his feet. The great audience hall was nearly empty this time. A few armed guards stood at attention among the pillars along the side walls, but none of Manasseh's courtiers was present, and the large room echoed with silence.

"All right, I'll listen," said King Manasseh, strangely acquiescent.

Naamah talked of Isaiah's lifelong commitment to Lord Yahweh and the kingdom of Judah. She spoke of his dreams for a future that would be far better than anything in mankind's history, the time when true peace would come on earth at last.

As Manasseh began to listen to his grandmother talk, he was suddenly reminded of his own mother, Hephzibah. Had she been like Naamah? He had often wondered about that but had never dared ask. He remembered that as a child he had heard one of his nurses say that Lady Hephzibah was more like her father, Isaiah. She had his high, aristocratic forehead, wavy light brown hair, high cheekbones and deep-set grayish-green eyes. Like him, too, she had that noble grace so noticeably lacking in her short, little mother.

Manasseh did not like to think about Hephzibah, for always with thoughts of her came the haunting memory of those words overheard in his childhood: "Killed his mother, and that's why his father doesn't love him."

Manasseh sighed. That was an accident of birth, but there were other killings that would not be accidental. Naamah was still talking, but he scarcely heard her.

From her seat on the stool at Manasseh's feet, Naamah looked up into her grandson's eyes. She realized how much he looked like Isaiah as he had been when he was young. "You are very like your grandfather, you know," she said impulsively.

"I am nothing like him," Manasseh answered. "Not at all!" The anger in his face erased the resemblance Naamah had noticed. "I will not have his name in my genealogy," he went on, aroused now. "In the book of the Chronicles of Judah, I have had it stricken. 'The mother of Manasseh was Hephzibah,' it now reads, but it will *not* say she was the daughter of Isaiah."

"You cannot change the past, Manasseh." Futile

words these were, to combat a new, ugly hurt, added to all the others. "Why do you hate us so much, my son?"

He shrugged, his mouth sneering in contempt. Manasseh had learned long ago that refusal to answer at all could be the most hurtful of all responses.

And what was there to say? He felt no kinship, no bond of any sort with the anguished but resolute old woman who sat on the stool at his feet. What was she anyway? And what was the old man in the prison cell somewhere below them? Manasseh wanted only to forget messengers of the God he could not comprehend.

"Isaiah must die," he said at last. "You have only persuaded me not to postpone it any longer. Tomorrow morning, he shall die. He shall be sawn assunder. You have heard me, woman! Now, go!"

Naamah did not go. Instead she clasped Manasseh's knees, weeping, sobbing inconsolably.

Manasseh gave a quiet signal, and from behind pillars at the opposite end of the hall, two armed guards came and began to drag her away.

Manasseh rose suddenly, "Wait!" he called out as Naamah and the guards reached the exit. "You shall see him again tomorrow," he said. "In fact, I command you to be present for the execution, but none of the rest of your household—not that pair of foundlings you adopted to take my mother's place! Just you, old woman. You'll be there to see him die. Guards, put her in a cell tonight so she can't run away."

"I won't run away, Manasseh," said Naamah. Her voice was firm and steady. "I will die with Isaiah if you will let me."

"Oh, no! For you it will be a far greater punishment to live without him."

Even now Naamah could scarcely believe the words she heard. How could there be so much hate, so much animosity in one human being—especially in one so young? "Manasseh," she cried out, "you will look for

270

forgetfulness, but it will not come! Through the years you will always remember this evil you are doing! In the dark of the night it will haunt you . . . forever!" She could not share Isaiah's willingness to forgive, only outraged anger, and her speech was fearless since she no longer cared what became of her.

"Take her away!" Manasseh shouted.

Naamah was taken to a cell somewhere near Isaiah's. Throughout the long night she lay sleepless, but as the hours passed, Lord Yahweh's presence seemed slowly to envelop her. Her anger subsided, and she felt a sense of purpose and new understanding. Though still outraged by Manasseh's actions, she grew ready to face the inevitable. She knew what she had yet to do.

TWENTY-THREE

The Last Farewell

As all available light in the prison dimmed, Isaiah lay on the dirty, threadbare mat in his cell, refreshing his mind with some of the words Yahweh had given him to write.

> Fear not, for I have redeemed you;
>> I have called you by name, you are mine.
> When you pass through the waters
>> I will be with you;
> and through the rivers,
>> they will not overwhelm you.
> When you walk through fire
>> you will not be burned,
>> and the flames will not consume you.
> For I am Yahweh your God,
>> the Holy One of Israel, your Savior.

Then the words he had spoken hours earlier to the people became a comfort, a personal promise from Yahweh to Isaiah himself: *You are precious in my sight, and honored, and I love you.*

Isaiah wept as he stared into the darkness, trying to comprehend Yahweh's love for him. Hadn't he failed to convince the people of their sin? Hadn't he failed in turning their hearts back to Yahweh? Again he recalled the words that the Lord had inscribed on his heart, and they made more sense to him now: *I give men in return for you, peoples in exchange for your life.*

"Oh, Lord Yahweh, is this your promise to bring salvation and restoration through the death of your servant?" he prayed in anguish. "Can even my death be used to accomplish your purposes?"

> Fear not, for I am with you;
> I will bring your offspring from the east,
> and from the west I will gather you.
> I will say to the north, Give up,
> and to the south, Do not withhold;
> bring my sons from afar
> and my daughters from the end of the the earth,
> every one who is called by my name,
> whom I created for my glory,
> whom I formed and made.

Isaiah's thoughts turned to his beloved children. Maher, whose mouthful of a name had predicted siege against Jerusalem—what tragedy had come upon his life! Even his attempt to rescue his brother had ended in sadness. Isaiah had had such high hopes for him as he had for Jashub, who seemed to waste his life on his single desire to be a potter. And yet what vivid illustrations Yahweh had given Isaiah, likening his people to the clay in the potter's hands.

> Yet, O Yahweh, we are the clay,
> and you are our potter;
> we are all the work of your hand.

> Woe to him who strives with his Maker,
> an earthen vessel with the potter!
> Does the clay say to him who fashions it,
> "What are you making?"

Indeed, Isaiah could not question the Almighty God in what was about to happen to him. He must focus on the glory which was to follow. Surely his daughter, Hephzibah, so delightful and gracious, warm and loving, epitomized the future glory of Israel.

> You will be a crown of beauty
>   in the hand of Yahweh,
> and a royal diadem
>   in the hand of your God.
> You will no more be called Forsaken,
>   and your land will no more be termed Desolate;
> but you will be called Hephzibah,
>   My delight is in her.

> You who put Yahweh in remembrance,
>   take no rest,
> and give him no rest
>   until he establishes Jerusalem
>   and makes it a praise in the earth.

Isaiah marveled that even his adopted yet dearly loved children, Ethan and Zina, seemed to have a place in Yahweh's revelation of a future hope.

> Thus says the Lord God,
>   who gathers the outcasts of Israel,
> I will gather yet others to him
>   besides those already gathered.

Still, as the blackness of night began to give way to the light of the new day, he became increasingly aware of his coming execution, now perhaps only hours away. *What will happen to my beloved Naamah, my faithful partner, my dear little prophetess?* he wondered. Tears rolled down the prophet's cheeks and he made no attempt to wipe them away. How grateful he was that Naamah had Ethan and Zina to look after her if Manasseh would but spare her life and theirs.

How can it all end like this? Isaiah wondered, a shadow of fear creeping over him. *Didn't anyone listen? Do they all hate me?* Isaiah remembered all too well his glimpses into the faces of the people as he pronounced his final message before visiting Manasseh. He shuddered at the memory of the fear, disdain, and hatred he saw there.

As Isaiah poured out his anguish to his God, he began to feel again the peace of Yahweh that erases all fear. Once again Yahweh reminded him of his bigger plan, his eternal plan to send another Servant who would fulfill his purposes and bring ultimate conviction, salvation, and peace to all men. Yet this Prince of Peace, too, would first be rejected before he could usher in the Kingdom of Peace.

> Surely he has borne our griefs
>   and carried our sorrows;
> yet we esteemed him stricken,
>   smitten by God, and afflicted.
>
> But he was wounded for our transgressions,
>   he was bruised for our iniquities;
> upon him was the chastisement
>   that made us whole,
>   and with his stripes we are healed.
>
> All we like sheep have gone astray;
>   we have turned every one to his own way;
> and the Lord has laid on him
>   the iniquity of us all.
>
> He poured out his soul to death,
>   and was numbered with the transgressors;
> yet he bore the sin of many,
>   and made intercession for the transgressors.
>
> It was the will of Yahweh to bruise him;
>   he has put him to grief.
> When he makes himself an offering for sin,

> he will see the fruit of the travail
> of his soul and be satisfied.

"Holy One of Israel," Isaiah prayed, exhaustion overtaking him. "If this is your will, I too can be satisfied."

A peaceful sleep enveloped him.

When morning dawned, Hanun, the kind young guard, came and unlocked Naamah's cell, leading her outdoors. His grasp on her arm was gentle yet supportive as that of a caring son.

"The king says you may speak to Prince Isaiah before—" He broke off, unable to complete the sentence, but Naamah understood.

So there would be one more visit, one chance to say the thousand things that cannot be said before the last farewell. Naamah almost wished it were not so, for the pain of the final parting was almost more than she could bear. It was Manasseh's way of making her suffer more.

"Your children, Ethan and his wife, have been outside the gate since daybreak asking for you," Hanun said as he walked along beside her. "I had orders not to allow them in. They wanted to see Prince Isaiah, too, but the king will not permit it. You, however, are to see him, and to be there until"—Hanun's voice broke again as he tried to pronounce the king's irrevocable decree.

"Yes, yes, I understand," Naamah answered.

"Then, I have the king's permission to let you go. Your children will be waiting for you outside the gate."

There was no chance to say more, for at this moment Naamah caught sight of Isaiah. He was standing in the covered walkway outside the guards' quarters, looking older and far more careworn than he had a few days ago, yet even now serene in the morning sunlight.

Naamah rushed to him. Throwing her arms around him, she buried her head on his chest. As best he could with the shackles that hindered him, he embraced her in return. And Naamah, the courageous one, wept for long moments while the words she wanted would not come. Then at last, drying her tears, she began to share with him something of the awareness from Lord Yahweh that had come to her in the long, long night.

"We do not know, my dear one," she said softly, "who will come after us. All through the night, I thought so much about Jashub and his family. I believe some of them may be alive yet. Perhaps somewhere we have great-grandchildren by now. If only we knew! But there are still Ethan and Zina—surely the children of our hearts. They will have a family some day and will keep your memory alive."

Isaiah nodded but did not respond.

"Besides," Naamah went one, "there are so many others whose lives you have touched. Lord Yahweh will not let his words return to him empty. They will accomplish his purpose. And I am going to organize all the things you wrote into a scroll."

"You, Naamah?" he asked, incredulous.

"Yes, my love, I promise. I have nothing better to do, and I know Ethan will help me."

Even in the face of impending doom, Isaiah smiled. The success of Naamah's venture seemed so unlikely.

"Isaiah," she said, reading his thoughts as she had so often done throughout their years together, "believe me. As Yahweh gives me the strength, your scroll will be written."

"You have been very dear to me, my beloved." He could say no more.

Hanun had been standing at a respectable distance, but now he moved forward. "It is time, my prince," he said. He gently grasped Naamah's arm and guided her away from Isaiah's side.

Naamah watched as Isaiah walked to the center of the courtyard and lay down in the hollowed-out log prepared for him. But when the two executioners came, carrying between them a heavy timber saw, Naamah turned away and sobbed. She could watch no more.

And Isaiah ben-Amoz, Prince of Judah and prophet of Lord Yahweh, died beneath the blade of his grandson's executioners. Overhead, the sun beamed down from the boundless blue of the summer sky as the old man's blood soaked into the brown, dry earth of Judah and his valiant spirit returned to the Lord who gave it.

What was it he always said? "Take heed, be quiet, do not fear, do not let your heart be faint." Isaiah's words, often repeated over the years, whispered within Naamah's consciousness on her homeward journey. For a moment she closed her eyes, and she could see him with the eyes of her heart, not so much as he had been this morning walking to his death, but as he had been in the years long vanished, young and strong, bending over his writing table, inscribing those wonderful fragments of his dreams on broken pieces of pottery.

And in the old wooden chest beside Isaiah's bed at home, those potsherds with the bits and pieces of his writing were still waiting, along with a few little scrolls.

And now, Naamah thought, *it is up to me, and with Lord Yahweh's help, I will not fail.*

The aged woman walked slowly beside Zina and Ethan, resolve and determination in her faltering steps. Though Isaiah was gone, she knew in a very real way, he was with her yet. He would always be with her as long as she lived.

Then beyond that, into the limitless reaches of time, Isaiah would live on in the words he had written, the messages he had proclaimed for Lord Yahweh. *I am certain of it,* Naamah thought, *for as long as there are human beings who dare to dream of peace on earth, Isaiah's memory will never die.*

Drawing strength from this assurance, Naamah proceeded homeward to the task before her.

AFTERWORD

The reign of Hezekiah presents certain problems of chronology, problems which have been debated by Bible scholars for years. Many scholars believe that the events in 2 Kings 20—Hezekiah's near-fatal illness and the visit of the Babylonian officials—probably preceded the events in 2 Kings 18 and 19. The phrase "In those days" used in 20:1 is a vague indication of time that does not necessarily place Hezekiah's illness after the invasion of Sennacherib. The author of 2 Kings, writing under the inspiration of God, may not have been particularly concerned to place all the events of Hezekiah's reign in strict chronological order. This in no way detracts from the authority of the Scriptures, but we mention it here as a way of explaining why the events in *Isaiah: The Prophet-Prince* do not exactly follow the order of events in 2 Kings.

Actually, many other problems surround the dating of Hezekiah's reign. Except for the well-established fact that Sennacherib besieged Jerusalem in 701 B.C., many of the dates in this period are open to question. Some scholars think that Sennacherib may have launched two

Judean campaigns, while others think there was only one. The dates of Hezekiah's reign are also debated. While it is fairly certain that he died in 687, it is not certain whether the year of his accession was 729 or 716. (He may have been a co-regent with Ahaz beginning in 729.) Again, these problems are mentioned only as an explanation of the difficulty in writing a work of fiction based on the Scriptures.

In the unfolding of a biblical story in the form of a novel, the author must draw not only on the known history of the era, but also on imagination and intuition. This may involve the weaving in of material found in sources outside Scripture, material that does not in any way contradict the biblical account. The story of Isaiah's martyrdom under Manasseh is not found in the Bible, but it is extremely old, and there is no reason the tradition could not be rooted in fact. Isaiah's family connections with the ruling house of Judah are not mentioned in the Bible, but, again, there are many traditions affirming his princely status. We do not know that Isaiah was the father-in-law of Hezekiah and the grandfather of Manasseh, but this is neither impossible nor opposed to the biblical account. Using imagination, ancient tradition, and, most of all, the accounts in 2 Kings, Isaiah, and 2 Chronicles, the author has attempted to tell the story of one of Judah's greatest prophets and one of Judah's greatest kings.

Other Living Books Best-sellers

THE ANGEL OF HIS PRESENCE by Grace Livingston Hill. This book captures the romance of John Wentworth Stanley and a beautiful young woman whose influence causes John to reevaluate his well-laid plans for the future. 07-0047 $2.95.

ANSWERS by Josh McDowell and Don Stewart. In a question-and-answer format, the authors tackle sixty-five of the most-asked questions about the Bible, God, Jesus Christ, miracles, other religions, and creation. 07-0021 $3.95.

THE BEST CHRISTMAS PAGEANT EVER by Barbara Robinson. A delightfully wild and funny story about what happens to a Christmas program when the "Horrible Herdman" brothers and sisters are miscast in the roles of the biblical Christmas story characters. 07-0137 $2.50.

BUILDING YOUR SELF-IMAGE by Josh McDowell. Here are practical answers to help you overcome your fears, anxieties, and lack of self-confidence. Learn how God's higher image of who you are can take root in your heart and mind. 07-1395 $3.95.

THE CHILD WITHIN by Mari Hanes. The author shares insights she gained from God's Word during her own pregnancy. She identifies areas of stress, offers concrete data about the birth process, and points to God's sure promises that he will "gently lead those that are with young." 07-0219 $2.95.

COME BEFORE WINTER AND SHARE MY HOPE by Charles R. Swindoll. A collection of brief vignettes offering hope and the assurance that adversity and despair are temporary setbacks we can overcome! 07-0477 $5.95.

DARE TO DISCIPLINE by James Dobson. A straightforward, plainly written discussion about building and maintaining parent/child relationships based upon love, respect, authority, and ultimate loyalty to God. 07-0522 $3.50.

DAVID AND BATHSHEBA by Roberta Kells Dorr. This novel combines solid biblical and historical research with suspenseful storytelling about men and women locked in the eternal struggle for power, governed by appetites they wrestle to control. 07-0618 $4.95.

FOR MEN ONLY edited by J. Allan Petersen. This book deals with topics of concern to every man: the business world, marriage, fathering, spiritual goals, and problems of living as a Christian in a secular world. 07-0892 $3.95.

FOR WOMEN ONLY by Evelyn and J. Allan Petersen. Balanced, entertaining, diversified treatment of all the aspects of womanhood. 07-0897 $4.95.

400 WAYS TO SAY I LOVE YOU by Alice Chapin. Perhaps the flame of love has almost died in your marriage. Maybe you have a good marriage that just needs a little "spark." Here is a book especially for the woman who wants to rekindle the flame of romance in her marriage; who wants creative, practical, useful ideas to show the man in her life that she cares. 07-0919 $2.95.

Other Living Books Best-sellers

GIVERS, TAKERS, AND OTHER KINDS OF LOVERS by Josh McDowell and Paul Lewis. This book bypasses vague generalities about love and sex and gets right to the basic questions: Whatever happened to sexual freedom? What's true love like? Do men respond differently than women? If you're looking for straight answers about God's plan for love and sexuality, this book was written for you. 07-1031 $2.95.

HINDS' FEET ON HIGH PLACES by Hannah Hurnard. A classic allegory of a journey toward faith that has sold more than a million copies! 07-1429 $3.95.

HOW TO BE HAPPY THOUGH MARRIED by Tim LaHaye. One of America's most successful marriage counselors gives practical, proven advice for marital happiness. 07-1499 $3.50.

JOHN, SON OF THUNDER by Ellen Gunderson Traylor. In this saga of adventure, romance, and discovery, travel with John—the disciple whom Jesus loved—down desert paths, through the courts of the Holy City, to the foot of the cross. Journey with him from his luxury as a privileged son of Israel to the bitter hardship of his exile on Patmos. 07-1903 $4.95.

LIFE IS TREMENDOUS! by Charlie "Tremendous" Jones. Believing that enthusiasm makes the difference, Jones shows how anyone can be happy, involved, relevant, productive, healthy, and secure in the midst of a high-pressure, commercialized society. 07-2184 $2.95.

LOOKING FOR LOVE IN ALL THE WRONG PLACES by Joe White. Using wisdom gained from many talks with young people, White steers teens in the right direction to find love and fulfillment in a personal relationship with God. 07-3825 $3.95.

LORD, COULD YOU HURRY A LITTLE? by Ruth Harms Calkin. These prayer-poems from the heart of a godly woman trace the inner workings of the heart, following the rhythms of the day and the seasons of the year with expectation and love. 07-3816 $2.95.

LORD, I KEEP RUNNING BACK TO YOU by Ruth Harms Calkin. In prayer-poems tinged with wonder, joy, humanness, and questioning, the author speaks for all of us who are groping and learning together what it means to be God's child. 07-3819 $3.50.

MORE THAN A CARPENTER by Josh McDowell. A hard-hitting book for people who are skeptical about Jesus' deity, his resurrection, and his claims on their lives. 07-4552 $2.95.

MOUNTAINS OF SPICES by Hannah Hurnard. Here is an allegory comparing the nine spices mentioned in the Song of Solomon to the nine fruits of the Spirit. A story of the glory of surrender by the author of *HINDS' FEET ON HIGH PLACES*. 07-4611 $3.95.

NOW IS YOUR TIME TO WIN by Dave Dean. In this true-life story, Dean shares how he locked into seven principles that enabled him to bounce back from failure to success. Read about successful men and women—from sports and entertainment celebrities to the ordinary people next door—and discover how you too can bounce back from failure to success! 07-4727 $2.95.

Other Living Books Best-sellers

THE POSITIVE POWER OF JESUS CHRIST by Norman Vincent Peale. All his life the author has been leading men and women to Jesus Christ. In this book he tells of his boyhood encounters with Jesus and of his spiritual growth as he attended seminary and began his world-renowned ministry. 07-4914 $4.50.

REASONS by Josh McDowell and Don Stewart. In a convenient question-and-answer format, the authors address many of the commonly asked questions about the Bible and evolution. 07-5287 $3.95.

ROCK by Bob Larson. A well-researched and penetrating look at today's rock music and rock performers, their lyrics, and their life-styles. 07-5686 $3.50.

THE STORY FROM THE BOOK. The full sweep of *The Book*'s content in abridged, chronological form, giving the reader the "big picture" of the Bible. 07-6677 $4.95.

SUCCESS: THE GLENN BLAND METHOD by Glenn Bland. The author shows how to set goals and make plans that really work. His ingredients of success include spiritual, financial, educational, and recreational balances. 07-6689 $3.50.

TELL ME AGAIN, LORD, I FORGET by Ruth Harms Calkin. You will easily identify with the author in this collection of prayer-poems about the challenges, peaks, and quiet moments of each day. 07-6990 $3.50.

THROUGH GATES OF SPLENDOR by Elisabeth Elliot. This unforgettable story of five men who braved the Auca Indians has become one of the most famous missionary books of all times. 07-7151 $3.95.

WAY BACK IN THE HILLS by James C. Hefley. The story of Hefley's colorful childhood in the Ozarks makes reflective reading for those who like a nostalgic journey into the past. 07-7821 $4.50.

WHAT WIVES WISH THEIR HUSBANDS KNEW ABOUT WOMEN by James Dobson. The best-selling author of *DARE TO DISCIPLINE* and *THE STRONG-WILLED CHILD* brings us this vital book that speaks to the unique emotional needs and aspirations of today's woman. An immensely practical, interesting guide. 07-7896 $3.50.

The books listed are available at your bookstore. If unavailable, send check with order to cover retail price plus $1.00 per book for postage and handling to:

Tyndale DMS
Box 80
Wheaton, Illinois 60189

Prices and availability subject to change without notice. Allow 4–6 weeks for delivery.